A SACRED PACT

A SACRED PACT

WAR OF THE ANGELS™ BOOK ONE

MICHAEL TODD   MICHAEL ANDERLE   LAURIE STARKEY

DISRUPTIVE IMAGINATION

A Sacred Pact (this book) is a work of fiction.

All of the characters, organizations, and events portrayed in this novel are either products of the author's imagination or are used fictitiously. Sometimes both.

Copyright © 2018 Michael Todd, Michael Anderle, and Laurie Starkey
Cover copyright © LMBPN Publishing
A Michael Anderle Production

LMBPN Publishing supports the right to free expression and the value of copyright. The purpose of copyright is to encourage writers and artists to produce the creative works that enrich our culture.

The distribution of this book without permission is a theft of the author's intellectual property. If you would like permission to use material from the book (other than for review purposes), please contact support@lmbpn.com. Thank you for your support of the author's rights.

LMBPN Publishing
PMB 196, 2540 South Maryland Pkwy
Las Vegas, NV 89109

First US edition, November 2018
Version 1.02, February 2019

eBook ISBN: 978-1-68500-378-4
Paperback ISBN: 979-8-89354-729-0

A SACRED PACT TEAM

Beta Readers

Dorothy Lloyd
Tom Dickerson
Dorene Johnson
Diane Velasquez
Timothy Cox
Sarah Weir

JIT Readers

Daniel Weigert
James Caplan
John Ashmore
Nicole Emens
Misty Roa
Peter Manis
Mary Morris
Kelly O'Donnell
Angel LaVey
Danika Fedeli
Paul Westman
Micky Cocker

If we missed anyone, please let us know!

Weapons Consultant
John Kern
Proprietor
Spurlock's - Henderson NV

Editor
Lynne Stiegler

DEDICATION

*To Family, Friends and
Those Who Love
to Read.
May We All Enjoy Grace
to Live the Life We Are
Called.*

1

"*Geu gaejasig. Jenjang,*" Sean mumbled in Korean.

Turner lifted an eyebrow at him. "Uh. What?"

Sean shook his head, his dark hair unruly. "Sorry. I tend to revert to my mother's side of the family when I get frustrated."

Turner chuckled. "I knew you were Korean, but I didn't know you spoke the language. You should teach me some so I can slam Brock and he'll have no idea what I'm saying."

Sean smirked. "I'll get on that as soon as we figure out how to combat these demons without ammo."

Brock kicked a pebble down the Romanian sidewalk, watching it roll down the street and hiss in the lava there. They carefully maneuvered up the old cobblestone walkway that cut through the village, surveying the white and black buildings. Scorched hand-painted signs hung above doorways, and small tables with half-melted legs wobbled in the hot wind. It was quiet, but that didn't mean danger wasn't close by.

Eddie pointed at a wilting flower in a planter outside of

a florist. "Well, this *was* a beautiful Romanian village. Now it's like a combination of a Renaissance festival after the crowd packs up and goddamn Pompeii. So much for picking up hot Romanian chicks."

Turner snickered. "Unless you like them skinless and sporting a demonic houseguest."

Brock ignored Turner and watched Sasha, their local guide, move down the street. Sasha had a curious calm which Brock chalked up to stress and shock.

They passed a bakery with pictures of various breads and cakes in the window. Turner stopped at the window and grabbed his stomach. They hadn't had much food since they arrived.

Sean put his face carefully up to the window and peered inside, trying to see if there was anything worth eating. A stream of lava poured down the counter. All that was left of the crusty creations were charred crumbs on the counter and a blackened corpse on the floor. Sean sighed. "I guess we won't be getting lunch there. I doubt that's up to code health-wise."

Eddie looked in and grimaced. "Jesus. Yes, I'd like a charred human body with a side of molten sweet bread. Poor guy. Should have saved himself first."

Sasha waved her hands to get their attention. "I bet the church has a food pantry. We can get some food there. People in this village take their breads very seriously."

Turner lifted an eyebrow. "No fucking kidding?" He followed her down the street.

They turned the corner, their guns out even though they were all completely out of ammo. Sasha stopped and gasped, then began sprinting up the hill.

Brock cursed. "Sasha, wait!"

The guys chased after her. She skidded to a halt and bent down, then tried to pry the top off of a manhole. "Help me here."

Sean chuckled. "I think she's lost it. They call women like her *neoteuga neomu manh-eun has lolppang.* Hot buns with too many nuts."

Turner and Brock knelt next to Sasha. The two grunted as they slid the manhole cover to the side. Brock recoiled from the smell. "Now what?"

Sasha nodded. "Go ahead, hurry and climb inside."

Turner stood up, wiping his mouth on the shoulder of his uniform. "Hold on. You want us to go down there? Into the sewer, with the shit and the rats? When we could walk easily around up here where the smell of sulfur isn't even close to the devastation that hole is causing my nose?"

Sasha put her hands on her hips. "I can lead you to the church through here. It's the main one in the village and will be safe."

Sean looked up as a minor explosion erupted in one of the buildings. "Uh, do you think this is smart? I mean, lava flows down, and we are going into a sewer. Which is down. Where there is no escape."

Brock looked up the hill. A slow wave of lava was creeping toward them. "I don't know if it will be much better up here. At least these are sealed."

Eddie stretched his tattooed arms over his head and frowned at the hole. "Death by sewage, that sounds fucking amazing."

Sasha rolled her eyes. "It's either go into the shit and have a chance or stay up here in the lava and burn to death.

It's your choice. Personally, I don't want to be a historical relic one day—just another pretty face trapped inside a cooled lava sarcophagus."

Sean put one foot on the ladder. "Chick has a point. I don't want to be the next Pompeii. Come on, guys, it's just shit. We've been covered in demon guts before. It can't be much worse than that."

They all climbed down into the hole, Sasha last. She pointed to the right and covered her nose. "Head that way. I'll tell you where to go next."

Brock made his way to the front of the group. They followed him through the sewage and trash floating at the level of their calves. They reached a fork and Sasha pointed to the right again. Brock made the turn and froze; four sets of bright red eyes stared at him from the end of the pipe. Without warning, the red eyes surged toward the guys.

Brock showed his teeth in a snarl. "Get ready. Go with hand-to-hand combat or any other weapons you have!"

Sean smirked and pulled a short sword from its sheath. Turner stood next to him grinning, holding a dagger in each hand. "Hell, yeah. I always wanted to fight shit in literal shit."

Eddie furrowed his brow. "You guys need to get a life."

Brock looked at Sasha for a moment, ready to comfort her. She didn't need it. She was calm and collected. He whispered, "Just stay here. We'll handle this."

The four guys ran and met the demons in the middle of the dirty sewer. Turner took the one in the middle, punching him hard in the side of the head. The demon stumbled back but caught his footing and growled. The beast lunged forward, but before he could slash him with his claws, Turner crossed both knives over its neck and pulled outward. Blood splashed the walls of the sewer and the demon fell into the sludge, the dark water splashing Turner across the face.

Turner grimaced as he wiped the shit from his cheek. "Come on, man, fucking *gross*!"

Next to him, Sean was kicking and boxing with a tall, thin demon. He jumped and spun with his leg extended. The demon stepped back, but not far enough; he got a boot in the side of his neck. Sean landed and immediately struck again, slamming his fist into the demon's throat. The demon's loud, screeching whine echoed down the tunnel.

"Fuck you. Get out of my sewer," Sean yelled. He leaped forward and grabbed the demon by the head, kneeing it in the face.

Before it could tug away, he twisted its head hard, ripping it from its shoulders. Sean dropped the head into the shit below and wiped his forehead with his sleeve. Farther down the tunnel Brock was battling a demon on one side, and Eddie fought on the other. Brock slashed his demon across his stomach, then shoved his long sword into the demon's heart. A girlish giggle floated to him. He glanced at Sasha, narrowing his eyes at her strange smirk. Suddenly a hand flew by his head. Turner was holding the demon's paw just inches from his face.

Turner wagged a finger in Brock's face. "You might want to watch what you're doing."

Brock glanced back at Sasha, but she had turned away. He jammed the sword harder into the demon's chest, and it turned to ash. He opened his mouth to say something to Turner when a loud shriek cut him off. They whirled to find Eddie holding the demon by the neck and pounding its face with the butt of his short sword over and over again.

Eddie screamed out in anger, "Fucking come to my planet. Fucking kill my friends, you sick sonofabitch. Go back to hell."

Sean walked up to Eddie and put his hand on his shoulder. "Bro. Just finish it."

Eddie breathed heavily, looking at Sean before reversing his sword and slicing the demon's head off. He mumbled to himself, "Fuck you, demon. Back to hell with you."

The four guys looked around, but there weren't any more demons in sight. As they walked back toward Sasha, Brock put his hand on Eddie's shoulder. "You all right, man?"

Eddie shook his head. "Yeah. I don't know what came over me. I just felt so *angry*. I'm okay now."

Brock clapped him on the shoulder, then the team formed around Sasha. She pointed down the tunnel. "Come on, I'll lead you to the church. Just keep your eyes peeled for anything else."

Brock stepped to the side as she walked past, feeling a cold chill run up his spine. He shook it off and joined the others. They were wounded and tired and ready for some food and sleep. The battles above and below the village had worn them down, but they had no choice but to keep going. They followed Sasha blindly, turning right and left through the maze of the ancient sewer system.

Turner looked down one of the long, dark branches as they trudged passed. "Do they know here in Romania there is a much better way to do this whole sewage thing?"

Sasha glared back at him. "Not everyone can be American. Sometimes we make do with what we already have. It works, yes? There is no shit running in the street."

Turner scoffed and kept moving. "Yeah, now there is lava, demon ash, and human remains. That's a whole lot better than shit, right?"

Brock elbowed Turner and shook his head. He just wanted Sasha to get them to the church. The tunnels were dark and unbearably warm, but the lava hadn't seeped down there yet. No more demons stood in their way, but something wasn't right. As hard as Brock tried, he couldn't seem to keep track of the route they were taking to the church.

Sasha stopped at the end of a tunnel and turned right. She grunted as she lifted a large steel bar from in front of an old wooden door, then opened it with a creak and disappeared inside. Brock and Turner looked at each other for a moment, and Brock shrugged. They followed her. They found themselves in a dank hallway. The walls were stone, dripping with what Brock assumed was water or condensation.

"We are below the church." Sasha closed and locked the door behind them. "You'll be safe here. This is holy ground. The door ahead will take us upstairs to the chapel. Down here are the sleeping quarters for the clergy."

The guys headed for the stairwell. Brock slowed down to walk beside Sasha. "How do you know so much about this church?"

Sasha smiled. "You live in a small village like this, you

explore everything. This church was the first thing built, even before the village popped up around it."

She hurried up the stairs ahead. When they reached the top, they walked through a large archway into the main chapel. Eddie stopped dead in his tracks. Brock hurried to him. They looked around the room, taken back by the carnage. Stacked all around the chapel were piles of dead bodies. Many of them didn't look like they had injuries, but they were all dead.

Brock covered his face with his hand as the smell of decomposition hit him. With the heat of the lava, the bodies were breaking down faster than normal. "All of these bodies. How did this happen? Usually when a demon attacks they tear a body apart and leave the pieces, if they leave anything. There have to be a hundred intact bodies here."

Sasha was unfazed. "Who knows? But it seems there are no survivors here. Probably for the best. It would be a mob with all these people. They would all want food and water."

Turner walked to the window and looked out. "We might as well get used to it. The streets have created a molten lava moat around this place. We aren't going anywhere anytime soon. I'm guessing that we'll have to wait until it cools before we can leave."

Eddie grimaced at a body slumped over the pew. "We should go back downstairs. I don't really want to hang with these guys. They don't seem like much fun."

Brock narrowed his eyes at Eddie. "Show a little respect. I don't know what happened here, but whatever it was, it wasn't good. These people died inside a holy place. They should have been protected."

Eddie looked at Turner. "Hey, where's Sean?"

Sean was standing at the front of the church looking at the large crucifix hanging from the ceiling. "It looks like Jesus is crying."

Sasha took a deep breath. "Yeah, well. Let's go downstairs. I know there were a couple of priests who lived here. Maybe they had some food or even a game. Something we can pass the time with."

Eddie rubbed his hands together, following Sasha. "Maybe we can play cards. I think I have some in my pack. Maybe strip poker?"

Sasha giggled as she reached the bottom of the stairs. She ran her hand down Turner's chest and his eyes glazed over. She winked at Eddie. "I think I might be down for that." She led them into a room.

As soon as they entered the priest's room, Turner started pacing the floor, talking super-fast and not making much sense. "The church is really nice. Tombstones on the ground. Demons, their red eyes. Making games, let's make games."

Brock furrowed his brow. "Turner, dude, are you all right?"

Turner chuckled nervously, rubbing his hands together. He looked straight at Brock. His eyes flashed red but showed their whites as they rolled into the back of his skull. He collapsed to the floor. As Eddie ran forward to catch him, Sasha moaned out loud in ecstasy. Brock stared at her for a minute. This whole thing was getting really strange, and for Brock, that was saying something. Sasha just shrugged.

Eddie and Sean lifted Turner onto the bed and began to

check his vitals. He was sweating and groaning, but his eyes were clamped shut. The vein on the side of his neck protruded, and his fists were clenched.

Brock walked up next to Sasha but kept enough distance so that she couldn't touch him. There was something strange about her—something that he couldn't quite put his finger on. "Tell me again how you ended up all alone out here? It was crazy that when we first met you, I missed the story."

Sasha kept her eyes focused on Turner. "Sure. I was here living with my cousin. He was really sick—dying, and then one day he was gone. I was left with all of his things and the responsibilities of the household."

Brock slowly rested his hand on the hilt of his sword. "Really?"

She nodded. "Yep. Why?"

Brock took a step back. "Well, I just find that odd. I thought you actually told us that your parents left town when the lava started coming down. You said they didn't realize they needed to wait for you. You didn't say anything about a cousin."

Brock carefully pulled his sword out and held it in front of him, but Sasha seemed to ignore him. "Sasha?"

He struck the ground with his sword, and it made a sound like a ringing bell. Sasha snapped her head toward him, her eyes glowing yellow. Brock swallowed and took another step back. Sasha tilted her head to the side. Brock thought she might lunge at him, but instead, she pulled her top over her head. "I knew that out of the four of you, you would be the biggest problem."

Eddie and Sean stopped checking Turner and looked at

the topless woman, their eyes wide. Brock put up his hand. "Don't move."

She began to laugh, quietly at first but then it became a booming, grating thing. Her skin shimmered and wiggled, pulsed, and writhed as it began to turn into a rough purple hide. "Turner was the easiest. I could tell he didn't want to be suspicious of me. I was a girl, and a pretty one at that."

Brock pointed his sword at Sasha. "What did you do to him? Undo it. Now!"

Her eyes flashed yellow like some jungle cat, and a smirk moved across her lips. She dropped her skirt to the ground and stepped out of it, then kicked off her shoes. The rough purple hide spread over her like a wave, covering her like a tight suit.

Brock's grip on his sword wavered. He put one hand to his temple, pressure pounding through his head.

Sasha easily pushed the sword out of the way. "Oh, poor humans. Inundated with hell demons and you just can't seem to catch your breath. Be careful, Brock, you might fall and hit your head. Why don't you take a knee?"

Sasha flipped her hand down his arm and Brock's legs buckled under him. He held tightly to his sword, but the pressure in his head was growing stronger with every moment. He blinked, his vision wavering. Sasha had completely transformed, now somehow wider and taller inside the small room. He looked for his guys but they too had taken a knee, both of them holding tightly to their heads.

The beast giggled in Sasha's voice. He swallowed hard as his sword fell from his hand. "Oh, shit."

2

One Week Later

Katie sighed as she looked out the window of the chopper at the small Romanian town. As soon as she was able, she had headed straight back to the lava-covered town. She had to continue to look for Brock and the team. One of the sergeants had kept her in the loop, but the last time she talked to him, nearly three days ago, there was still no sign of the team. There was every reason to believe the team was dead, but there was something about that theory that didn't sit right with her.

Through Katie, Pandora peered out the window. *You okay?*

Katie sat up straight in her chair, forgetting she wasn't alone in her thoughts. *Yeah, just ready to get out there and start searching again. Every day I'm not looking is one more they might be hungry, wounded, or worse.*

Pandora didn't say anything. Katie knew why. She was starting to lose hope just like everyone else. Katie refused to see it in that light. She refused to allow things to just go unanswered. As far as she was concerned, Brock and the team were just as important as anyone else in her life. Especially Brock. She wouldn't say it out loud, but there was a burning in her chest. A gaping wound at the thought of Brock being dead.

The shuddering of the chopper's descent shook Katie from her thoughts, and she pulled her bag into her lap, clutching it in front of her. They knew she was coming, but it didn't make much difference at that point. There weren't any demons for her to fight. She was there for the search.

The chopper touched down, and she opened the door. The sergeant was there to greet her. "Katie, I'm glad you're back."

Katie nodded, ducking as she followed him away from the chopper. They stood to one side and waited for it to take off again. Once it was quiet, Katie turned to the sergeant. "Any word? Did you get the tattoo description I sent you?"

He put his hand on Katie's shoulder. "I got it—the tattoos of guitars. Unfortunately, we have looked everywhere we can think of. We've got plenty of wounded, but nobody matching Brock or the other team members' descriptions. All of our wounded soldiers have been identified by dog tags or by telling us who they are."

Katie looked out over the town. Steam rose into the air above the ruins. "I'll keep looking. I know they are out there somewhere."

The sergeant waved his hand at a couple of soldiers. "Make yourself at home, then do what you need to do. These soldiers will take you to your tent. We made it up today so you wouldn't have to wait for us. I'll be here when you're ready to head out."

Katie shook her head. "Thank you, Sergeant. It won't take me long."

She followed the soldiers through a long line of tents. They stopped and stood at attention until Katie entered her tent and shut the flap behind her. She looked around at the cushioned cot, desk, and sheets neatly folded on the chair.

Sighing, she put her bag down and unzipped it. *This is the first time I have actively wished that I was not in this situation.*

Pandora understood. *You're doing the right thing, though. Beyond the fact that they are family, we need them now more than ever.*

Katie sat down in the chair and pulled a dagger from her bag. *I know. Calvin is still pretty fucked up from the fight.*

Pandora sighed. *Yeah, and he lost Marty, that taco-loving freak of a demon. He may not have been close to any of us, but he protected Calvin. It's a shame he was lost.*

Katie stuck the dagger in the sheath on her calf. *It is a shame. He's pretty messed up about it, but I know Sofia will be supportive. Right now, I'm just glad I still have Korbin there to protect the base. With everything going on, I don't know what will happen next.*

Pandora perked up. *Don't forget you have Juntto. I still think you should have let him come with you.*

Katie pulled Tom and Harry from her bag. *I know, but Angie just got him back. He came out of a coma not that long ago. It means a lot that he would have dropped everything on a second's notice to come with me, but I made the right choice.*

They need time together, time to remember what we are fighting for.

Pandora snickered. *You mean time to bow-chicka-bow-wow. Time to get some giant Leviathan loving on. I wonder if his wang stays the same size in human form? If it does, Angie is going to be walking funny for life.*

Katie wrinkled her nose. *I don't want to think about what they do with their quality time if you don't mind. I would much rather focus on finding Brock and the team.*

Pandora laughed. *Shit, I'd focus on* anything *else, like bumblebees, demon feces, the general's dick—*

Katie's shoulders shot up. *Whoa, there. I don't want to think about all that.*

Pandora shuddered. *Yeah, maybe you're right. Old wrinkly balls and a flaccid pecker aren't really better than Juntto's giant morphing pants ranger.*

Katie finished suiting up and headed back outside. Soldiers were there waiting to escort her to the sergeant. As they walked back through the camp, several soldiers saluted Katie. It was not an honor normally given to civilians, but at that moment, Katie didn't feel like she had done much to deserve it.

When they came to the sergeant's tent, they found a dozen young, fresh-faced soldiers standing at attention listening to the man give them orders. He stopped when he saw Katie. "These soldiers have volunteered to go with you. They are your protection unit, just in case. They will also be there to help you if...*when* you find the soldiers you are looking for."

Neither Katie nor Pandora liked the idea of that. Katie shook her head, lowering her voice. "I appreciate this, but I don't know what I'll find. These are regular soldiers. Good men, but without demons. I would rather not put their lives on the line. I can handle this on my own."

The sergeant looked at her for a moment and gave her a kind smile. "While you are here, you are under my protection. These soldiers may not be Damned, but they are brave and trained. Besides, General Brushwood gave strict instructions that we are to watch your six at all times. They won't get in the way; you'll barely know they are there."

"Sergeant, I really must insist."

He ignored her, waving his hand at the troops. "Fall in, boys. Katie will be working ahead of you. Watch her back at all times. If there is any kind of attack, you know what you need to do. Keep low, go with the plan, and don't get in her way."

He turned back to Katie and saluted her. "Good luck out there. Let us know if you need anything. We can keep an eye on the whole village from up here."

Katie sighed and reluctantly nodded, then headed down the hill. Her dozen shadows moved with her. Every few steps she glanced back at the soldiers. She stopped halfway down, out of earshot of the sergeant. "Look, guys. I really appreciate the comradery, and I bow to your bravery, but you don't need to follow me. Just tell the sergeant that I accosted you, then flew off."

The soldiers looked at each other, and the one in the middle cleared his throat. "With all due respect, ma'am, we have our orders. We are to escort you around the village and assist in the search and rescue of four Special Ops brothers."

Pandora chuckled. *At least they're fucking hot.*

Katie rolled her eyes. *Not now, Pandora. For Christ's sake!*

Oh, sorry. You're still struggling with the whole Brock thing. I get it.

Katie summoned her wings. *Uh, duh. That's one of the reasons we are in fucking Romania right now. I swear you are about as bright as a white crayon sometimes.*

Pandora didn't understand. *They make white crayons?*

Katie sighed and turned back to the soldiers. "Well, boys, you'll need to catch up on foot unless you're half-pigeon or something. Anybody? Half-pigeon? No. Okay, then. If you lose me, just go back to base and be safe."

Katie spread her wings, flapped them once, and took off. The soldiers chuckled and kept going down the hill, following her as best they could. They were in for a tough time.

Down in the catacombs beneath the church, four fat cocoons were stuck to the stone walls. Three of them wriggled and moved as Sean, Turner, and Eddie struggled inside them. Thick silken fibers wrapped tightly around them, and ooze dripped down the walls and pooled on the floor. The fourth cocoon was split open, sections of the cocoon hanging in jagged flaps. It was empty.

Two rooms over, Brock huddled in the corner with his longsword, breathing heavily. He tried to wipe the goop from his arms. He had found a quiet and calm place to think. He squatted in the shadows and tried to figure out his next move. He had managed to cut himself out of the cocoon, but he was sure he was dying. He was weak and tired. It had been a week since Sasha had turned on them, a week without food or water. The cocoon had kept him alive, but now that he was free? He didn't know.

He wiped his hands on a tablecloth he had pulled from the center of the room. He ran it down the handle and blade of his longsword, trying to make it possible to grip.

In his head, he could hear Sasha taunting him with her melodic voice.

Brooock. Where did you go, sweet human? Those cocoons were for your own good. Now look what you did—ruined all my hard work. You've been a bad boy. Why don't you come back so we can play? I want to hold you and suck you dry. Sasha laughed menacingly, and Brock cringed at the thought.

He took a deep breath and slunk across the floor to the edge of the hallway. He looked both ways, then hurried down the hall. He stopped and knelt in front of the door. His friends were inside. He carefully pushed the door open. There they were, hanging trapped in their cocoons. They were moving around, trying to get out. That was good. They were alive.

Sasha was nowhere in sight.

Brock breathed heavily and shook his head. "Fuck it!"

He pushed the door open and made a run for it. He pulled his sword back and struck at the tops of the three cocoons. They fell to the ground with a thud. Brock wasted no time. He tried to get them out as fast as he could.

A thud from above froze him in place. It sounded like a huge, galloping horse running around on the floor above them.

A loud crash sent boards falling to the ground, and Brock put his arm up. The thing that had once been Sasha dropped in front of him, then swatted him, sending him flying to the other side of the room. "Do you think you can actually trick me? I am Teyollucuani, the mighty warrior! I am not so easily defeated."

Brock pushed to his feet, dust coating his sticky arms.

She was ten feet tall and covered in rough purple hide. Eight muscular legs carried her body across the floor. She was something like a spider but had the body of a supermodel and the personality of a demon. Her eyes glowed brightly as she advanced on him.

Brock pulled up his sword and snarled, "Fuck you, Teyo."

With that, they charged one another.

Mania sat perched on her lesser throne, surrounded by magical black crows. She smirked, her long black hair curling over her shoulders and resting on her heaving breasts. She stood and walked to the side of the room, catching Beelzebub's nervous eye. Oh, Lucifer wouldn't like that.

Lucifer snapped his fingers in front of Beelzebub's face. "Stay with me, fool. Mania is just the advisor. Pay her no attention."

Beelzebub nodded nervously. "Of course. I'm sorry."

Lucifer let out a soft growl. "What were you doing on Earth?"

There was a loud bang to one side of the throne room, and Beelzebub tried not to look. He was trying desperately to come up with the right words, but his nerves had gotten the best of him. After all, the last time he'd stood in front of Lucifer, torture had been the name of the game. That was the last thing he wanted to do was think about it, so of course, it was the *only* thing he could think about.

Mania held up a long-handled club with long, fiery spikes. "What about this one?"

Lucifer looked over, smiling. "Ah, I was wondering where that had gone."

She giggled and put it down on a table, then vanished into a dark alcove just off the main throne room. When she emerged, she grunted and heaved as she pushed out a tall casket-like structure. It had a small window at the top and a large metal latch across the front. When she pushed it against the wall, the front of the casket swung open and half of a body fell out, full of holes. Inside, the casket was covered with long metal spikes coated with blood.

Lucifer put his hand on his chin. "*That's* where I left that body. Mania, would you be a dear and find the soul who used to belong to that one? We can have him clean it up. And he should clean the inside too. I hate it when the spikes get all clotted. It makes the dramatic slam of the door so embarrassing."

When Mania smiled, and the black tattoo-like markings of tree limbs across her cheeks seemed to move as if they were swaying in the wind. She clucked her tongue and put out her arm. Beelzebub watched as a large black crow with yellow eyes flew overhead. It circled once and landed on her wrist. She nuzzled her nose against its beak and nodded to Lucifer.

Lucifer turned back to Beelzebub and chuckled. "She never fails me, as the rest of you do. Though I have to share her with her other diabolical duties. No matter, partial time with her is better than none."

Beelzebub pointed at the devices in a pile. "I, um, what are those for?"

"Oh, torture most foul." Lucifer grinned evilly. "Do not fear, old friend, she is simply cleaning out a closet. Now, where were we?"

Nerves twisted Beelzebub's stomach.

"That's right. You were going to tell me why you visited Earth."

3

Beelzebub rubbed his claws together nervously, taking a moment to collect himself as Lucifer took a seat on his throne. "Your Grace, I was trying to help. Moloch was out of control, and I was attempting to stop him from making any more stupid decisions. I wanted him to rethink what he was about to do, so I let him know there were better ways to go about it. Unfortunately, by the time I got to him, it was too late."

Lucifer ran his claws down his long black goatee. "As in, the event had begun?"

Beelzebub shook his head. "As in, his head had been cut off in the middle of New York City by that human and Lilith."

Lucifer narrowed his eyes and gritted his teeth. "I don't know why you thought it was your place to step in. If you think I didn't know where things were heading, you would be wrong. I gave Moloch the opportunity to redeem himself, knowing full well my lovely...*ex*-wife would take his head before she let him anywhere near her human. Still,

Moloch was not a weak demon. If he'd planned correctly, he might have had a chance."

Beelzebub nodded. "Yes, your Grace. I knew he might. I wanted to make sure that he made the right choices to get the job done. Not only for his sake but for yours as well."

Lucifer looked Beelzebub up and down. "The problem I am having here, Beelzebub, is that when you inserted yourself on Earth, you took on the responsibility of killing these human sacks of shit. You took that into your own hands. But in the end, you and Moloch both failed, which makes me look very bad. I look incompetent. I can't go around letting my own demons being defiled and killed by demons on Earth."

Beelzebub's hands began to shake again. "I understand. I had no ill intentions toward you, Master."

Lucifer tapped his chin thoughtfully. "Since you went to help, I will not torture you for a thousand years, not this time. Besides, as you saw, my torture room is undergoing some serious renovations. I don't have the space right now."

Beelzebub let out a deep breath. "Oh, thank you, Master. You are as gracious as you are evil."

Lucifer glared at his servant, taking a cup of something thick and red from the tray. He crossed his legs and took a sip, letting Beelzebub stand there awkwardly. He wanted him to think about what it felt like to stand before him. Beelzebub was doing just that, remembering the last time he was tortured. It had taken him a century to grow back the scales on the lower half of his body, not to mention the limbs that'd had to be reattached. It had been more than a mess. The last thing he wanted was to go through that all over again, even if he was one tough sonofabitch.

Lucifer sighed and shook his hand. "If you can't win, you shouldn't play the game. So don't play fucking games on Earth. Do you get it?"

Beelzebub nodded. "Of course. As you wish, Master."

Lucifer waved him off. "You can go, but remember, I am keeping an eye on you."

Beelzebub bowed but paused before he left. "Did you wish to see Baal as well?"

Lucifer chuckled. "No, of course not. I know what Baal is up to, which is nothing. The demon follows orders and stays in the background. He is the least of my concerns right now."

Beelzebub bowed again and turned to hurry from the hall. As he walked out of the Dark Lord's chambers, he smiled. He had actually gotten away with something for once.

Lucifer took a deep breath and leaned back on his throne. Mania came back into the room, a smirk on her face. "Are you all right, my lord?"

Lucifer glanced at her. "As always, I am on top of everything. Silly Beelzebub. You would think by now he would know I see everything. I run this realm from top to bottom. One day he will remember that. It might be too late when he does."

Mania took his hand and sat on the empty throne beside him. "As your advisor, should I worry about him heeding your warning?"

Lucifer shook his head. "I don't think so. I have dealt

with that fucking fool for millennia. He knows what I am capable of. The thing is, he gives zero fucks."

Mania sighed and crossed her legs, petting the crow on her shoulder. "Do you think that he will listen?"

Lucifer smirked, not speaking a word but saying volumes. Mania began to laugh, her crow calling out and flapping off. "I have dead to lead down here."

Lucifer lifted an eyebrow. "Straight to hell?"

Mania chuckled, standing up with her staff. "You know I must lead them to the fork. They will choose their path based on their souls' need. I'm sure death will keep you full."

Lucifer scoffed. "Human greed and fucking egos will keep me in business for the rest of time. They can't seem to get their shit together, even when faced with annihilation by demons. I am not worried in the least. If nothing else, we should see an influx in the coming years. Have you seen the hate going on up there?"

Mania smirked. "That I have. And you are welcome."

Lucifer smirked and kissed Mania's hand. "See you soon."

Mania stepped down and waved, disappearing from sight. Lucifer finished what was in his cup and walked to the pile of torture devices. He picked up the club and swung it, laughing loudly. He looked around for a demon to try it on, but they knew better than to remain close by. He shrugged and carried it back to his throne. "Sometimes you have to handle things old school. Right, Beelzebub?"

Katie soared over the village. All of the bodies had been cleared from the streets below, and the lava had finally hardened. It looked like a sea of asphalt with crumbling structures protruding through the black waves. Fires still smoldered in some parts of town, and smoke was billowing upward. Pandora did her best to clear the air Katie breathed.

As they approached the church in the center of the village, Katie slowed down. *There is the main church. We checked the smaller one, but we didn't do this one. The troops are approaching it now.*

Pandora sniffed. *You should probably slow them down. We both know that these days holy ground doesn't hold the same weight it used to. They can be havens for lost souls, or they can be sanctuaries for the innocent. You don't ever really know until you enter.*

Katie sighed and dove to fly in front of the soldiers. She touched down, folded her wings back, and spread her arms, stopping them at the front steps. "I think it would be best if you guys stopped here. We aren't sure what is inside, and I want to make sure that you stay safe. Wait outside until I have a chance to do an inspection."

One of the older soldiers stepped forward. "We were instructed to watch your back."

Katie smiled. "And you will, just from outside of the church. You have seen me fight. I would much rather take care of any riffraff first than have to jump in when one of you finds yourself in a sticky situation. I'm sure it's clear, like the rest of the town. I'll just check."

The soldier nodded. "And how will we know if you need us?"

Katie's wings disappeared, and she pulled out her pistols. "I will yell for you. If you hear fighting, hold off until I holler. I know it will be hard for you to do, but it is the smartest thing. The distraction could get all of us killed. Can I have your word on that?"

The soldier looked at the others. "We will do the best we can, but we won't make any promises. I'm sure you understand about orders."

Katie chuckled. "That I do."

Pandora sniffed. *There is something strange about this place. It's almost a familiar feeling. I just can't place it.*

Katie turned toward the door. *Is that a good thing or a bad thing?*

Pandora snickered. *With my track record, I wouldn't bet on it being a good thing, that's for damn sure. Get ready for whatever creature may be behind those doors.*

Creature? Well, shit. Katie groaned and readied herself. *I am not excited about this, especially when you're describing it as a creature.*

Katie shook her head and kicked the door hard. It flew open, snapped off its hinges, and crashed to the ground. Katie rushed in with her guns drawn and looked around the entryway. She grimaced as her feet caught in muck. She raised her foot, which was covered with a stringy gray substance. *Ew, gross. What the fuck is that?*

Pandora laughed. *Like you are afraid of a little stickiness!*

Katie wrinkled her nose, ignoring Pandora. She walked around the corner and stopped dead in her tracks. Along the walls of the chapel were piles of dead bodies. In the center, hanging from the crucifix, were four large gray cocoons. They swayed slightly. Katie stepped forward, watching whatever was inside those cocoons move and pulse. *What are they?*

Pandora sniffed. *Wait, what? Holy shit. That's Brock and his team!*

Katie's eyes went huge. *What?*

Pandora sniffed again. *Go! The one all the way to the right is Brock!*

Katie rushed over, pulling her knife from her belt. She jumped up on the altar and sliced through the thin gray webbing. Ooze plopped to the ground as the cocoon split open. Katie grasped the sides, ripping it apart. She pulled Brock from the disgusting thing, both of them falling to the slick floor. Ooze covered him from head to toe. He grunted, then heaved, coughing as he hacked the crap from his lungs.

Pandora was getting nervous. *Oh, man. This is not good. Not good at all. You need to get these guys out of here pronto.*

Katie cupped Brock's cheeks and her eyes glistened blue. *He was alive.* Before she could say a word, the strange sound of galloping horses echoed in the space. Katie stood and looked around. A piece of long gray webbing shot down and hit the floor in the center of the church. Katie's eyes slowly moved up as Sasha dropped to the floor and landed on all eight of her legs, her four arms waving.

Katie jumped, pointing her knife at the thing. "Holy shit, what the fuck are you?"

Sasha raised herself on her lower legs and tossed her hair. Her bright yellow eyes flashed, and her lips curled into a smile. "Why, I am Teyollucuani, also known as Sasha. And you are that angel with Lucifer's wife in you. How cute."

Pandora growled. *Ex-wife, you fucking freak.*

Katie's eyes went wide. *Oh great, another goddamn weird-ass creature.*

Pandora snarled. *Don't hesitate. Attack her now!*

Katie pulled Tom and shot at Sasha, striking her in the chest and neck. The bullets slammed into her thick purple hide and fell to the ground. Sasha's lip twitched into a snarl, and she saw something shining on the ground—Brock's sword. She grabbed it with two of her arms and swung around, then scurried quickly toward Katie.

Oh, balls, balls, balls.

Katie holstered her weapons. Sasha slashed at her with Brock's sword, a hard, cruel blow.

Katie summoned her angel armor. Gold armor gleamed on her body, and her angelic sword appeared in her hand. Katie brought it up to block Sasha's blow just in time.

Katie swung low, trying to hit one of her legs, but the spiderwoman used her webbing to lift her off the ground. With another of her arms, she slapped Katie across the face. Katie grabbed her cheek, her eyes flashing from blue to red and back again. "You fucking *freak.*"

Sasha charged her and slashed at her again. Again Katie blocked the blow, but Sasha did not relent. She used three of her arms to push down on the sword, forcing Katie to one knee. Pandora gave her a spike of energy, and Katie pushed herself back to her feet. Sasha fell back. The creature growled and hissed, jumping back up and charging Katie with all her might. She knocked Katie's sword aside and slammed into her, sending the angel flying back into the pews.

Pandora growled. *I'm coming out, Katie. Fuck this.*

Before Katie could say a word Pandora stepped out, her skin so dark the red scales were almost black. "No one fucks with my human and gets away with it, bitch."

Sasha chuckled but stopped when Pandora summoned her angel. Her wings were white, with threads of silver and gold running through them. Her robes were pure white, and the crown of thorns on her head was gold.

Katie looked at the feathers and grunted as she pulled herself from the pile of wood that had been a pew. "You could have given me a moment."

Pandora chuckled. "Sorry. I just want to take this bitch down."

Sasha moved fast. She bolted to Pandora and grabbed the angel by the throat, smiling at her. "Which bitch are we talking about?"

Pandora gasped as Sasha pulled her close, wrapping her legs around Pandora from head to toe. Sasha's eyes glimmered bright yellow as she took a deep breath, pulling the energy from Pandora's body.

Pandora's eyes wavered between blue and red. She was being drained, and fast. She gasped and gurgled, trying desperately to free herself. "She…is…some…sort of succubus. My energy—it's my demon…energy."

Katie's eyes went wide, realizing that not only was the creature pulling the demon energy out of her, she was quite possibly killing her.

The sword fell from Pandora's hand, clanking to the floor. Her body began to twist as she attempted to push away. "Get…off…me, bitch!"

Sasha's ecstatic moans echoed through the church and Katie grimaced at the sound. She dusted herself off and swung her angelic sword around in front of her, and the blade shimmered. It was now or never. She couldn't let Pandora die, not when she had just achieved her redemption. Demon or an angel, it didn't matter. Pandora was her friend, and she had vowed to protect her.

Katie stepped forward, eyes flashing blue. "Hey, bitch, you forgot something."

Sasha smirked. "What's that, little human?"

Katie growled. "Consent."

4

Juntto looked like Channing Tatum again. He had his feet on the coffee table and his arm around Angie. She gripped her controller, smashing the buttons while her tongue stuck partway out of her mouth. Her whole body was into the game. She moved to the right and left before throwing her hands up in the air. "Dammit, he came out of nowhere!"

She set the controller down next to her and looked down at her naked body, realizing she had a bit of an orange sheen. She was confused for a moment, then saw the dozen empty bags of cheesy poofs. Right. Cheese dust.

Juntto cursed as he finished his game with a loss as well. "That guy is good."

Angie glanced up. "Who? Onion4578? Yeah, and he's probably twelve fucking years old."

Juntto reached over and groped Angie's breast. "I guess we should turn the camera off then, huh?"

She grabbed a pillow and pulled it in front of her. "What?"

Juntto chuckled. "Just kidding. I'm the only one who gets to stare creepily at the goods."

Angie hit Juntto with the pillow, chuckling. "Not if you keep that up."

Juntto gave her a pouty face and leaned over, kissing her on the cheek. As he rose, he flicked her nipple. She gasped and slapped him on the arm, wiping the cheese poof dust off her boob. "We really should pick some other snack when we have a naked day."

Juntto popped another cheese poof in his mouth. "But you taste extra good this way. And I like leaving cheesy fingerprints on your body."

Angie giggled, shaking her head. "I guess it's better than bruises."

Juntto grimaced. "Sorry about that again. I got a bit carried away. It's the Leviathan in me."

Angie smirked and jumped up on her knees, pressing herself against Juntto's side. "Don't apologize, I liked it."

Juntto looked at her with a raised eyebrow. "Oh, yeah? Don't tell me that. I need a rest."

Angie laughed and sat back down, grabbing the controller. "How about we go head to head on Destiny instead of playing teams? I'll go easy on you."

Juntto scoffed. "Please, I could beat you with my eyes closed. What do I get when I win?"

Angie clicked the game on. "If I were you, I would be thinking about how not to lose so badly that you embarrass yourself. Winning is setting your sights a little high."

Juntto wrinkled his nose and mimicked her. "You know, one of these days I'm going to stop letting you win."

Angie's mouth fell open. "You do not let me win, asshole. I beat the pants off of you, literally."

Juntto looked down. "That you do."

As the game loaded, Angie leaned her head against Juntto's shoulder and let out a sigh. He looked down at her and rubbed her shoulder. "What's wrong?"

Angie shrugged. "I just hope Katie is doing okay out there in Romania by herself."

Juntto waved his hand. "Of course she is. The last time we were there the threat was almost completely over. I'm sure everything is fine."

Angie nodded. She hoped he was right.

Everything was about as far from "fine" as it could get. Pandora continued to struggle against Sasha, but the spider-woman was too strong. Six of her legs were wrapped around Pandora, and two of her arms were busy fighting off Katie's advances.

Pandora mustered her strength and pushed with all her might, which was enough to break the connection with Sasha for just a moment. "Katie, a little help here. I'm literally dying. I'm too hot to die, especially from being killed by some creeper with eight legs and four arms."

Sasha moaned, pulling Pandora back into her grasp. She pressed her mouth to Pandora's. Pandora grunted as the creature pulled more energy from her. Pandora broke off the terrible kiss and turned her head to spit. "Oh, fucking…gross, lady. Keep your…mouth to…yourself."

Katie screamed a war-cry as she slashed one of Sasha's legs off. "I'm trying!"

As soon as the leg fell, another grew in its place, too fast for Katie to move on it. The newly grown leg slammed into Katie's chest, clanging against her armor.

"They grow back as soon as I cut them off."

Pandora wheezed. "Go…for…the gut."

Katie leveled her sword at Sasha but all those legs moved quickly, pulling Pandora in and out of the way. "If I do that, I just might stab you."

Pandora shook her head. "Abort…don't do that. Fucking hell."

Sasha latched onto Pandora's neck and sucked hard, pulling an immense amount of demon power from Pandora. Pandora's eyes shimmered, going gray, and her body went limp. She was losing everything, and Katie was powerless to stop it.

Katie looked at the door and raised her voice. "Okay, boys, now would be a good time!"

Almost instantly some of the soldiers standing outside threw themselves into action. The squad leader put up his hand and waved them in. They flew through the door in a four-man team, their guns pointed ahead of them. As they entered the church they stopped, taking in the madness that was Sasha.

Katie waved her arms. "Shoot her!"

They snapped out of it and began to unload their bullets, but nothing so much as penetrated her skin. Sasha hissed, irritated by the intrusion. She tilted her head back and wrapped one of her legs around Pandora's neck, holding her upright. She slammed another leg into Katie, throwing her against a pile of bodies. The soldiers continued to fire, trying not to shoot Pandora.

Sasha was not having it; she wanted to enjoy her meal in peace. She gripped the sword in one hand and flung her arm out. It grew in length as it raced across the room. With one large swoop, she decapitated all four of the soldiers. Their bodies hit the ground in a clump, and their guns slid beneath the pews. Katie got herself quickly out of the decaying bodies, gagging as she stood up.

She wiped her arms and sheathed her sword, narrowing her eyes. "Okay, bitch, now you've *really* gone and done it. Hey, Octopussy!"

Sasha's yellow eyes turned to Katie and the angel bolted forward, throwing herself into the air. She slammed her left elbow into Sasha's face and kicked her sword-hand. Brock's sword flew from her hand and slid across the floor.

Katie fell to the floor, then picked herself up and grinned at Sasha. "Please, you think some freak sorority girl dressed in purple leather is going to scare me? You haven't been to Earth in a while, have you? It's a fucking frightening place to live."

Sasha shot webbing at Katie, catching her arm, then pulled the angel across the floor and stuck her to the wall. Katie growled loudly, trying to get her arm back. "What the fuck is this shit? You know, instead of devouring everyone, you could probably market this stuff and make a shit-ton of money."

Sasha grinned. "I don't need money. I need fucking souls. Stay there, little angel. Momma's almost done. You're next. I've never eaten the energy of an angel before."

Katie snarled, "I promise it's bitter, especially one like me."

Across the room, Pandora struggled to rise. Her eyes were now dim gray and her wings drooped, feathers molting. She was dying, and Katie knew it.

"There has to be something! I can't let Pandora go down like this."

Katie could already feel the hollow place in her mind where Pandora had once lived. She curled her hand into a fist and pulled against the monster's webbing.

"What do we do?" One of the remaining eight soldiers looked at the squad leader for an answer.

The squad leader took off his cap and wiped off the sweat on his forehead. The church loomed tall before him and the sounds of fighting raged inside. "Our duty is to watch her back."

Another soldier shook his head. "It's hard to have someone's back when you don't have a fucking head!"

Several of the soldiers nodded and the squad leader grimaced. "We can't just stand here and do nothing."

One of the soldiers at the back cleared his throat and pushed to the front. He was young, with huge muscles and a square chin. He had his gun at the ready, and he stood at attention and nodded at the squad leader. "I'll go in. One man will be less conspicuous than a team."

A loud, erotic moan sounded from inside the church, followed by the breaking of glass. The squad leader rubbed his chin. "You may have a point. There is no way to sneak in there right now. Sending in multiple people at a time is obviously not the answer. You *do* know that if you walk in there, there is a really good possibility you won't walk back out?"

The soldier lifted his chin. "I was ordered to protect Katie, and I am prepared to do that, no matter what the cost."

The squad leader nodded. "All right, soldier. Everyone give him a magazine of your ammo. Once you are safely in position, call us in. We'll meet you one at a time. Good luck, soldier. May the angels be on your side."

The soldier took a deep breath and pulled the strap of his gun over his head, then stood in front of the doorway and gathered his courage. He gave his teammates a nod, then took off into the fucking madhouse the church had become. He tried to be stealthy, carefully coming around the corner and putting his gun up. His eyes grew wide.

An eight-legged beast was sucking the life out of an angel.

He crept behind a row of stone columns. He took a step forward and paused, stepping on a broken piece of glass. The glass cracked under his foot, catching Sasha's attention. As soon as her yellow eyes were on him he opened fire, stepping out from behind the safety of the columns. She hissed and was on him, slapping the gun from his hands and grabbing him by the neck. She lifted him and began to squeeze. The soldier gasped for air. His face turned beet-red and his legs kicked beneath him.

Katie tugged harder on the webbing but wasn't able to pull away. "Fuck. If I leave here with one less hand, I'm going to be pissed!"

Her eyes shifted to the pulpit. Brock, gooey and bloody, was rising on all fours. His arms buckled, but he pushed himself up again. He crawled along the floor until he made it to the choir bench. He put one hand on the bench and lifted himself to his feet. He steadied his shaking legs. Katie saw what he was going for—his longsword, cast aside under a pew. Katie wanted to yell and tell him no, but she knew he wouldn't listen. By doing that she would give away the element of surprise. She knew he might be the only hope they had left.

Brock caught Katie's eye and nodded. He quietly moved across the church, wiping his hands on a cloth on the altar as he passed it. He bent down to reach under the pew. Goo dripped off his head, and he wiped it from his eyes. His fingers touched the sword, and in a moment it was in his hands again. The sword's handle was covered in webbing, but it gave Brock something to grip.

Good. He only had one shot.

He snuck around the debris and bodies and came up behind Sasha. He raised the sword above his head and slammed it down swiftly, cutting off one of her arms. She wailed, and the brave soldier she had been holding fell to the ground and ripped Sasha's severed hand from his neck. The soldier leaned back, breathing heavily. The hand disintegrated as he dropped it onto the ground.

Brock stumbled but caught himself on a chair. He was weak, but he could feel the energy slowly seeping back into him.

Katie pulled her knife with her other hand. She carefully placed it by her stuck hand and began sawing through the webbing. Sasha's eyes shifted to Brock and she snarled.

She grew bored with Pandora and threw her across the room. Pandora hit the wall and slid down it, groaning. Her eyes flashed light blue. As soon as the beast let her go, the restoring energy of the angels began to flood back into her.

Sasha turned her attention to Brock, bringing him quickly into her arms. She ran a hand down his cheek, smiling at him. "You're going to get sucked after all, Brock. See? It would have been easier to give in from the beginning."

Sasha took a deep breath, sucking the energy from Brock's demon. Brock shivered, trying to hold onto his sword. Katie ran up to Sasha, poking her in the shoulder. Sasha snapped her head toward Katie and hissed. "Hey, bitch. Get your hands off of him. I don't like it when a bitch creeps on what's mine."

Katie reared back and slugged Sasha across the face. Immediately the creature's leg flew up, knocking Katie across the church. In the moment she wasn't paying attention to Brock, he was able to pull his sword up.

He gasped, "You are a really shitty kisser."

With that, Brock jammed the sword into her stomach. She howled in pain, and her remaining three arms fell. She released her hold on him and dropped him to the floor. She stumbled back, frantically grabbing the hilt of the sword. With three arms, she still wasn't able to yank it out. Purple blood spilled from the wound, and her yellow eyes raged. She took a step toward Brock again, but Katie and Pandora were already by his side, angelic swords drawn.

Sasha wrinkled her nose and shot some webbing up to the hole in the roof. "Don't think this is over."

With Brock's sword still buried in her stomach, she sprang up and through the hole. There was the sound of horses galloping as she ran over the roof. Pandora shook her head and spread her weak wings. "Fuckity fuck. Come on, guys, she's getting away."

Katie looked at Pandora's wings, which had shed their feathers and were struggling to regrow them. She gently put her hand on her shoulder. "We are all hurt. You and Brock don't have the energy to defeat her. If you chase her and she gets hold of you, she will kill you."

Pandora glared at the hole Sasha had disappeared through. "Then what? We just wait? She killed all these people."

Brock nodded. "That's right, she did, but you know three people she didn't kill? Turner, Eddie, and Sean, who are currently stuck in those cocoons and running out of time."

Katie followed Brock to the cocoons and glanced at Pandora. "Come on, help us cut them down. We found what we came to find, Pan. We will exact revenge, but now it is not the time."

Pandora snarled at the hole, but she hefted her sword and followed them. She swiped one of the cocoons down. Katie floated up, wings wide, and hovered just below the crucifix. She sliced through the thick webs holding the other guys and the cocoons dropped to the ground beside Brock.

Their eyes met, and Katie smiled. "Let's get your guys out of here." She ran her angelic sword over the cocoon, and it split. Inside, Turner was covered in gray, viscous fluid.

The squad leader paced in front of the church. Everything had gone silent, which either meant that they had won or the situation had just gone from bad to a shitstorm. He looked at the remaining six soldiers and sighed, shaking his head.

One of the soldiers stepped forward. "What is it?"

The squad leader glanced at the church. "This isn't right. We're here to protect not just Katie, but the guys in Special Ops as well. We are being cowards, standing out here. Men, get your gear together. We aren't sitting this out."

The soldiers immediately readied their weapons. They weren't sure if it was the smartest idea the squad leader had ever had, but they had their orders. The leader stepped to the door and waved the guys through, covering the area with his rifle. A loud crack sounded through the roof and they hurried into the chapel, ready to fire.

As they entered, the leader help up his fist, looking around in awe at the bodies piled everywhere. At the pulpit were Katie, Brock, and Pandora. They were standing around three huge cocoons.

The squad leader swallowed hard. "Katie, we are here. What can we do?"

"Get me some donuts." Pandora flashed her claws and started ripping through another cocoon. "These late-to-the-party motherfuckers..."

Katie shook her head. "The weird spider bitch got away. We have to get these soldiers out of these cocoons. We don't know what kind of shape they are in or what kind of medical attention they will need."

The leader whistled to his medic. "Delahunt, get up here and get your med kit ready."

The rest of them just stood there staring at the devastation. They had never seen anything like it. It was like a scene from some sort of science fiction movie, which wasn't that far off. Pandora ripped a piece of cocoon away and rolled her eyes. "Well, don't just stand there, numbnuts. Drop your cocks and grab your socks. Help us get these men out of here."

The leader jumped to and started barking orders, sending men to each cocoon to help with extraction. He knelt next to Brock. Brock pulled a shred of cocoon from Turner's body. The squad leader peered at Brock for a moment. "Hey, I recognize you now. You were a hero during the incursion."

Brock's red eyes had a gray tint. "That was ten lifetimes ago." Brock looked up at the hole in the ceiling. "Aw, shit."

"What?"

"She stole my goddamn sword."

5

Katie leaned against the wall of the mobile med plane, looking at the bruises covering her arms. Pandora was doing the best she could to heal her, but her powers were weak from Sasha's attack. She stared across the bay at Brock, who was strapped to a bed, his eyes closed. The medic had given him a sedative to help him rest. Katie figured it was the best thing for him and the other guys. Their demons were weak too, and it would take extra effort to heal them.

The plane shook, and Katie looked up. *Maybe we should have just gone through hell after all. It would have been in and out. This plane is shaking all over the place from turbulence. The guys need to be stable.*

Pandora sighed. *Katie, this is the best way, trust me. I did not feel good about taking four wounded men through that shit. It would have been incredibly hot and unstable, and they wouldn't have been able to walk. There was just too much that could have gone wrong with that scenario. We made the right choice.*

Katie crossed her arms and shook her head. *I guess you're right. I just don't want to see anything else happen to these guys. They have been part of our family for a long time now. I care about all of them.*

Especially Brock, and don't lie, I can feel it.

I suppose so. We did have a connection I didn't share with anyone else here.

Pandora snickered. *You might be less stressed out if you did.*

Wouldn't this be an interesting situation if I had slept with all of them? Lord.

All of them? I just meant maybe Turner.

Turner? I was thinking Eddie. He's no Brock, but he's a reasonable runner-up.

The tattoos have you bamboozled. Brock is the only Brock. Pandora laughed. *Listen, I know you're worried. It's not crazy for you to worry about people you love. But they are alive, and they still have their demons. It could have been a hell of a lot worse. From the looks of things, if we had gotten there even a day later, they would all most likely be dead. Their human bodies were not meant to withstand something like that.*

Katie nodded, staring at Brock. *He just looks so weak and tired. I'm used to him being a badass. I feel helpless.*

Pandora chuckled. *Don't worry. He is a fighter. He will be back and ready to ride before you know it.*

I really hope by "ride," you mean get back to work.

Pandora sniffed. *I mean whatever you want it to mean. Ride him, him riding you, you riding all of them. Hey, live your life, baby!*

Katie rubbed her face. *You are impossible.*

Beelzebub walked up to the crest of Mount Iniquitous and stared out over hell. He rubbed his hands together and turned to the plateau, where droves of demons were waiting on his words. They howled as he slashed a portal open and pulled it wide. He put his hands out to the rushing demons and shook his head. "Patience, my beauties. Patience."

Beelzebub stepped out of the portal, immediately growing to enormous size. An incoming helicopter swerved to miss him but smashed into his shoulder. Beelzebub glanced down at the minor explosion and flicked debris from his scales. He looked around the city of New Orleans, smiling at all the people running like ants below him. He marched across the city, his big feet crashing through buildings and destroying cemeteries along the way.

He reached the Superdome of the Saints and smirked. What a stupid name. The cheering fans made him grimace. He lifted his fist high and slammed it into the dome. It went through, sending chunks of the roof down onto football players and fans alike. The fans screamed and ran over one another in a rush to get to the exits. The football players on the field below stared at him. He leaned forward and looked around for a moment.

He spotted one he liked.

Beelzebub bellowed laughter as he reached down and plucked #43, Marcus Williams, from the field. He tossed the man up and caught him in his open mouth like he was a piece of popcorn. He swallowed the player in one gulp.

The demon glowered down at the rest of the team. "Don't play games if you can't win. Ha!"

Beelzebub stuck his large paw down into the stadium and ripped open a second portal, letting a barrage of lesser demons loose. They rushed onto the field, screeching wildly as they attacked everything that moved. Several of the demons hopped into the stands and began tearing through the people trapped there. Body parts flew everywhere.

A squad of bulky demons turned on the football players.

Drew Brees looked at Manti Te'o, and the two nodded. They slammed their helmets on and rushed at the demons, tackling them to the ground. Te'o gripped a demon around the waist and slammed him into the wall behind it. The beast screeched and fell. Te'o chuckled and began to walk away, but the demon grabbed his leg and sank his teeth into the big man's calf. Te'o went down, scratching at the dirt. The demon stood up, pulling him closer and ripping off body parts.

Garrett Hartley roared as he ran straight at the demon. He kicked hard, hitting the beast in the nuts. As he lay moaning on the ground, Hartley kicked again, breaking the demon's neck. There was a wet crunch, and the demon burst into dust. Hartley put up his hands and did a little victory dance, then moved on, practicing his kicking on every set of demon balls he came across. They were fighting back, but they only had helmets and cleats. The demons had teeth and claws.

Angie jabbed the buttons on the controller with lightning speed, shifting her body right and left. She had really gotten into it. "Come on, Ahamkara are such badasses."

Juntto furrowed his brow. "That's not an ahamkara." He was sitting next to her in a smaller version of his frost giant form, relaxing as he watched her play.

Angie nodded. "Yes, it is. They are shapeshifters like you. They can become whatever they need to be."

Juntto smiled. "A character like me."

Angie smirked, biting her bottom lip as she dodged the ahamkara. "Except they are evil and you are the sweetest shapeshifting alien I have ever met."

Juntto chuckled. "And you've met so many."

Angie's phone rang, and she looked down to see Katie's name on the screen. She handed the controller to Juntto and picked up the phone. "Katie! I've been worried about you. Did you find the guys yet?"

Katie sighed deeply. "We did."

Angie put her hand to her chest. "Thank God. How are they?"

Katie was silent for a moment. "They are still alive. We found them in the church wrapped in alien cocoons. They had been captured by some creature named Teyollucuani. She was this eight-legged, yellow-eyed bitch covered in purple hide. I'm not sure why she put the guys in cocoons, but she did. They are all badly hurt and barely conscious. I am taking them to my base."

Angie looked at Juntto. He saw the concern on her face and paused the game. "Shouldn't they be healing by now? I mean, they have demons in them. I thought that was one of those instant things."

"I know. Their demons aren't healing them as quickly as they should. Pandora tried to talk to the demons, but they aren't answering. Something is seriously wrong with both them and their human counterparts."

Angie crossed her arms over her chest. "Wow, this isn't good at all. Has Brock said anything?"

"No, but he did save us by putting himself in danger. He was the one who stabbed the bitch and put her on the run."

"Wait, did you just say 'on the run?' So this thing escaped?"

"Yeah. It almost killed Pandora. We were all too weak to chase her, so we focused on getting the guys out of there."

Angie glanced at Juntto. "You should call Dr. Ozu. He took care of Juntto when he was a popsicle."

Katie smiled. "Already on it. He's meeting us at the base. I really hope he can help these guys. I am getting all the help I can. Dr. Thorough and Dr. Alice Cromwell are on their way to the base as we speak as well. With their knowledge of hell and demonic energies, they may be able to help us. I have to just sit back now and hope that together they can help Brock and the guys."

Angie shook her head. "Well, keep me updated. If you need us to come out there, we will."

"Thanks, Angie. Honestly, there isn't much you *can* do at this point. You might as well stay and enjoy each other's company. You know downtime is rare in our line of work."

Angie walked over and took Juntto's hand. "Okay, but call me as soon as you know anything. Give the team my love."

"Will do." Katie hung up.

Angie was about to update Juntto when her phone rang

again. She sighed and put up one finger as she brought it to her ear. "This is Angie."

The general sounded serious but happy. "Angie, it's General Brushwood. I'm glad to hear you sounding better."

"Thank you. You sound a bit better as well."

He sighed. "Just trying to keep up with everything. Gotta keep a positive attitude, or it'll start to get to you."

Angie chuckled. "I know that all too well. What can I do for you?"

"I actually called to speak to Juntto." The general cleared his throat. He almost sounded nervous. "Is he close?"

Angie's eyes trailed down Juntto's naked body. "Yep. He's here. All of him."

"What?"

"Hold on."

She handed the phone to him. "It's the general."

Juntto sat up. "General, this is Juntto."

"Yes. How are you feeling?"

Juntto glanced at Angie's naked cheese-dust-coated body. "I have nothing to complain about."

"Good," the general replied. "Listen, I didn't want to bother Katie with this since she has enough on her plate. I'm not sure if you know, but Brock and the team have been found. Unfortunately, they are much the worse for wear, and I can't imagine them being ready for combat any time soon."

Juntto wrinkled his forehead. "Will they be okay?"

"They will be looked after by the best doctors in the world. We will do everything we can for them. That being said, between Brock's team and Calvin being out of commission, possibly permanently, we need a new strike force. I hate to jump on it this quickly, but unfortunately, the war does not stop or even slow down when our men are injured. In fact, the enemy pounces on these times of weakness."

Juntto scooted to the edge of the couch. "Yes, as would any enemy. You still have Katie, though."

"I do, but Katie can't be everywhere all the time. She is only one—or two—people."

Juntto narrowed his eyes, cautious but interested in what the man was saying. "What do you need from me?"

"I need to know where you are with all this."

Juntto thought about it for a moment. "I am willing to fuck up demons any day of the week."

The general chuckled. "That's damn good to hear. I was really hoping when I called you that it wouldn't be a problem. I know you've been through quite a bit, and you just got back into the swing of things. Thanks for the assurance that you are still with us."

Juntto squeezed Angie's hand and stood up, his face becoming quite serious. "But, General, I have a serious problem. I am only at my best when fully myself."

He grunted, thinking about it for a moment. "I agree with that statement. There is no denying that a twelve-foot blue frost giant is a hell of a thing in battle. You fill the role of at least a hundred of my soldiers, not to mention that your mere presence in battle seems to scare the hell out of demons."

Juntto nodded. "Yes, it does. But the problem is, I fear my size may not be enough against the larger demons. I need Juntto-sized weapons."

"Like what?"

Juntto thought about it for a moment. "Well, I love spears, but I could use something a bit more modern. You don't bring a spear to a second-level demon fight. You are bound to lose."

"Okay, okay. Did you like any of our current weapons that we could create to suit your size?"

Juntto gestured to the television. "I didn't see quite what I'm looking for in your arsenal. I could use something with power, you know? Like a gun that shoots hydrogen bombs, or grenades that turn enemies into skeletons. Something strong and sturdy that annihilates the enemy. Something with lasers."

The general was silent for a moment. "Uhh, Juntto? I am pretty sure those are weapons from video games. In fact, I am pretty sure I just got one of those when playing Destiny 2 the other night."

Juntto gasped. "You play Destiny 2? What's your screen name?"

The general hesitated. "BadAs$General69."

Juntto laughed. "That is a good one, General. I'll send you a connection. We can play teams."

"That doesn't solve our weapons problem. Those weapons are in the games. They're created and drawn by an artist, not a military factory."

Juntto wasn't catching on. "Exactly. I need Juntto-sized weapons, General. In the meantime, you point me in the right direction, and I will smash."

The general sighed. "Right, Juntto-size laser guns. I will see what I can come up with. In the meantime, make sure you either are close to Angie or you have your phone on.

There is sure to be an incursion any day, and I want you to be my first point of contact. You will roll in with my guys, but you won't be military. You can remain under Katie's supervision."

Juntto nodded. "I'm ready."

6

Katie's jet raced through the sky on its way to the base. The guys were comfortably situated in a makeshift med area in the main part of the plane. They had switched planes once they were back on American soil. Katie decided she would much rather go back in her jet than the giant mobile med plane. The guys were in rough shape, but they had two medics with them. Besides, her jet would make better time than the clunky mobile med plane.

She looked out the window as they flew over the desert. They were already very close to her base. *I need you to think long and hard. Do you have any idea what that creature was? That information could save these guys and anyone else she attacks.*

Pandora clicked her tongue. *I honestly have never seen anything like her before. A crazy spider bitch who managed to fuck up Brock's entire Special Forces team? She's an anomaly to me. Not to mention as the former queen of the Damned, I should have heard of her but I never even got a whiff of anything that powerful and dangerous.*

Katie gritted her teeth and shook her head. *She couldn't have hidden this entire time. Is she a demon?*

Pandora sighed. *I honestly have no idea. I have to say, though, if she were a demon I would have known about her. Lucifer would have had to put in a ton of work to keep her hidden from me. She sucked the energy out of demons, so I doubt we would keep her locked up in hell. Don't want to keep the bitch right next to a food supply, right? They may be assholes in hell, but they aren't stupid.*

Katie clicked on her seatbelt as the plane began to make its descent. *Then could she be something else? Some creature from another dimension? Something they maybe created here on Earth?*

Pandora groaned. *I mean, it's possible.* Anything *is possible at this point. There is something about her—something vaguely familiar. I'm just not sure what it is. I'm sorry I don't have the answers that you need.*

Katie held the arms of the seat as the jet touched down on the runway. When it came to a stop, the ground crew opened the door and pulled a rolling staircase up to it. She stepped into the light and squinted, shielding her eyes with her hand. *At least we are home now, and Brock and the others will get the help they need. I knew all along he was alive, no matter what the rest of them said.*

Pandora cleared her throat. *Understand, that wasn't a jab at you or the team. It just looked hopeless from the outside.*

Katie nodded. *I know, and if it had been anyone else, I probably would have thought the same thing. I would have told myself I was crazy for even* thinking *they could be alive. Maybe it was the angel powers boosting my intuition, but I knew it was true. All I know is, we are not done with her. I will find her, and I will fuck her up.*

Katie walked down the steps of the jet as a security detail from the base readied themselves to carry the guys off the plane. Her friends were there to meet her. Stephanie broke free of Timothy and Korbin and wrapped her arms around Katie. "It's so good to see you. I'm sorry this has happened. We all know how much Brock means to you. I made sure the med wing was all set up. The doctors helped me get everything we would need to take care of the guys."

Katie kissed her on the cheek. "Thank you."

Korbin gave Katie a strong hug. "You look good, kiddo. And hello, Pandora. We haven't forgotten you."

Damn straight they better not forget me.

Katie turned to Timothy, who was looking at her with a tilted head. He put his hands out and pranced to her, giving her a pat-hug and a kiss on each cheek. "Girl, you go out fighting demons in lava and rescue four soldiers, and you still look like a million damn bucks. I just don't know how you do it. You need to share your secrets because this bitch is feeling like an overworked hag."

Katie laughed, shaking her head. "Don't be ridiculous. You look amazing."

"You are flattering me. Don't stop."

Katie laughed. "How have you guys been faring out here?"

Korbin shrugged. "It's been quiet, which is good. All the defenses are set up, and the front gate is being installed in a couple of days. We went with concertina on the top. It won't stop the demons, but it'll slow them down. Joshua came up with a way to make it out of the special metal. Makes it difficult to install since we gotta leave it up to the non-infected, but it will be a major asset."

Katie nodded. "Good. That sounds good."

The soldiers brought the guys down one by one and rushed them to the medical bay. All four of them were still asleep, and hopefully, they would stay that way for a little while. The longer they rested, the better chance their bodies had of healing.

Katie let out a deep breath and looked at Stephanie. "How is Calvin?"

Stephanie smiled. "Why don't you grab your stuff and come inside? You can see for yourself. I'm sure he will be thrilled to see you."

Katie nodded with a tight-lipped smile. "He better be."

The joke broke the tension, and they headed into the building. Everything was running like clockwork inside; even better than the last time she was there. That felt like forever ago, and Katie had to remind herself it only been about a week. They made their way down the hall to the med unit. Everything was bright white and chrome, and there were several more people there helping.

Korbin nodded to a station where a few doctors were speaking quietly. "The general sent us some bodies, too. He knew we wouldn't be able to care for five people without a bit of help."

Katie waved at Dr. Alice Cromwell, who smiled and waved back.

They led Katie down the hall to a room at the end. Korbin stood to one side, letting Katie go in on her own.

Calvin was sitting in a chair by the window, his body frailer than the last time she had seen him. Katie smiled at the sight of him. "Hey, there. 'Bout time you got out of that damn bed."

Calvin saw her and grinned, the gesture accentuating his bruised and battered face. He lifted himself slowly out of the chair. Katie ran over and grabbed a pair of crutches from the bed. "I'm assuming you need these."

Calvin put out his arms. "Not to hug my partner in crime."

Katie smiled and hugged him gently. She pulled back and looked at his shiner. "You look terrible."

Calvin chuckled and took the crutches from Katie. "You're not looking too hot yourself."

Pandora cleared her throat. *I don't care if he is a demon short, I'll still kick his ass.*

Katie smirked. "You're stuck with crutches?"

Calvin looked down at them. "For now. It's a hell of a lot better than having to be rolled around in a fucking wheelchair. I told Joshua to add some metal spikes to that bitch and send me to war. They refused."

Katie laughed. "I think I support their call. Sucks to have crutches, though. I had them when I was eleven. Pain in the armpits."

Pandora snorted, pushing through in Katie's voice. "This is Pandora speaking. I took over this broad for a moment. I have a question."

Calvin put up an eyebrow. "Well, hello, Pandora. I saw your wings. Very nice."

Pandora smiled. "Thanks. I think they suit me. So, back to my question."

Calvin crutched to his bed and took a seat. "Oh, boy, this should be a good one."

Pandora laughed. "So, do you need those crutches when you're horizontal?"

Calvin leaned his head back and bellowed. "No, I have a good woman who will do the physical work for a while. Definitely don't need a crutch for that." He chuckled and grabbed his side in pain.

Katie pushed Pandora back. "Okay, that's enough, you two. Can't have Calvin getting overly excited here. I'm still in the damn room. Pandora, act like an angel."

Pandora snorted. *Yeah, that was never part of the deal.*

Calvin pulled his legs up on the bed and threw the covers over himself. "I missed you two. I heard about Brock, and I'm sorry. How are things looking?"

Katie glanced over her shoulder at the hallway. "I don't really know yet. We just got here. They've been sedated to try to help the healing process. Luckily Pandora had her angel wings going, so even though the creature got her, she was able to get her energy back really fast. Can't say the same thing about any of the guys."

Calvin shook his head. "It's a damn shame. Those guys are heroes. Brock has been part of the fam since the first time Korbin was here."

"Well, within a few hours of Korbin being here. They retired not long after." Katie walked to the window and peered out. "Speaking of retiring, have you given any thought to what you will do next?"

Calvin opened his mouth to reply, but he was interrupted by Timothy running into the room. He tried to stop, but his patent leather square-toed Calvin Klein shoes had a slick, flat sole. He slid into the room, out of control, so Katie put out her arms and caught him. She stood him upright. "Slow down, you're going to kill yourself."

Timothy put his hand to his chest. "Girl, I just about broke my leg coming down the steps. There is an incursion in New Orleans."

Katie looked at the phone on the wall. "That call out?"

"They all do."

Katie picked up the receiver and dialed the general. It rang a few times before he finally picked up. "General Brushwood."

"General, it's Katie. I'm at the base, and Timothy just told me there is an incursion in New Orleans. What do you need?"

The general was calm and collected. "You deal with what you got going on over there, though I appreciate you being on the ball like that."

Katie was confused. "No matter what is going on here, I can't just take the day off when there is an incursion."

Calvin switched on the television. "Holy shit."

Katie backed up, staring at Beelzebub on the screen. The giant demon broke through the roof of the Superdome and began his terrible assault. "Uh, General?"

The general groaned. "Yeah, he ate some really prominent football players, then left. The rest were pulverized, or are currently getting pulverized by a rush of demons."

Katie shook her head. "I'll get the plane ready."

"No need. I'm pretty sure I have it covered. At least I hope I do. A new tactical team was mustered when I heard about Brock. As much as I hoped he was still alive, I had to prepare for something just like this. I hope you understand."

Katie looked down at the floor. "I understand. The world doesn't stop when we are not functional. In fact, this is the time to double down, especially if they know the majority of the team is incapacitated."

"Exactly. And I also wanted to give you a bit of a breather."

Katie exhaled, relieved. She pursed her lips, suddenly very curious. "So, who is heading up this team?"

Juntto was normal-sized, so he could fit on the military plane. He looked like Brick Bazooka from Small Soldiers, down to the cropped blond hair and dog tags around his neck. Even his smile looked slightly cartoonish. The other soldiers kept staring at him, trying not to get caught looking. They were walking around the back bay as the plane made its way toward New Orleans.

A large table was bolted down in the center of the floor and covered in weapons. The sergeant pointed to a tactical shotgun. "You interested in using anything here?"

Juntto picked up the shotgun, but it barely fit in his hands when he was Brick Bazooka. He knew it would never work for a twelve-foot-tall frost giant. "The general promised me Juntto-sized weapons."

The sergeant nodded. "He told me he had. Unfortunately, the process to make something like that is pretty extensive. Right now, they are in development."

A few of the other soldiers began to load up on weapons and ammo. Juntto stepped back and watched them. "So, what is this New Orleans all about?"

One of the soldiers chuckled. "It's fucking amazing. They have this huge holiday, Mardi Gras. It's technically Fat Tuesday, the last day you can eat before some big fast. But that isn't really what they focus on. You walk down Bourbon Street, and there is a massive parade. Food everywhere, and music, costumes, and shows."

Another soldier smirked. "That's not the best part. The most important thing is that women will show you their tits for beads."

Juntto looked at them curiously. "Beads?"

"Necklaces with beads on them."

"You give them beads, they show you boobs?"

The guys laughed. "Yep. Pretty amazing."

Juntto was conflicted. On the one hand, he loved the idea of a sea of tits as he ate food and drank tequila. On the other, he was dedicated to Angie and had no desire to be with anyone else. He cleared his throat and looked down, kicking idly at the deck. "You know, maybe we kick the demons' asses really quickly. Then we stop by Bourbon Street for a moment. You know, just to explore."

The soldier nodded, understanding completely. "Yep. I got you. To make sure there's no demons there, right?"

Juntto blinked and caught on. "Oh! Yes! Good idea. We will make sure there are no demons on Bourbon Street. You are a smart man. We have to keep the tits, I mean, people, safe from harm."

The soldier chuckled and clapped Juntto on the shoulder. "You got it, big guy. We will go protect the fuck out of those boobies, I mean, people. It's been a while since I've been there, so it should be a hell of a time."

Juntto nodded, clearing his throat. "I love kicking demon ass, that's for sure."

Another soldier laughed loudly. "Fuck it. *I* love boobies."

Baal walked into Beelzebub's cave, swiping the ash off his shoulder. He snarled as he shut the door behind him. He hated being that far out from his home. He walked into the living room and called for Beelzebub. "Hey. Come out. I didn't just march through hardened lava, pass all my favorite spots, and get the outer-ring chills for you to hide in the fucking shadows. You're like the hunchback of Notre Dame."

Beelzebub was digging through a stack of books in the corner of the room. "I'm over here, you mound of shit and cockroaches. What's got your tighty-whities in a bunch?"

Baal walked farther in and glanced at the water dribbling across the ceiling of the cave. "I was curious how everything was going. I guess I wanted to know how the meeting with Lucifer went."

Beelzebub let an evil smirk cross his lips before hiding it and turning around. He shrugged nonchalantly and walked to his bar, pouring a glass of whiskey. He held the glass out to Baal. "Drink?"

Baal shook his head in irritation. "I don't want to give up halfway back to my home and end up sleeping in some dark cave like this."

Beelzebub laughed. "Wow, you've gotten quite sophisticated. You sound like Moloch."

Baal growled. "I resent that remark. Moloch was an idiot who got exactly what was coming to him. Tell me, what did you and Lucifer talk about? Was he angry? I don't see any torture marks on you, so you must have gotten away without it."

Beelzebub sat down in the chair and took a long sip of whiskey. "He wasn't angry with me in the least. In fact, Mania was there, and they were showing me the different retro torture tools they had pulled out of storage. He was actually glad I attempted to go after Moloch. That demon was making a mess of everything, and Lucifer appreciated that I had his back. He told me that it wasn't my fault, and he wasn't going to punish me for something Moloch had done."

Baal narrowed his eyes. "Lucifer wasn't angry with you?"

Beelzebub sighed and shook his head. "When will you realize, dear Baal, that the Dark Lord has never been really angry at me? He is disappointed when I go off the rails, but when it comes down to it, he knows I am really good at what I do."

Baal clenched his fists, furious. "That's bullshit. You opened portals of lava and got Moloch captured and beheaded by angels, who are now hot on our tail. How could you just walk into that and not even get reprimanded? I don't understand."

Beelzebub shrugged. "I guess after all these centuries Lucifer sees that I am not the threat, but possibly the answer to all this. In fact, he shook my hand and thanked me for the work I have been doing. He told me that I was the epitome of 'do it right or don't do it at all.' Pretty cool, right?"

Baal's eyes reddened further. He couldn't believe what he was hearing.

7

Sofia stood outside Calvin's room in the main part of the barracks, straightening her lacy top. She had been away from Calvin for a long time. Now she was going to see him for the first time since he'd lost his demon. Nerves fluttered through her stomach.

"Psst," she heard to her right.

Timothy was standing in the hall. He grinned and gave her a thumbs-up. She laughed as he slapped his ass and strutted off. Twisting the handle to Calvin's door, she opened it slightly. The door came out of her hand and opened on its own. Calvin stood in the doorway and smiled. "I thought I smelled your perfume. Come here and give me a kiss."

Sofia beamed and put her arms gently over his shoulders, pressing her lips to his. She pulled away and giggled, but Calvin's eyes were still closed. He sighed, staying in the moment. "That is exactly the medicine I need."

Sofia pouted as she eyed the bruises covering his body. "Baby, you look like you got hit by a bus."

Calvin chuckled and steadied himself on his crutches. "That's what you get when you lose your demon and then get your ass kicked."

Sofia stuck out her bottom lip and closed his door. She followed him into the room, helping him into a chair. "Korbin told me you lost your demon. I'm sorry. I know you've been with him for a long time."

Calvin breathed deeply. "Such is the life of the Damned. Or un-Damned, now. It's strange; everything is so quiet, and I no longer crave tacos."

Sofia giggled, sitting down across from him and scooting the chair closer. "I'm not so sure that is a bad thing. You never did handle spicy very well."

Calvin chuckled. "True. You always see the bright side of things. How was your trip?"

Sofia stretched. "It was good. Katie sent the jet for me, so I got to fly in luxury. I just wanted to get to you."

Calvin just watched her. "You are so beautiful. What can I get you?"

Sofia laughed, shaking her head. "Nothing. Stop trying to take care of me. You have done so much. You have saved my life many times. First from Manuel, then other people and demons after that."

"I had to. You're my girl. You have to be safe."

Sofia leaned forward and took his hands in hers. "I know, and you are my knight in shining armor."

Calvin shook his head. "Knight in shining bandages atop my trusty crutches."

"And sexier than ever. Baby, you have been fighting for so long. Before you were Damned, you were fighting. You never stopped. Even on your only vacation ever you saved my life and killed a ton of demons. Maybe you could use a break."

Calvin's eyebrows went up. "I wouldn't argue with a break. There's no way I can fight anything in this shape. I struggled with brushing my teeth today. When I'm down, I have no problem saying so."

Sofia snorted. "Yeah, right. The only reason you are saying that now is because there is no way anyone would let you do anything but get better."

Calvin smirked. "Okay, you got me. I have been forced into a corner on this one, that's for sure. But what else would I do?"

Sofia shook her head. "To start, you could let me take care of you. Now that your demon is gone, you are on your own, and that's not okay with me. You deserve to be treated like a king. I grew up with Mexican parents, so my mother taught me a thing or two about taking care of a man. I never thought I would be interested in doing so until I met you. I want to take care of you like you have taken care of me."

Calvin squeezed her hand. "But who will take care of *you?*"

Sofia shrugged. "Me, until you are better. Then we will take care of each other. That's how it works, right? We are there for each other and make sure that each is successful."

Calvin grinned. "That's a pretty old-fashioned way to look at things. I like it. Continue."

Sofia scooted to the edge of the seat. "Well, you can finish getting through the worst of it here, then I can take you back to San Diego and we can share my home. We can spend our days walking on the beaches, watching the sunsets, drinking fruity drinks and visiting Mexico. Just visiting, this time, without the threats we had to deal with before. We can actually spend time together without looking over our shoulders or wondering if you will get called to an incursion."

Calvin leaned back, hiding a smirk. "So, live like the cluelessly innocent do until we come to save their asses."

Sofia nodded hard. "That's right. And you fucking deserve it—you know that. You have been on guard for too long. It's your turn to live cluelessly."

Calvin rubbed his chin, looking out at the base. "You know, that doesn't sound so bad. I have to admit that I could use some sand between my toes. Even more than that, I could use some time with you. Just you."

Sofia smiled. "I hoped that you would say that."

She grabbed her purse, pulling out a black jeweler's box. She pushed the chair back and got down on one knee, revealing a black ring with a tiny diamond set into it. "Calvin, will you make me the luckiest girl in the world and marry me?"

Calvin grinned. "That's *my* line."

Sofia laughed, shaking her head. "Yeah, but you're so beat up you can't get down on one knee."

A low hum of voices chattered across the main room of the restaurant. The white tablecloths covering each table were held down by a cluster of candles lit in the center. Light instrumental music played in the background as Belphegor sat down across the table from the Romanian president,

Dragos. The man was large, with a double chin, very little hair, and a complete disregard for manners when it came to eating.

Belphegor placed his napkin on his lap to cover his expensive suit. He was still in his human skin, masquerading as an important attorney, and he had finally gotten a meeting with the president. Dragos had his cloth napkin tucked into the front of his white button-down, and his tie was thrown over his shoulder. He picked up an oyster and slurped it noisily, then tossed the shell on the tablecloth.

"*Ce vrei aici?*" Dragos grunted.

Belphegor cleared his throat. "Do you mind if we speak English?"

Dragos shrugged. "Whatever. What are you wanting from me?"

Belphegor tightened his tie. "First, I want to thank you for allowing me to come to Bucharest to meet with you. I know you are a very busy man, especially with everything going on in your country. I am a lawyer working on behalf of the World Council."

Dragos glanced at him, inspecting his expensive suit. "Council Member Bringham said nothing about a visit from a lawyer. Especially not one like yourself, obviously American."

Belphegor rubbed his cheek, secretly pushing his skin up. This human skin didn't fit him all that well. He spent more time pulling the skin into place than he did acting like a human. Dragos didn't seem to notice, which was good. Belphegor didn't want to blow his cover so soon. He had always been good with disguises, but this particular human skin had turned out to be an unfortunate fit.

Belphegor cleared his throat and nervously took a sip of his water. "We did not go through Bringham. We are representing the Council as a whole in an investigation."

Dragos slammed down the last oyster and wiped his mouth, then chugged a full glass of champagne. "I know nothing. I do not know what you want to ask of me. I keep my business in Romania. The World Council could have called me and I would have told them the same thing."

Belphegor nodded. "I understand. However, this specific subject has everything to do with you. In fact, you are the only one I will be contacting for this case. Your participation is critical to this matter."

Dragos's bodyguard leaned down and whispered in Dragos's ear. The president waved him off, leaning back as a waitress replaced his empty plate with one holding a large steak and mashed potatoes. "I love American food. You make this so good. That is why I come to this restaurant. American-owned."

Belphegor looked around. "Yes, it feels very much like being at home."

Dragos sighed at his food and waved his hand for Belphegor to proceed. "Okay, let us hear this. What do you want me for?"

Belphegor pulled out a thick file and set it on the table. "I have been given custody of a file of complaints against mercenary organizations. Though there are several different merc groups listed in this file, the majority of the complaints are against Katie of Katie's Killers."

Dragos's eyebrow lifted as he opened the file. The first

picture was of Katie in her black leathers, dressed for battle. "I have heard that she helped us during our recent crisis."

Belphegor wrinkled his nose. "Let me ask you this, Mr. President. What if you had an assistant you trusted completely? What if he led you to believe that if you turned the gas in your home up higher, you would save money? But, one day there is the slightest spark, and your house explodes from the sheer amount of gas. That's a tragedy. You would blame your assistant. He might have been helping in one way, but in reality, he was the person who caused you to lose everything."

Dragos tilted his head, listening. "And you are saying Katie caused the demons to attack?"

"I'm saying something very like that."

"But she rescued many men."

"Sure. After the fact, she rescued people, when she could have prevented the whole thing in the first place." Belphegor made sure he had Dragos's attention, then continued, "Katie is an angel. Her demon is also an angel. They have been fighting and taunting demons for a long time. Those demons came here to piss you off and to hurt her."

Dragos's eyes narrowed, and he gritted his teeth. "This is a grievous charge. I have hundreds of people dead, and now a town full of hardened lava. It is practically hell on Earth there. You are saying that Katie had something to do with that?"

Belphegor nodded sympathetically. "And through all that, what is Katie doing to help?"

Dragos slammed his fist on the table. "Nothing. She

came to rescue her people but left even more dead in her wake. She did not come to help us, she came to help herself. Then she left without another word. She is not good, like the American troops. She is a liability."

"A threat, maybe?"

"A *traitor*!"

Belphegor could see that Dragos was growing angrier by the second. Belphegor was having the time of his life. "I heard that she took her injured to safety and got them top-of-the-line medical attention. She did everything she could to save them while your troops, your people, lay injured and dying in the streets." Belphegor poured two full glasses of champagne. "Katie's a rich woman. She probably fed her friends caviar while your brave soldiers buried their dead."

Dragos took the glass of champagne and downed it quickly. He grimaced and burped. "She must be stopped. She cannot be allowed to reap the rewards our brave dead have sown. She must be punished for bringing these demons down upon my country. Whatever you need me to do, I will do it."

Belphegor grinned. "President Dragos, lucky for you I'm an idea man. And I've got some ideas about Katie."

Juntto jogged behind the soldiers. He had to duck as they ran through the tunnel that led from the locker rooms to the open field. When he broke out of the tunnel and brought himself up to his full height, his eyes went wide. People were banding together against demons all over the place, but the demons were pouncing from body to body.

Two men hurried past him with a stretcher. Drew Brees gave him a thumbs-up from the stretcher. Juntto nodded and took off across the field. As he ran, his blue skin morphed and became a football jersey and helmet.

He raced toward a demon standing in the center of the field. "Ready, set, hike!"

He pulled his leg back and punted the demon across the field and through the goal posts. He put up his arms, making a cheering sound in the back of his throat. He looked around at the others, who were using their weapons to blast through a half a dozen demons at a time. Juntto wrinkled his nose. A snarling demon leaped for him and he batted the creature away with one meaty fist, sending it to the upper part of the stands.

"I need Juntto-sized weapons," he grumbled, then shrugged. "I will rack up points in the meantime. Yes."

He grabbed a charging demon and wadded him up tightly, crushing his bones until he was vaguely ball-shaped. Juntto threw him in the air and punted him downfield. The hell-beast turned to dust between the goal posts, and Juntto pumped his fist. Fucking with demons was fun. He ran down the field, tackling and slamming into any demon he saw. One fat demon hissed at him, and Juntto ran forward and kicked him in his stomach. The beast soared over the field, slammed into the goal post, and split apart. Juntto cackled.

Two security guards came running up with their guns out. "Hey, Juntto, we're here to help!"

Juntto got down on one knee and shook his head. "You guys have balls the size of the moon, but you shouldn't be here. Get the innocents to safety. You have no demons in you. No need to die. I am here to clean up the mess."

The security guards chuckled and tipped their hats to him before running off.

Juntto loved how kind the security guards were. Being in a coma had changed him. He now fed off empathy and compassion, and with every innocent life he saved, he became stronger. He continued to bash demons right and left, ripping some apart and punting others. Juntto chuckled as he grabbed a skinny demon and threw him like he was passing a football downfield. The demon landed on his head and rolled into the end zone. Juntto froze, then grinned and put his hands in the air, doing a victory dance. "Touchdown! Or touchback! I'm not sure. Either way, I score!"

When the last demons were ash, Juntto jumped over to the soldiers, and the ground shook as he landed. One of the soldiers looked at him with a smirk as Juntto shook his fist in the air. "Now we go to Bourbon Streeeet!"

8

Katie leaned against the wall with her arms crossed as Dr. Thorough and his assistant Dr. Cromwell inspected Brock, Turner, Eddie, and Sean. They were all still unconscious, and they didn't seem to be healing any faster than a human would. In the shape they were in, they desperately needed to heal faster or there was a chance that they wouldn't make it. Katie didn't know if the demons inhabiting their bodies were injured, or just not there anymore.

Pandora sniffed. *I can't tell anything at this point. All I sense are injuries. I can't tell if they are all the guys', or if the demons are injured too.*

If their demons were in there, the guys would be up and around by now. Just from the bruises and cuts on them, you can tell that they aren't healing fast. Pandora, talk to their demons. Tell them to get their asses in gear!

They're not responding. They're probably busy healing the guys.

But the guys aren't *healing!*

Pandora could tell Katie was starting to get antsy. *Take a deep breath. I'm sure there is something these doctors can do. I mean, one of them saved Juntto or at least was smart enough to know what to do with his sleeping body.*

Katie shook her head. *This isn't the same. They don't have tough-ass Leviathan bodies. They are human, and human bodies are fragile. Just look at them. They are broken and bruised. When I find that bitch, I am going to rip all eight legs off and shove them right up her ass.*

Pandora grimaced. *Ugh. Even* I'm *not into kinky shit like that.*

Dr. Ozu walked into the room pushing a cart in front of him. He smiled and nodded at Katie as he positioned the device into the center of the floor. Katie looked down at it. "What is this?"

Dr. Ozu pushed some buttons and a screen lifted from the device. It was a cross between an x-ray and a radar screen. "This is a modified version of the sensor that you use to detect demonic incursions. Basically, what we are hoping is that it can detect the lifeforce of the demons inside these guys. Dr. Thorough and Dr. Cromwell have spent many hours working on this with me."

Doctor Thorough pushed the glasses up his nose. "Yes, yes. You can think of this as a detector for demons."

Katie nodded. "And how many times has it worked?"

The doctors looked at each other and Alice smirked. "In reality, they have never used it. It was supposed to go into testing next week, but with these injuries, they decided that they couldn't wait. We really need to determine their status and figure out what to expect from their healing."

Katie took a step back and lifted an eyebrow. "Please don't melt or mutate or shrink-ray my team, okay?"

Alice chuckled but Dr. Thorough nodded, not seeing the humor in it. "Oh, this isn't related to the shrink ray. Ozu, did we use any shrink ray parts?"

Katie? Is he joking? I can't tell.

I don't think so, Pan.

Katie was about to say something, but Alice waved her hand. "Best not to ask too many questions."

Dr. Ozu pushed the device next to Turner and flipped it on. Dr. Thorough carefully handed him a long wand that resembled a three-hole punch. Katie watched nervously as the doctor ran the wand over Turner. The machine made a chorus of beeps and buzzes.

Dr. Thorough printed out the report, and they moved on to Sean. They repeated the process with him, pausing around the belly and moving all the way up his chest, then did the same with Eddie. Katie waited with bated breath as they moved to Brock. The doctor looked like he was getting more nervous by the second.

He ran the machine over Brock, his face firm. Dr. Ozu sighed and handed the wand back to Dr. Thorough. They were silent as the report printed.

Katie stepped forward. "Well?"

Dr. Ozu nodded at the soldiers and shook his head. "I have to admit I am not picking up any demonic activity in any of them. It looks as if their demons are no longer there."

This nerd can't be right.

Katie looked at Brock. "Could it be a mistake? You said yourself you have never tried it on a human before."

Alice grabbed the machine and rolled it to Katie. She flipped it on and pulled out the wand. Katie stood perfectly still as she ran it over her body. As soon as the wand was inches from Katie's skin, a low warbling sound rang out. Alice turned the screen toward Katie and showed her a fuzzy scan of her body.

She pointed at the swirling red inside of Katie. "This is your demon. See?"

Look at my fine-ass self.

Not now.

Alice brought up stills of Brock and the other guys for comparison. "If you look at the guys, there is just nothing there. You see? These guys are all alone now."

Katie felt her voice waver. "So, what does this mean?"

The doctor looked at the guys. "Even without their demons, the guys are incredibly strong. Eddie, Turner, and Sean's injuries are no longer life-threatening. I foresee them healing very slowly, but they will recover."

Katie could feel a lump in her throat. "And Brock?"

They both turned toward Brock. Doctor Ozu sighed loudly. "Brock is in critical condition. He was beaten and drained worse than any of the others. His demon was most likely taken early on when she pulled the energy from him. Any injuries after that had to be dealt with without the help of his demon. All we can do at this point is stand by and hope he can pull himself through."

The doctor put his hand on Katie's shoulder. "I'm sorry about this. It would take a demon infecting him and being willing to heal him for me to give you any kind of positive report. We'll keep fighting for him. Don't give up."

The front door of the barracks shot open and slammed into the wall. Katie rushed outside and stopped in the open air, closing her eyes and taking a deep breath. She felt like she was having a panic attack. She could barely keep herself together.

Pandora tried to calm her. *Just simmer down. You cannot control this, and I know that makes it hard for you. You can't control everything.*

Katie listened. She gritted her teeth. *This is insane. Where are these crazy demons, or whatever she was, coming from? I don't understand. Just when you thought you had seen the worst, something crazier comes at us.*

Pandora breathed deeply. *Why don't we go for a walk in the desert? It's a bright night, and the wind will do you some good.*

Katie took off across the base and passed through the front gate. She walked down the gravel road a short way, then turned off and strode out into the desert. When the sand weighed down her feet, she slowed. She climbed to the top of a short dune and sat down. She pulled her knees to her chin and looked out over the landscape. The moon was bright in the sky, and the stars twinkled wildly.

Katie felt like nothing was within her control. *What I want to know is how this thing managed to take the Special Force's team's demons? She left them alive, or at least alive enough, but exorcised them. But it really wasn't an exorcism. At least I don't think it was. I guess when they wake up we will be able to tell. Their minds should be reset if that was what* happened. But with how Calvin's is, I suspect they will remember everything.

Pandora listened to Katie, trying to remember anything she could about this. *To be honest with you, until recently I thought that when a demon was ripped from a human they died. Calvin showed me differently, and Turner, Eddie, Sean, and Brock have confirmed that. I thought the only time humans stayed alive was during an exorcism.*

Katie groaned, leaning back on her hands. *What can we do? We don't know where she is. We don't know* what *she is. And we don't know what other powers she may have.*

What to do is not clear. When she was holding me, it felt like she was sucking the demon right out of me. I am not a human, though, so she couldn't take me down. My angel prevented that.

Katie calmed herself. She couldn't keep flailing. She needed a question she could answer. *What about the guys? How do we help them? We can't just let Brock die.*

I could always go down to hell and grab some demons. We could re-infect all four of them, which would help them heal. I can put the fear of Lucifer into any pain-in-the-ass demon. It would be a quick swap.

Katie thought about that for a moment. *I mean, that is an option, sure. But I'm not so certain that's the right thing to do. The guys on that team didn't make a conscious choice to be Damned in the first place. They were all Damned by force. Is it right for me to re-infect four human beings just because we need them?*

Pandora grumbled. *I've never been very good at answering tough questions like that. Morality was never my strong suit, even as an angel.*

Katie shook her head and stood up. She walked down

the hill and out into the sand. It had gotten cold since the sun went down, and clouds were starting to move in. She didn't feel cold, though. In fact, Katie could only feel her anger and helplessness.

I have a hard time making life-changing decisions for people. They should have the right to choose whether they want to be Damned. For all we know, none of them wanted to be. They might want their lives back.

Pandora agreed. *What would you do if you were them?*

I don't know. I don't know how to be normal anymore. On the other hand, I wouldn't want some random demon hitching a ride for all eternity.

Pandora chuckled. *Yeah, having some rando after having the queen would be a bit of a letdown.*

Katie scowled at the stars. *I need someone to help me with this. What is the good of being an angel if you can't call on the others for help?*

She shook her head, feeling the lump in her throat again. She began to walk, but her knees felt weak. She stopped and turned in a circle, clenching her jaw tightly. When she stopped she looked at the sky and screamed in anger and desperation, "Gabriel, come down here!"

She was silent for a moment. She wondered if he would actually answer. Pandora sniffed. *He's not here, Katie, and I don't think he's coming.*

Katie let her arms drop to her sides and expelled a deep breath from her lungs. *Basically, it's up to me to make a decision with both hands tied behind my back.*

Pandora was silent for a moment. *What about Brock? The doctor said the others will recover, so you don't have to put a demon in them. They can make that choice when they wake up, but for Brock, it might be a matter of life and death. What do you think he would want?*

Katie tilted her head back and looked at the stars. *I wish I knew. I wish that I had gotten to know him as a person more so this decision would be simpler. He might have made the decision to become infected again on his own. At the same time, he had a hell of a life before this all. I'm not sure he wouldn't want to go back to it.*

General Brushwood walked into his office, took off his trench coat, and hung it on the back of his door. He tossed his hat on the coffee table. He walked to the bookcase, opened a hidden door, and pulled out a glass and a bottle of whiskey. He poured himself two fingers and went to his desk, sitting down and sighing.

He held his glass in the air. "To the success of the new team, and no more complications."

It couldn't be that easy. His secretary's voice came over the speaker. "General, you have a call holding on line three. It's the president of Romania."

Brushwood groaned and picked up the phone, pressing line three. "President Dragos, it's good to hear from you. What can I do for you?"

Dragos grumbled something and the general sat straight up in his chair. The last thing he needed right now was an angry world leader. Dragos coughed a lung out, then cleared his throat. "When the demons began spilling into that village, you told me to send American troops in because they knew how to handle them. You told me that I would lose too many of my own men because they were not trained to handle those monsters."

"Yes, sir. And that was what we did." The general gulped down some whiskey. This conversation was already going downhill.

Dragos snarled, "But that is *not* what happened. I do not know what they did out there. The town is covered with lava. Destroyed. There are reports of demons roaming the countryside, and this morning piles of bodies were found in the main chapel of the larger church. The number of survivors dwindled quickly, and I am left with an absolute mess on my hands."

The general cleared his throat, bringing the troop numbers up on his screen. "President Dragos, I apologize if you were not satisfied with the protection our troops provided. I am not sure, even if we tripled the number of troops, that we could have stopped the lava flow. Many people were killed before we had time to react."

Dragos snapped, "And once you got there, what did you do? You patrolled, you looked for lost soldiers, and you helped a few of your own survivors. There are still troops there from what I understand, but all they do is roam the lava streets looking for what? Ghosts? These people can't go back to their homes; they can't leave. They can't even seek medical treatment in their own country. My people are suffering, General."

Brushwood rubbed his face, trying to understand where this was coming from. Just two days before, the president had lauded them for their efforts. "I don't know what I can do at this point. We only have so many troops, and they are already spread thin. Here in the States, we are having daily incursions just like yours. I don't have any more men to send to you. We lost a lot of our noble troops in the Romanian battle."

President Dragos scoffed. "That was not my fault. You made a promise, and I expect you to fulfill it. I could have done this my way from the beginning, but instead I trusted you."

"President, I have tremendous sympathy for the people of your country. I promise I do. I just don't know how to make things easier for you. I could recruit Katie again. I could send a team back over there to search for rogue demons. That would at least allow people to leave their homes and get medical attention."

Dragos growled, "Your Katie is absolutely unreliable. She came here to find her team, and that was it. She got in some sort of battle in the church where a half a dozen soldiers were killed, then she left. This happened in my country, but I didn't get that report until now. You should have informed me."

The general nodded. "You are right, I should have contacted you immediately. I was trying to figure out what we were dealing with before we called. As far as Katie, she was not sent there on assignment. She went of her own accord to save our Special Forces team. She is one of the most reliable fighters and bravest people I have ever met. If you are not comfortable with her, I won't send her. The problem then becomes, I have very few people to send." The general hesitated, then stated, "There *is* Juntto, I suppose."

Dragos barked bitter laughter. "I ask for help and you want to send me a monster? He is worse than Katie! No.

There has to be something you can do. The major fight is over, but we are still being attacked. A child was killed yesterday by a rogue demon. She will not be the last, General. That is unacceptable on all counts."

The general winced. "That is terrible news. I'm so sorry for that loss. It is inevitable that when you have a crisis of this magnitude you will lose people. Not everything will be simple."

"I am not looking for simple, I am looking for effective."

Brushwood pulled up his schedule and began making himself a note. "I may not have extra troops to send over, but that doesn't mean we are out of ideas. Let me see if I can help the people of Romania in some other way. Give me a little bit of time to put the pieces together and I'll send you a plan. I won't leave you stranded, President Dragos. The American word, a least through me, is still worth something."

Dragos calmed a bit. "Good. Call me when you have a plan. I will be waiting by the phone."

The president slammed the phone down in the general's ear. Brushwood grimaced and hung up. No big hitters, fine. He didn't like the ungrateful tone in Dragos's voice, but he couldn't let innocent people go without defense. He leaned back in his chair and rocked, sipping his whiskey thoughtfully. After a moment, he sat up straight and grabbed his phone. He dialed Korbin's number.

It rang a couple of times before it was answered. "This is Korbin. How can I help you, General?"

Brushwood was relieved to hear his voice. "It's been a long time since the two of us have tackled a problem together."

Korbin chuckled. "Is that what we are about to do?"

The general growled, "I sure as hell hope so."

"Hold on." There was a shuffling sound as Korbin walked into a quieter room. "What can I do for you, General?"

"I just got a call from the Romanian president. He is not happy with the way that things have gone. There are demons in the countryside, and survival rates are plummeting. There's a lack of decent medical care, and he is pissed that we didn't let him know about what happened in the church."

Korbin was surprised. "Really? I just saw him giving a rousing speech of thanks to the United States two days ago. What changed?"

"Stress. Pressure from the rest of the country. I'm not sure."

Korbin was quiet for a minute. "Why don't you send Katie back there on an actual hunt? She is great at smoothing people over, too. I think Pandora could have old Dragos eating out of her palm by the end of it."

The general shook his head. "Apparently Dragos does not believe she did an adequate job of protecting them last time. He rejected my offer to send her, and there is nothing I can do about that. I am calling because I need your help designing fortifications. Weren't you interested in designing modern castles? Fortifications for a new era?"

Korbin perked up. "I was, sure. We've only implemented my ideas at the base so far."

"Well, if I can't send any more troops, I need to do something else to help protect these people."

"You want fortifications for the Romanian town?"

"In all honesty, we are going to need these all over the world. Right now, though, yes. Let's set up a test facility outside the recently destroyed Romanian town. Hopefully we can make the president happy and repair our relationship."

Korbin chuckled. "You can't win for losing, can you, sir? I can fly out there and help them set up their defenses. While I'm there, I'll check on those rogue demons. I just need to get a few things in order before I can leave. As you might imagine, it's been a mess around here."

The general rubbed his chin. "I heard. I'm sorry about the guys. They did their duty."

Korbin looked out the door and down the hall. "They did. Now we're all praying that Brock lives to see the end of the war."

"In that, I will join you."

9

Timothy swiveled in his chair and stretched his arms out, showing off the control room. "Do you like what I've done to the place? Figured it would be nice to have a comfortable area."

Stephanie leaned against the doorframe of the control room. It was decorated in purple and black, much like her home before she joined the mercs. "I like it! Very gothic and sexy."

Timothy beamed at the Victorian clawfoot couch on the righthand side of the room. "I put a sitting area in so I can get away for a second without losing track of what's going on. I even have the alarms set up so I can plug in and listen to music in my headphones. If an alarm goes off, it will interrupt the music and let me know. I foresee many a good nap happening on that couch. Smooth out the wrinkles I've acquired working this job."

Stephanie laughed as he grabbed her hand and pulled her to the couch. She sat next to him and he crossed his legs, putting his hands on his knees and batting his eyelashes. Stephanie ran her fingers over the mahogany coffee table, shaking her head. "You went all out. I'll have to have you design some rooms in my home if we ever go back there."

"Yaasss, queen. Then we can have girl time; do hair, drink tea, and all that good stuff."

Stephanie smiled sweetly as she leaned back on the couch. "So, what did you want to chat about today? I was so happy you called me down here. It's been forever since we had one of our gab sessions."

Timothy rolled his eyes. "I know. Good God, it's been ages. But, I'm not here for the juicy gossip this time. I was actually hoping I could talk to you about something a bit more serious."

Stephanie sat up immediately. "Of course. Are you all right?"

"Yes. Well, no. I don't know. To be honest with you, despite the beauty of our sisterhood, I've been pretty miserable since I became infected. I make do with what I have, of course. I buy new clothes and keep myself busy with decorating, but there is just something missing."

Stephanie shook her head. "I understand. You're lonely."

Timothy sighed. "You could say that. I have been unable to have any sort of real relationship since all of this happened. I may talk a juicy game, girl, but I crave that companionship."

Stephanie bit the inside of her cheek. "Well, I'm sure there are other gay men who have been infected, or maybe someone like Sofia who doesn't mind it. In fact, I think she finds it sexy."

Timothy put his palms flat together and pressed his

fingertips to his lips. "There is no drought in men, but my demon is not the least bit interested. In fact, he loathes the idea of it. He's a complete homophobe. He pitches a fit every time I get feelings. It's not very conducive to a relationship. Think about it this way: what if your demon prevented you from being with Korbin?"

Stephanie's heart dropped into her stomach just thinking about it. "Oh, Timothy, I'm so sorry. I never thought about it in that way. I would absolutely die if I couldn't be with Korbin. He is the person for me. But what are the options here? The world is a frightening place for the mere mortal."

Timothy groaned. "Oh, I know. I fully understand just how dangerous it can be for the non-infected. Their bodies are fragile, they are all alone, and they can't fight off the demons even with our special weapons. It's like walking onto a battlefield in a bathing suit. But still, I can't help but remember what it was like before this. It's all a bit foggy, though."

Stephanie's heart went out to Timothy. "Did you like your life before this?"

Timothy scoffed, slapping Stephanie's knee. "God, no. Please. I lived in my mother's basement hacking shit all day. And don't even get me started on my fashion choices. Girl, it was a dark dungeon disaster. But now I know what the world has to offer. I grew into myself. Now I think I've outgrown the demon inside me. What was it like for you without a demon? You spent quite a long time free from the shackles."

Stephanie sat back again and looked at the ceiling with a small smirk on her lips. "Things were definitely more colorful. The silence in my head was amazing. It wasn't always perfect, though. Thinking about how fragile I was, I can't believe I took the risks I did. It was tough sometimes, but most of the time it was really nice."

Timothy leaned his head on the back of the couch, staring at Stephanie. "And what was it like to control your body?"

Stephanie laughed. "That was the best part. I couldn't do all the cool shit I can do now, of course. Demons have their uses. But I had full, uninterrupted control of my body. I could make whatever choices I wanted, and I would either reap the benefits or suffer the consequences, but the choices were all mine."

Timothy shook his head, closing his eyes. "Oh, to have my body back. To have control. It would be so amazing. I could touch anyone I wanted, do anything I pleased, and just be me. I don't do a lot of cool tricks like the rest of you, since my demon is a bit of an ass. For me it would be almost a clean sweep. It would be me just being me and no one else."

Stephanie lifted an eyebrow. "Why are you asking all this, anyway? You've never brought it up before. Does it have something to do with Brock and the guys losing their demons? If you're feeling jealous, just remember that the grass is not always greener on the other side. They are in serious pain."

Timothy stood up, leaning over and kissing Stephanie on the cheek. "Right now, I don't know what will come of me thinking about it. It's probably nothing. I don't want to say anything until I have talked to Katie a bit. I'm going to go look for her. Have you seen her recently?"

Stephanie narrowed her eyes. "Just don't do anything rash. Think it through."

Timothy swatted his hands. "Duh, this queen will never sacrifice her body or soul. Nope."

Stephanie chuckled. "In that case, I think she is in the dining area upstairs."

Timothy stopped in the doorway. "Love you."

Stephanie put her legs on the couch. "Love you too. Gonna hide out in here for a bit."

Timothy winked and took off down the hall. He leaped up the stairs two steps at a time, then walked down the hall and stuck his head into the kitchen. Katie was sitting at the kitchen table with two full boxes of donuts and one empty one. She had sugar and icing all over her fingers and the remains of countless donuts crusted on her lips. She was slumped forward in the chair with a morose look on her face.

Timothy raised both eyebrows. "Good Lord, child, you look like you shouldn't even be wearing pants."

Katie glanced at him and groaned. "I'm stress-eating."

Timothy walked to the table and handed her a napkin. "Start with this. I think we might have to hose you off later."

She pushed aside the empty box and offered a nearly empty box to Timothy.

"I'm all right, girl. You go ahead."

Katie dug in. "Don't judge me. This is my go-to in really crazy times. It's been a while."

Timothy sneered. "Uh, that's probably a good thing."

Katie's belly was sticking out slightly from the sheer number of donuts she had consumed. Pandora wasn't helping. She was already comatose, victim of a sugar crash.

Timothy reached out and took Katie's sticky hands in his. "I love you so much I'm going to ignore the way your skin sticks to mine right now. Look, I know Brock means a lot to you. I'm sorry that you are having to go through this. I think I might have a solution."

Katie lifted an eyebrow. "What's that?"

Timothy sat up straight, clasping his hands in front of him. "I've decided to give up my demon for Brock."

Katie's face slowly fell. "What? But what about you?"

Timothy waved his hands. "I'll be fine. I mean, seriously, I've been in this post forever now. All I ask is that when Pandora takes him out of me she figures out a way to keep my memory intact. I still plan on staying here in this position as a non-infected. It is important to me to do this."

"I don't know what to say. I can't promise your memory will remain intact."

"Calvin is a bit fuzzy, but he seems fine, so it's possible."

"I need to talk to Pandora." Katie rubbed her chin and made her demon wake up. *Can you do that?*

Pandora thought about it for a moment after she was firing on all cylinders again. *Pretty sure I can. I just have to concentrate a bit. Keep my focus from spreading. Shouldn't be an issue. With my angel powers, things are a bit easier these days.*

Really?

Shit, I don't know. Probably. This isn't an exact science, sweetheart.

But probably?

Probably.

Katie squealed. She jumped up from her seat and ran

around the table to throw her arms around Timothy. She squeezed and shook him like a rag doll. He patted her on the back and wheezed slightly. "Honey? Oh, God, honey, you are going to kill me."

Katie smiled and let go. "Sorry. This is just so amazing. My only thing is, I feel bad for infecting him without his approval."

Timothy waved her off. "Girl, bye-bye with that bullshit. He loves what he does. If he woke up and was told that he wouldn't be allowed to do it, he would be devastated. Besides, Brock needs a demon to heal. You're just giving him medicine. You can always exorcise him if he doesn't want it anymore."

Pandora smirked. *This* chica *has a point.*

Katie pondered it for a moment, then grinned. "Let's do this."

Down the sterile white hallways and inside of one of the surgery areas, Timothy lay on one of the tables. A satin sheet was stretched under him, and a cashmere blanket covered his body. His hands were harnessed at his sides and straps held his legs at the ankles. "I told them tying me down wasn't necessary. He wants to go as much as I want him gone, but they insisted." Timothy lowered his voice. "Have you been strapped down like this before? It's amazing."

Katie chuckled, but Pandora was intrigued. *It's been a few thousand years since I was into rope play. Something to keep in mind.*

Katie smiled. "I'll have Pandora come out to do this. You two have met."

Timothy pursed his lips. "Yass, girl. She is fabulous."

Pandora laughed as she stepped out of Katie's body. She wore a tight white strapless bodycon dress with red heels.

Timothy whistled. "Look at those heels."

"Look, but don't touch." She leaned over Timothy and sniffed, rubbing her hand over his forehead. "Just hold still, princess. Momma's gonna take care of this."

Pandora focused hard. She tried to separate the demon from Timothy's memories. She would usually just yank the whole thing out at once, but she wanted to keep Timothy intact. In reality she wasn't sure she could do it, but she figured it was better to keep that to herself. Timothy wanted the demon to go either way, and if he forgot, they would remind him. Besides, Katie had proven good at restoring memories thus far.

Pandora's hand moved down Timothy's chest. He clenched his eyes shut. When she reached the center of his body, where his demon's energy was strongest, talons grew at the ends of her fingertips. She whispered to herself as she slowly pushed her hand into Timothy's chest and grasped the demon. When she pulled the snarling creature from his body, Timothy groaned and passed out.

The thing immediately began to curse, but not at Pandora.

The demon held tightly to Pandora's hand. "You fucking douche bag. I am so happy to be rid of you. All I want is a little trim! Is that so wrong? An eternity in hell would be much better than a human life in *that*."

Pandora narrowed her eyes. "Be nice. He is our friend."

The demon spat and cursed some more. Pandora scowled. "Be cool or be fucked, little one."

The demon shivered when he realized who was holding him. "Sorry. Where to now?"

Pandora turned with the demon and walked over to a second hospital bed. Brock, beaten and bruised, lay on the white sheets. Pandora held the demon over Brock. "You are going to save the day. Heal this one double-time, or else."

"Oh, fucking great." The demon rolled his eyes but screeched as she slammed him into Brock's body.

Pandora smirked and pulled her hand out. "Get to work, fuckhead."

Katie was already questioning Dr. Thorough. "Okay, time to get to work. Let's get Brock back to health. What can I do?"

Thorough pushed up his glasses and shrugged nervously. "I'm not sure how long this will take, but it should work. Maybe if the demon had a bit of motivation?"

Katie nodded. "Pandora? Can you get this demon going?"

Pandora snickered. "It would be my pleasure."

She took a deep breath and centered her focus on the demon inside Brock. *Look, bro. I am here to tell you that this isn't a free ride. If this man dies, you are going to be my new personal punching bag, then you'll go back to Timothy.*

Aw, come on!

Shut the fuck up. After I knock the shit out of you and put your dick in a vice, I have no problem putting you back in him.

The demon shivered. *I know. Trust me, I know. I'm looking around right now. I will do my best, but it's nuts in here. It's like whatever took him hollowed him out. It's insane. I've never seen anything like this before.*

Pandora could tell he was being honest. *Well, work with what you have. If you feel like giving up, remember I am watching you, lover boy.*

Pandora turned to the doctors. "Later, nerds." She slid back into Katie's body and sighed. *He is doing what he can. Having that demon just might save Brock's life.*

I hope so. Do me a favor, stop calling the doctors 'nerds.' They're trying to help Brock, too.

That's a tough one. I'll see what I can do.

Timothy moaned, and Katie turned to him. She could feel the tears of gratitude welling in her eyes. She put her hand in his and leaned over him. "Timothy? Are you awake?"

Timothy blinked his eyes twice and took in Katie's face. His eyes floated down to her tits, over her curves, and then rested on her ass. He looked back at her face, expressionless. Katie stood up straight. "Oh God. I think you un-gayed him, Pandora. How do you even do that?"

I told you, this shit isn't an exact science.

Timothy smiled mischievously. "Just kidding. I was just double-checking. Making sure I had that damn demon out of my head once and for all. See, normally when I glance at your ass or your tits, the demon would make some sort of crude remark about you. This time there was nothing but glorious silence."

Katie burst into laughter. "Oh, my God, it worked! You can remember everything?"

Timothy looked at the ceiling with his hand to his cheek. "Mmmhmm, every little detail. The color of my control room, and all the words to the Hamilton musical. That night with Willy Blackburn. It's so good not to have that pussy-hound demon voice yapping in my skull. Oh, God, girl, it's almost orgasmic."

Katie giggled. "Do you feel free?"

"Like I could hide from danger with a Mai Tai and my computer for the rest of days. I will have to watch my body fat, though. That was the only thing the asshole did for me."

Timothy sat up and looked across the room at Brock. "I hope he does more for you, man."

Katie nodded soberly. "Me, too."

"Come one, come all, enter my No More Hound in My Head coming-out re-release party!" Timothy stood in the doorway to the living area, his arms raised like a carnival barker's.

Timothy had gone all-out for the event. He was wearing his favorite pleated pink dress pants, matching vest, black button-up, and a tie with flamingos on it. His hair was gelled to perfection, his eyeliner was on fleek, and his yellow-tinted glasses had Hollywood glam-sized frames.

Stephanie had helped with the decorations, including a flamingo-shaped ice sculpture for shots, balloons everywhere, and of course as much glitter as humanly possible. They would be living in a sparkly snow globe for the next decade. Timothy had gotten special permission from the general to allow the security detail to come to the party. They were all stunned by the inside of the place.

One of the soldiers used his beer to point to the huge flat-screen on the wall. "Shit, if we're gonna be fighting, we should join the mercs. At least we would get a badass pad."

Stephanie overheard this and walked up. "You boys enjoying yourselves?"

The soldier with the beer stood at attention. "Yes, ma'am. We were just talking about how nice it was in here."

Stephanie sipped her drink through a flamingo straw. "Your housing isn't like this?"

The guys chuckled, thinking about the military housing on the other side of the base. "No, ma'am. We have standard military-issue insane-asylum-gray walls and decades-old bunks, but it's what we expect in the military."

Stephanie shook her head. "That just won't do. You are protecting one of the most important assets in the world. You need to have a good place to lie down at night. I'll see what I can do."

Katie came through the door and stopped. She marveled at the decorations. Timothy ran over and gave her a kiss on each cheek. "Oh, my lady. How are you? You look fabulous."

Katie looked down at her leather stretch pants, stilettos, and the white t-shirt tied at the waist. Her hair was down and pulled to one side. She had let Pandora give her smoky eyes. "Thanks. They said look trendy, so here I am. It's the best I can do."

Timothy giggled. "Well, come in. There is food on the table, drinks against the back wall, and if you want to hear anything special, just let me know. I have the iPod plugged in."

Katie smirked. "I will. This doesn't even look like the living room."

Timothy put his hand to his chest. "I know, right? Stephanie did a fab job, as always."

Katie got a drink and waved at Stephanie, who was talking to a couple of the guards. Pandora sniffed. *Okay, what is wrong with you? You are pouting at a party.*

Katie swallowed her drink. *Nothing. I mean, I guess I just feel bad for partying while Brock is laid up in the med unit.*

Pandora groaned. *Man, you are* hooked. *He would want you to have fun. Besides, the doctors say he is already getting better. He will be up to boning in no time.*

Katie's eyes fell on Calvin, who was sitting uncomfortably on the couch. She walked over, helping him lean his crutches on the wall. She sat down next to him and whispered, "You look like you are incredibly uncomfortable."

Calvin chuckled. "Who knew being human and having a few broken bones would be so difficult?"

Katie laughed. "I don't even remember what it was like. I'm sure it feels strange. How are you doing with it all?"

Calvin took a deep breath and shrugged. "It's different. It's been over a decade since I was infected, and that's a long time. In reality, I miss Marty. He was a taco-loving asshat, but it was like having a pain-in-the-ass brother by your side. You can't stand him while he's in your face and sharing your room, but when he moves away for college, you miss his shitty antics."

Pandora took over Katie's voice. "I'll come inside you."

Katie clamped her hand over her mouth, shocked. "That wasn't me."

"Oh, I knew who that was." Calvin laughed. "Thanks, Pandora. I think I'm okay. There's no way I am rocking this life with someone like you inside me."

Pandora pouted. "Come on. You could share me with Katie. It'll be fun."

Katie pushed Pandora out. "I think he's good with the silence, Pandora. No offense."

Pandora peeked back in. "I don't mind sharing you with Sofia."

"I think I'm good without the constant body makeovers and donut obsession. Never really liked donuts." Calvin shrugged.

Pandora gasped. *What? I am disowning this man. That's the last straw.*

Katie shook her head. Calvin looked at Sofia, who was in mid-conversation. She caught Calvin's eye and winked at him, smiling slightly. He smiled back, and something unspoken passed between them. Katie loved seeing her friend so happy. "Now you get to spend some quality time with Sofia, right? You guys can redo your Mexican vacation or something, minus the drug cartels."

Calvin chuckled, but stopped. He went wide-eyed. "Oh, shit. I should tell you that Sofia popped the question."

Katie was stunned. "What? When? Oh, my God!"

Pandora made a gagging sound. *All this fucking love is giving me a headache.*

Calvin nodded. "When she first got here."

"And?" Katie was practically standing on the couch. The suspense was killing her.

Calvin snorted. "Of course, I said yes!"

Katie threw her arms around Calvin. "*What*! Oh, my God! That is so exciting. Congratulations!"

Timothy popped over to the couch next. "What are we congratulating him for?"

Katie glanced at Calvin. He nodded, letting her know it was okay. "Calvin and Sofia got engaged!"

Timothy clapped his hands together. "Ohh, I love weddings. This is so fantastic." His face grew dark. "But, really, Calvin? You had to break this news at my coming-out party?"

Calvin held up his hands. "I didn't mean to intrude!"

"Just teasing you, darlin'. Well, fuck it." Timothy clapped his hands three times. "Attention, everyone! I want to thank you all for coming out to celebrate my fabulous self, but we are scratching the No More Hound in My Head Party. It is now an engagement party for Calvin and Sofia!"

A cheer went up from the crowd. Timothy rolled his eyes. "Ugh! We're going to need a lot more champagne."

10

Belphegor leaned down as if he were tying his shoe. Instead, he pulled back on the skin on his cheeks, situating the flesh. He had yet to pick an appropriate body for his size, but he supposed it was too late. The leaders of various countries already knew his face and assumed everything he said was true. He had to stay the course, even if that meant a slightly saggy face.

The Chancellor of Germany, Adler Schroder, tucked his napkin into the front of his shirt. "I was told, but remind me of your name."

Belphegor tried his best human smile. "Belfast. Just call me Belfast."

"Belfast, then. You are a lawyer for the Council?"

Belphegor pulled at the neck of his shirt. "Yes. I'd like to speak to you about the mercenaries and this war."

Just then the food arrived. The server placed two large plates of sauerkraut in front of Belphegor and an array of meats and sausages in front of Schroder. The chancellor gave his plate an admiring look, but Belphegor dove in. He shoveled sauerkraut into his drooping jaws like he hadn't eaten in weeks. He burped softly as he finished one plate and moved on to the next.

Schroder chewed a piece of sausage and sipped his lager. "What do you wish to discuss with me?"

Belphegor wiped his face with his napkin and looked across the table at him. "I would like to discuss Katie and her team of mercenaries. Specifically, her overreach. She has unlimited power when it comes to the demon war. No one to answer to, and no one to control her."

Schroder sat back, wiping his hands. "I disagree with you on that. I believe she has proper oversight. General Brushwood in the States directs her. Katie and her teams have saved many German lives over the years. I would be hard-pressed to muzzle her now."

Belphegor narrowed his gaze. "Understandable, but maybe you haven't given it the right amount of thought. Romania was also very supportive of Katie and her team until a few tough questions were asked. The more questions we asked, the more suspicious her activities looked."

"Questions like what?"

Belphegor smiled. "Like, does this Katie end up doing more harm than good in the long run? Who does she answer to? Shouldn't she be answering to the World Council?"

Schroder thought about it for a second. "The World Council has only recently been formed."

Belphegor nodded. "Yes, and it should have been the first business on the agenda. The Council should have pushed to gain control of these mercenary forces. She is able to travel the world, destroying cities and towns and bringing demons into countries. Oh, yes, she brings them. They look for her specifically. And if they can't find her, the demons destroy cities as retaliation for her actions. If she were on a tighter leash, how many incursions could have been prevented?"

The chancellor waved his food away and waited for the waitress to refill his stein. He took a big gulp and wiped his lips. "Yes, but she will be less inclined to help us if we pile on restrictions."

Belphegor took a deep breath and put his napkin on his plate. He pushed his chair back and leaned toward the chancellor, putting both palms on the table. "I can see you need to think about what I'm saying a little more."

Belphegor nodded to the next table, where three scantily-clad women were watching them closely. "Please enjoy. I took the liberty of booking them for the night. I figured they could help you relax and think about the situation at hand, and perhaps in the morning you will come to a clearer decision on Katie and the mercenaries."

The chancellor smiled at the prostitutes and looked at Belphegor, shuffling in his seat. "This is a bribe."

Belphegor grinned and quickly straightened the chancellor's tie. "No, no! I just want to give you time to think. To relax, so you can understand the seriousness of the situation. The world must have laws, and this Katie, well, she thinks she is above the law. You don't believe anyone should be above the law, do you?"

Schroder looked at the girls, then back at Belphegor. "I suppose without laws we have pure chaos."

Belphegor stood up. "Exactly. And with chaos comes terror. I can see Katie's red eyes glistening in the German night sky as we speak. She swoops down and delivers her own form of punishment to those she feels aren't living up to her expectations. We wouldn't want you to be ripped from your home and carried off by a demon angel who thinks she is better than you, would we?"

Schroder shook his head. "No one tells me how to act in my own country. I make the choices, and we as an authority punish those who do not live up to our standards. We do not go by the rule of some girl."

Belphegor stood up with a smile on his face. "You are starting to see where we might have a problem. The World Council is looking out for the best interests of the world. No one said we cannot harness the power of Katie and her angel-demon, but we will need to use her powers in a restricted manner. She cannot be allowed to continue this reign of terror over the citizens of the world."

Belphegor waved the prostitutes over. "Think about these things. Mull over your choices as you enjoy an evening of relaxation on me."

Belphegor picked up his briefcase and walked from the restaurant. Schroder looked at the prostitutes, then waved at his assistant. "Clear my schedule for the rest of the day. I suddenly feel the need to rest up."

Wild webs of gray swirled around Brock. The sound of Sasha's moans echoed through his head and he gasped for air, trying to work his way out of the thick goop surrounding him. He pressed his hands against an invisible shell encapsulating his body. All at once a terrible pain shot through his body. It was his demon dying inside him.

Brock gasped lightly and opened his eyes. The room was too bright. It took a moment for his eyes to adjust. He put his hand to his chest. He could feel the presence of a demon inside of him. He knew it was there, but for some reason everything felt different. He couldn't put his finger on the reason, but it was drastic. His hands slid down to the edge of his cotton blanket and looked around the room. A steadily beeping EKG machine was hooked up to his chest, and a clear fluid of some kind was being dripped into his arm.

With some effort, he turned his head. He had to put his hand on the railing of the bed to steady himself. Katie was curled up in an armchair next to him. Her face was still, and her hair fell over one shoulder. The skin of her face was pale, and her cheeks glimmered and glistened in the bright lights of the room. She clutched the edge of his blanket in her outstretched hand, and Brock wondered just how long she had been there. He wondered how long he had been there, too. His mind was foggy, but slowly, bits and pieces came back to him. The last thing he remembered was being face to face with the monster who called herself Sasha, but he could not remember what happened next.

Brock rested his head back on the pillow and stared at Katie, warmth gathering in his chest. He hadn't forgotten just how amazing she was, but until that moment, he hadn't realized how much he cared about her. She was not only gorgeous and, honestly, amazing in bed, but she was kind. Despite having the wife of Lucifer inhabiting her body, she was one of the best people he knew. It didn't hurt that she was one badass bitch when it came to kicking demon ass.

A voice began to speak in Brock's head, but he didn't recognize it. *Man, there is a lot more room in here. No more of that cramped shit. And the strength! You are one strong dude.*

Brock narrowed his eyes. *Who are you? Where is my demon?*

The demon chuckled. *She was sucked out by the eight-legged freak you keep dreaming about. Of course, if you want her back, I could look around?*

Brock shook his head. *No, I don't want her back. How did you get in here?*

Wild fucking story, brother. That crazy chick over there? A badass demon popped out of her. Lilith, I recognized her right away. She pulled me out of Timothy, threatened my balls if I didn't heal you, and shoved me in here. Bro, you were on the verge of death. I used all my powers and skills to fix you up. My name's Wormwood.

Brock swallowed hard, still not fully comprehending. He had to set some ground rules, that much he knew. *Wormwood, I want to make one thing clear. I'm in control of this body and my mind, no matter what you're capable of. I think by now you know I have ties to some demons who could kick your ass.*

Wormwood hissed. *Calm down, dude. I don't want to take over. I just really hope you like chicks. I haven't gotten laid in a very long time.*

Brock thought about it for a second. *Yeah, I guess not. Timothy isn't a chick kind of guy. None of that matters to me, though. My demon might have been a pain, but she understood the boundaries.*

Wormwood sighed. *Fine, fine. I don't want anything to do with controlling this meatsack. I've never been very good at the wheel. It's embarrassing. I really couldn't get the whole control of the body while controlling the bladder thing. Last dude I tried to control pissed himself at least four times a day. Not cool. Timothy? We pretty much kept to ourselves.*

Brock wrinkled his nose. *Yeah, I got my bladder. Don't worry about that.*

Okay. I'm still fixing your liver, but you're almost good to go. By the way, you like chicks, right? I need a firm answer here.

I like women, yeah.

Wormwood was relieved. *Good. Now that we got that settled, how about we pick up that guitar you keep thinking about and get us some ass ASAP? Okay?*

Brock couldn't help but laugh. He tried to cover his mouth so as to not wake up Katie, but he failed. Katie opened her eyes and sat up quickly. Brock lay there smiling at her. "Brock! You're awake!"

Brock nodded. "Seems that way."

He grunted as he pushed himself to a sitting position. Katie moved over and put down the rail on the bed, perching on the edge. Before he could say another word, her arms were wrapped around him.

Katie had to hold herself back or she was afraid she'd squeeze him to death. "I'm sorry. We just weren't sure it was all going to work out."

Brock smiled as she pulled back. "What the hell happened?"

Katie shook her head. "I have no idea. You were missing

for a long time, but we found you in the old church in Romania. There were these cocoons, and you and your team were in them. We cut them down, but then this beast came down from the rafters. I don't know how else to say it. She started to suck the energy right out of Pandora. We tried to fight her, but for every leg I cut off, another would grow in its place, and fast. You ended up stabbing her in the gut with your sword and she ran off. We brought you and the guys back here to recover. She had done her energy-sucking trick on you, too. All of your demons were lost. They were just gone. Timothy sacrificed his demon so you could heal. Without it, you would have died."

Brock immediately sat up further. "And my guys? Are they okay?"

Katie pushed him gently back. "Turner, Sean, and Eddie are all recovering very nicely. They don't have demons anymore, but their injuries were far less serious than yours. They are awake, though, and really want to know how you are doing."

Brock relaxed once he knew his guys were okay. "I've never felt anything like that before. She latched on, but she didn't even have to touch me. When she breathed in there was pressure in my chest, and it felt as if my entire body was lifting off. All the good, the bad, the ugly, and the beautiful was coming right out of my mouth into hers. I wanted to stop it, to scream and fight her, but the more she pulled, the less I was able to fight back."

Katie put her hand on his. "I don't know what to say. I can't imagine. Pandora was out of my body when Sasha attacked. After, she told me it was like Sasha drained her. Like she made an empty place inside of her."

Brock nodded. "That's a good description of it. It was like being hollow. Like my soul had been deflated."

Pandora sighed. *When we put Wormwood in there, he said it looked like he had been hollowed out. I bounced back fast, so I know he will feel whole again. It will just take a bit of time.*

Katie squeezed his hand. "Pandora says you will be back to normal, but it will take time. Do you remember much?"

Brock shook his head. "No. I mean, what I do remember comes in flashes. When I remember her taking my energy, seems like it was days before you arrived. Then I remember flashes of stabbing her with my sword, but that's it. Like a dream sequence almost. When I woke up a minute ago, I saw you lying there asleep." Brock's lips curled up into a smile. "I have to admit, it seemed to fill my soul back up again."

Pandora scoffed. *You sure that wasn't your pants?*

Wormwood couldn't hear Pandora but made a comment of his own. *Filled up more than my soul, if you know what I mean.*

Brock tried not to make a face. *Are you already ruining moments with other people? Don't make me have Pandora muzzle you.*

Wormwood grumbled. *Fine, I'll say it more nicely. I like this chick. She seems cool, calm, level-headed, and together. Not the kind of* chica *who would stab you in the middle of the night or burn your house down for the insurance money.*

Brock twitched. *Good fuck, what kind of girls have you been hanging out with?*

Wormwood chuckled creepily. *Oh, you wish you knew. Wild women, brother. Wild.*

Katie watched Brock's face twitch. She figured he was

probably talking to his new demon. Pandora yawned. *Did you see his eyes twinkle when he fucking saw you? It was gross. This dude has it bad for you. Like, so bad.*

Katie let a little smirk cross her lips and looked down until she could straighten her face. She stood up and kissed Brock on the forehead. "Get some rest. Trust me, you're gonna need it."

With a sly wink, she sauntered from the room, leaving Brock speechless and Wormwood cheering.

Angie turned her head away from the window of the plane and looked at Juntto, who was playing his Nintendo DS. His chiseled chin twitched as he clenched his teeth, pressing the buttons hard. Angie had requested he look like Channing Tatum again, but anything would have been better than the creepy-eyed military guy from the cartoon movie. That look freaked her out. Having Channing Tatum next to her definitely kept her warm. Then again, having Juntto in any shape or size made her happy.

"Sonofabitch!" Juntto yelled, dropping the DS in his lap and slamming his head back against the seat.

Angie giggled and reached over to turn the thing off. "It's okay, sweetie. We're almost there anyway. I'm just glad that New Orleans went well and you are back safe and sound. I don't know if I'll ever get used to being in love with a warrior."

Juntto turned his head and smiled. "No need to worry. I am the size of twenty men, and I can kick ass. New

Orleans was simple, and come to find out, Bourbon Street has absolutely no demons. I was very relieved."

Angie lifted an eyebrow. "Oh, I'm *so* glad Bourbon Street is safe."

"Not to worry. Everything is in order."

Angie laughed at him. "Please. You think I don't know you went there to catch a glimpse of tatas?"

Juntto snarled his lip. "Come to find out, women don't like it when you stop them on the street, hand them beads, and stare. I was slapped three times."

Angie giggled, putting the DS in her bag. "That's what you get. You should be glad none of them gave you a black eye. Can you believe, not long ago you would have thrown one of them over your shoulder, or maybe over the side of a mountain? You have come so far."

Juntto leaned in and kissed Angie. "And all because of you. Are you sad to leave New York?"

"Not really. I love the people here, but I'd like to see everyone again. I also heard that Timothy is demon-free now. I am curious to see how that has changed things for him."

Juntto nodded. "I am anxious to see how Brock and the rest of his team are doing. I heard they took quite a beating from a mysterious monster. I will ask them the details of this creature. I have been here long enough that I may recognize who it was."

Angie's face went serious. "Yeah, Katie is really pissed about it. She didn't say much on the phone, but I'm curious to hear everything when we get there. It's not often that our guys go down that hard, not to mention the demons they lost in the process."

Juntto shrugged. "I did not know you could lose your demon and stay alive, unless you were exorcised."

Angie chuckled and Juntto raised his eyebrows at her. She straightened her face. "Sorry, it's just so weird to see Channing Tatum's face and hear your accent. Totally throws me off, but I like it."

Juntto laughed, kissing her again. Just then the plane began its descent, and the two stared out the window until the wheels of the plane hit the runway. It was the first flight Angie had taken where she wasn't afraid. Then again, she had a man who could just jump out of a plane with her and land safely below. How could she be afraid of flying when she had Juntto?

When the plane came to a stop, Juntto and Angie walked down the steps with their bags on their shoulders. Angie kissed Juntto on the cheek. "I'm going to go find everyone and see what's up."

Juntto took a step with her but stopped. "I'd like to go the med bay and check with the doctor. I want to make sure everything is on the up and up."

Angie nodded and kissed his cheek. She headed into the main building and strolled down the hall, then poked her head around the corner into the living room. Stephanie, Katie, and Timothy were crowded onto the couch, talking excitedly to Sofia. Katie looked up and smiled excitedly. "Hey, girl! I didn't realize you were going to be here so fast."

Angie skipped into the room and kissed Timothy on the cheek. "We were ready early, so we headed on over. What are you guys doing?"

Timothy patted the seat next to him. "Talking about the wedding!"

Angie clapped her hands. "That's right! Congratulations! Do you know what you want your dress to look like?"

Sofia gave her an "of course" smile. "Something tight and strapless that flairs out at the bottom."

Angie cooed as Timothy showed her a picture. "You would look fabulous in that. *My* boobs would fall right out."

Sofia giggled. "That's why you tape those suckers down."

They talked about the cake, the music, and all the details. Angie shook her head at all the excitement. "So much to do. When are you thinking? Next year?"

Sofia looked at Angie and grinned. "Actually, that was what I wanted to talk to you all about. We want to do it at the end of next week."

Everyone freaked out. Timothy put his hand to his head and pretended to faint. Sofia laughed and folded her hands in her lap. "The thing is, I feel like Calvin and I have spent enough time waiting for each other. I could have lost him on this last run, but he survived it and was given a second chance at a normal life. I don't think there is any more time to lose."

Stephanie giggled excitedly. "I don't blame you. You never know what tomorrow will bring."

Sofia pointed at her. "Exactly. We are ready to start living our lives together."

11

Juntto walked into the med bay, slowing down as he rounded the corner. Doctor Ozu looked up from his desk and tilted his head to the side. "Channing Tatum?"

Juntto looked down at himself and chuckled, morphing his body into a smaller version of the blue frost giant. "Sorry. I get less attention when I don't walk around like this."

The doctor laughed. "I was utterly confused for a moment, Juntto. You look healthy. How are you feeling?"

Juntto sat down on the other side of his desk. "I feel good—really good. Things are different. I seem to get more powerful the more people I save. Positivity really gets me going."

Doctor Ozu closed the file in front of him. "You could start a business as a motivational speaker."

Juntto shook his head. "Don't like crowds much, especially the ones who stare at me."

"Me either. What can I do for you? I am assuming you came to see the guys."

"I did, but I wanted to stop by and thank you for taking care of me. I never got a chance to say that after waking up."

Ozu took a deep breath. "Of course. You were one of the most interesting patients I have ever had. I will be right here, or somewhere close, if you ever need me again."

Juntto chuckled. "I hope that's not necessary. As nice as the nap was, I don't think I want to go back into that freezer again. Hopefully, life starts to settle down a bit."

Ozu clapped his hands together. "I hope for that too. And I don't blame you; it *was* a bit chilly in there. It's actually funny that you stopped by at this moment."

"Why is that?"

Ozu pulled out a sheet of paper and glanced down at it. "Well, General Brushwood contacted me a few days ago. He has asked me to fabricate some experimental weapons for you. Of course, I would be using Joshua as my main man."

Juntto pumped his fist. "That is amazing news. When I am full-sized, I struggle when I use anything but my fists. I usually get torn up because I have to be close to be effective. A ranged weapon is what I need. It will be nice to fight without demons clawing my legs. Little bastards hurt."

"I imagine that would be uncomfortable. We are doing our best to accommodate you and the general. Just remember, weapons don't solve everything. There will still be times you have to throw your body into it."

Juntto smirked. "Oh, I know, and maybe I'll actually look forward to those times again."

Ozu stood up. "Let me get you in to see the boys. They are all in one room right now so they can have some time together, but we're trying to limit their visitors. They need their rest."

The doctor led him to a room down the hall and opened the door for Juntto. Dr. Ozu didn't go in. He knew the guys had more than enough to keep them busy. As soon as Juntto entered the room the guys cheered, happy to see him alive and well.

Juntto looked at Eddie, Turner, and Sean in the beds and Brock in a wheelchair and shook his head. "Should have known you would be over here taking a nice vacation while the rest of us did the real work."

Brock pulled himself up and grabbed some crutches. "Good to see you're still an asshole."

Juntto slapped hands with Brock and laughed. "I wouldn't have to be if you guys were still around. You fill up the asshole ticket fast."

Turner smirked. "You out there landing all the women and kicking demon ass?"

"Not this Leviathan. Kicking demon ass, yes, but I am a one-woman Leviathan now."

Eddie booed, and Sean laughed at Juntto. "Angie's got you all kinds of twisted up, doesn't she?"

Juntto shrugged. "What are you gonna do? She's hot, she puts up with my bullshit, and she plays Destiny better than half the guys online."

Eddie sighed. "Dreamgirl status right there."

Brock nodded at Juntto's bag. "You just get here from New York or from a fight?"

Juntto dropped his bag to the floor and sat down in one

of the chairs. "Both, actually. I went out on an assignment for the general, then grabbed Angie and headed over here. We were in New Orleans."

Eddie shook his head. "Dude, did you go to Bourbon Street and get any fucking amazing food?"

Juntto smiled. "Yeah, I did. I thought there would be a side of tits with my gumbo, but apparently, that's only during Mardi Gras. I settled for the food and the coffee."

Sean wrinkled his nose. "Coffee? What about whiskey? It's New Orleans and you drank coffee? What are you, an old man now?"

Juntto frowned. "I was on assignment. I didn't have time to properly drink and fight all the demons in the city."

Eddie put his hands behind his head. "I remember my first time at Mardi Gras. There were beads, boobs, and beer all over the fucking place. We were dancing in the streets, drinking everything and anything, and having a fucking blast. One day I'm gonna go back."

Turner snickered. "Yeah, 'cause it's the only place he gets to touch titties without getting slapped into next week."

Eddie sneered at Turner. "Very funny. Better than that chick you took home from the Halloween Party last year. We all thought she was in costume, but it turned out she was just that fucking ugly."

Turner shrugged innocently. "Hey, sometimes you just gotta get it done. She was willing and I was able."

Juntto leaned back and bellowed with laughter. He pointed a blue finger at Brock. "How about you? You are up and around. Women love scars and war-wounds. I should know."

Brock looked up but Turner chimed in first. "Nah. This guy done been snatched up by the queen bee herself, Miss Katie. She must have something special, because boyfriend here is whipped."

Brock rolled his eyes. "Not whipped. I just like her."

Juntto nodded. "There is no shame in that. I get it. Ignore these douchebags." He pointed at Eddie. "Especially him."

Eddie shrugged. "What did I do?"

"This is a true warrior! You would be lucky to snag his leftovers."

Sean cackled. "Eddie would be grateful for sloppy seconds."

Juntto was giving them a hard time, but it was seriously boosting their morale. Being stuck in bed without demons to help them heal had taken a real toll on them. They had all thought about what life would be like without their demons, and Juntto's visit was a welcome distraction.

Brock cleared his throat. "You were in New Orleans, so are you working for the general now?"

Juntto leaned forward and pressed his hands together. "That is one of the reasons I'm here. I'm going to be out there fighting in the field until you guys either come back or another task force is deployed. I have been fighting all my life, but you have been fighting demons for a long time. If I am to take over your duties, I would like any advice that you can offer."

The reality of the situation was that Juntto didn't need their advice in the slightest. He had been fighting for centuries and had taken on creatures that would give these men nightmares, but he knew it would make the guys feel better if they were in the loop. He wasn't going to hold back from them. Who knew, maybe something they said would help him.

Turner put his hand up. "Stay away from the claws as best you can. That shit hurts."

"Oh, that's a big one. Very important. You should write that down." Sean grinned at Turner, who flipped him the bird.

Eddie offered, "Always clear out the little demons before going for the big guy. Otherwise, they will nag you to death. Little bitch claws take your attention off the giant swinging fists."

"That's good. Yes. Kill little bitch demons."

"Exactly."

"Okay, okay, that's great advice. Anything else?"

Sean cleared his throat. "Yeah. If you got a weapon, get good with it. Shoot them in the head first to save bullets. Shooting them in the body doesn't do much good unless you explode the heart. Easier to go for a headshot."

"I am still waiting for Juntto-sized weapons, but I will take your suggestions to heart."

The room went quiet for a moment and Turner looked up from his lap. "Any word on the bitch who did this?"

Juntto shrugged. "I don't know. I just got off the plane and came right here."

"She was something else. Like no demon I've ever seen, and I've seen some shit." Eddie let out a deep breath and relaxed back on his bed.

Turner shook his head, letting out a deep sigh. "I sure as fuck hope that the sword Brock stuck in that spider bitch's belly did her in. Hopefully, she shriveled up in a corner somewhere and died."

Juntto perked up. The term spider bitch struck him for some reason. It sounded very familiar.

Korbin looked down at the map in the soldier's hand. They were walking along a perimeter and discussing the line for the new reinforced fence.

The soldier gave him the current status. "We'll start here at the back and work ourselves around. We are hoping to have the back and right side done in one week, then the other two sides done in another week. Two weeks will also give us time to get that barbed wire top finished. Joshua is working on it, but he had to come up with a machine to wind it like thread. He's a smart cookie."

Korbin chuckled. "That he is. That all sounds good. I just wanted to do a last-minute check before I leave."

The soldier smiled. "I know it's hard for you to leave this unfinished."

Korbin took a deep breath. "It is. It's really hard, but I have to trust that my team will complete the base security while I'm gone. Of course, you know how to contact me if you have any questions."

The soldier folded the map. "We do, but all that's left is the fence. That, and a few new guns we are mounting on the towers. The rebuild after the latest attack set us back a couple of weeks, but we're moving full steam ahead, now. There shouldn't be any problems. Besides, your boss lady will be here to help."

"That's right," Stephanie said, walking up behind them.

Korbin kissed her on the forehead. Stephanie looked at the folded map. "Going over the plans one last time?"

The soldier patted Korbin on the shoulder. "I'm gonna go get the men in gear. Let me know if there is anything else you need before you go."

Korbin nodded. "Will do."

Stephanie narrowed her eyes. "Go? Where you going? You didn't finally decide to run off with some Damned yoga instructor, did you?"

Korbin laughed and pulled his wife close. "I got all the limber Damned I could ever want right here in my arms."

Stephanie kissed him but pressed him for answers. "So? Where you going?"

Korbin put his hands in his pockets. "The general called me the other day."

"Really? And what did he want?"

Korbin looked toward the horizon. "He offered me a gig. He wants me to go around to different cities, starting in Romania, and help to fortify them. Set up protections, weapons, fences, and anything else they need. They have to be able to hunker down and fight on their own when the mercs can't be there. We have to start protecting people, you know? There are ten times more demons than fighters."

Stephanie groaned. "Don't remind me. Those things multiply every time there's a new incursion. This last one with the lava was brutal, or so I've heard from the guys. I can't even imagine what that must have been like."

Korbin turned back to Stephanie. "I know, and that's

why we need to get this done. We need these places to be strongholds. I mean, cities all over the world. We can't have the rest of the world falling to demon control. There are a lot of lives left to protect."

Stephanie rubbed her hands on Korbin's arms. "And I think you are the perfect man to do it. You have the know-how and the training, and you can fight if you need to. I know it's something that you have been wanting to do for a long time. I'm glad the general was smart enough to call on you. Will you have a team?"

"It will probably be military. I didn't get all the details, but I know I can't do it alone. I was actually thinking about asking Calvin if he wanted to go with me when he is well enough."

Stephanie tilted her head to the side and giggled. "You might have to pry him out of Sofia's hands. She is chomping at the bit to start a real life with him. They are getting married, then they are gonna relax and enjoy each other. You know, just like we used to do once upon a time."

Korbin smiled. "That we did. We will get back to that point again, trust me. Right now, we just gotta get this war under control."

Stephanie pursed her lips. "Maybe you could ask Timothy. It would probably be a good idea to have someone there who is tech savvy. I know he could probably use some time out of the dungeon."

Korbin thought about it for a second. "What about the comm center?"

Stephanie shrugged lightly. "I know how to work the basics and all of the protections. There's no reason he couldn't go with you. Besides, I want to make sure someone is keeping an eye on you."

Korbin laughed. "So you send the guy who has more scarves than I have socks? His hat collection takes up two closets."

Stephanie nodded. "That's true, but he is also fiercely loyal, and very brave when he needs to be."

"You know what? You're right. Maybe I'll ask him to go along. Lord knows I could use help with all the tech stuff."

"When are you guys going to be leaving?"

"After the wedding. Calvin would kill me if I left before then."

Stephanie giggled. "*Timothy* would kill you. He has a lot invested in this wedding. He is like bridezilla and he's not even the one getting married. God help us all if he ever does. He will drive us all crazy."

Korbin laughed. "Then definitely after the wedding. Maybe even two days after, to let him come down off his high. I'll see what the general needs us to do."

Stephanie sighed. "Well, I'll hold down the fort for you while you're gone. Might be watching a lot of soap operas."

Beelzebub dragged his twisted body through the hall of Baal's castle and slammed open the double doors to his dining room and office. The demon servants scurried in ten different directions, but Baal sat still with his back to the doors. He didn't move a muscle, just continued eating.

Beelzebub walked over in front of him and slammed his hands on the table, knocking a Chihuahua head onto the floor. Baal frowned down at the fallen morsel. "That wasn't nice. Do you know how expensive these things are? They are miniatures. Perfect for an afternoon snack."

Beelzebub puffed air from his scaled nostrils. "I want to know what the fuck is going on!"

Baal popped another head into his mouth and stared at him, emotionless. "Well, right now I am enjoying a snack, and later I will catch up on the news, beat a few demons, then possibly take a walk."

Beelzebub growled. "You know that's not what I mean, Baal. Are you fucking around on Earth? I want the Lucifer-loving truth here. I don't need any more of your bullshit. You act like you're not involved, but I know better than that. You can't bullshit a bullshitter."

Baal rolled his eyes. "Will you calm the fuck down, please? You are going to give me indigestion. I am not fucking around on Earth. As far as I am concerned, I'm retired. Moloch is dead, and my hands are clean. I don't want to be the next one called to Lucifer's chambers. We all know it's never good to be the last demon called into the throne room."

Beelzebub sat down, shaking his head. "Why do I feel like I can't believe you? I know you are up to something here, Baal."

Baal sighed, wiping his hands. "I am done trying to take over Earth. That's a fool's errand. It was not my idea anyway. It started with that moron T'Chezz and spread like wildfire after that. Then Moloch got involved and became obsessed. I'm not stupid. I know where it leads, and I like my head firmly attached to my neck, along with all my other limbs."

Beelzebub watched him closely. The other demon walked to the bar. He poured himself a glass of whiskey and handed one to Beelzebub, who shook his head. Baal shrugged and drank the first in one gulp. He took the second glass to his large leather lounge chair. He crossed one scaled foot over the other and swirled the whiskey in his glass. "You know what is wrong with you, Beelze? You are too stressed out. You have all of hell to roam in, but you are worried about capturing Earth. Give it to Lucifer, is what I say. He'll take the worry and stress right off your shoulders."

"He'll take the *head* off your shoulders if he finds out what you're doing."

"I'm not doing anything. If you are supposed to be on Earth, he will let you know."

Beelzebub snarled. They were playing games with each other and they both knew it. Neither of them wanted to admit the plots they had in motion for Earth. They definitely didn't want to work together in any way, shape, or form. The anger between them was still there and Beelzebub hated the fact that Baal didn't seem to be afraid of anyone—especially not him.

Beelzebub stood up and marched to his leather chair. "I know you are lying, Baal. Stop holding back from me. You are plotting something, I can smell it. You know how else I know?"

Baal sighed. "Because the crazy voice in your head told you so?"

Beelzebub growled. "No, because the only time you are this calm, you have something in the works."

"Have you ever stopped to think that my calmness had

to do with Moloch being gone?" He took a leisurely sip of whiskey. "I am no one's errand boy or nursemaid anymore, sewing on limbs when they are sliced or exploded off? I can relax without all the mumbling and roaring in my ears, at least when uninvited guests don't come throwing doors open like you just did."

Beelzebub growled louder. "Cut the bullshit!"

Baal sighed and put his drink down. He stood up from his chair and walked to the fireplace, looking at the fire of souls he had taken from Moloch's office. The souls flickered, casting shadows on the stone hearth. "I will give you a bit of information if you are nice."

Beelzebub gripped his fists tightly but did not speak. He knew Baal was baiting him.

Baal smiled into the fire. "As we speak, Katie's entire team, the Damned, that asshole Juntto, and Katie, are all gathered at her base. There is some disgusting human wedding about to take place."

Beelzebub perked up at this news. He relaxed his muscles. "How do you know this?"

Baal turned toward Beelzebub. "That information is not of any note. No need to give up my sources. I was just saying that it's a very interesting bit of information that I came across. I figured if someone came along looking for it, I would give it to them. Luckily, you stormed into my life unannounced and angry."

Beelzebub rubbed his hands together and began to pace the floor. "All of them together in one place? This couldn't have worked out any better. What are those fools thinking, gathering at that base? Maybe the mercs aren't as smart as they seem. That sure is a lot of eggs in one basket."

Baal grinned. "That it definitely is. It would be a mighty shame if somebody came along and smashed them all to hell."

Beelzebub began to laugh maniacally. "Oh, Baal, you never cease to disappoint."

12

It had been a long time since Katie had been shopping in Las Vegas. She had tried to talk the girls into letting her fly them to New York, but Angie and Sofia had told her she was nuts. So there she was in one of the high-end boutiques, staring at herself in a deep-blue spaghetti-strap sequined dress. She turned her head and lifted her arm. There was a crazy amount of side boob showing.

Angie rounded the corner with a stack of dresses in her hand and stopped in her tracks. "Holy tits, Batman. I think maybe you should try something with a smidge more fabric in the front."

Katie didn't say anything, just plopped into the chair. Angie slowly hung up the dresses. "Hey, or not. You can totally just paint a dress on and be done with it. Can't pop a boob out if they're not held down by anything."

Katie didn't laugh or act like she heard Angie. Angie sighed and walked over, sitting on the arm of the chair. "What's up with you? You are not here for this. I know this isn't your thing, but usually, you at least fake it like hell for your friends."

Katie let out a deep breath. She slapped her hand on top of Angie's and nodded. "God, I know. I'm being a total bummer right now, aren't I? I'm so glad Sofia is at the tailor with her dress and is not seeing this."

Angie grabbed another chair and pulled it up in front of Katie. "Hey, what's going on with you? Is it Brock?"

Katie wrinkled her nose. "Yes, and I know that it's stupid. I know that I need to get my head out of the clouds, but I can't help worrying."

Angie shook her head. "I thought he was getting better, and doing it at a record pace."

Katie swallowed hard and picked at the sequins. "He is, and that's the problem. I mean, I want him to get better, but I'm afraid that once he does, he is going to dive right back into fighting. His last demon was a piece of shit, but she was fucking strong. She gave him speed, strength, accuracy. His current demon Wormwood is not any of those things. Apparently, he can heal like a champ, but Brock is going to be rolling out in battle with a lesser demon."

Angie pulled her lips into a straight line. "And you are afraid that he isn't going to take that into consideration, and sooner or later, he'll end up in a situation where his demon can't help him."

Katie slowly nodded. "Yep. We tend to feel invincible when we know someone is making us bulletproof. His demon is less bulletproof and more like a light rain jacket. I don't know. I want to protect him, but I know if I focus on that in battle I could get myself killed."

Angie felt for Katie. It was obvious she cared deeply for Brock. "I want you to know that no matter what, we are behind you. You have a whole family there for you."

Katie looked at Angie and smiled. "Thanks, girl."

Angie shook her head and stood up. "Now, let's get some fabulous dresses so we can support our friends in their new lives."

Angie went off to the dressing room to slip into her next dress and Katie did the same. Pandora sniffed. *When you've stopped being a whiny bitch, I'm going to need you to make sure you pick out two dresses.*

Katie scrunched her eyebrow. *Two?*

Pandora plumped Katie's breast further and put an extra curve on her hips and ass. *Yep. You didn't think I was going to miss Calvin's wedding, did you? Put on the next one. I like that one for me.*

Katie chuckled and threw on the dress. She twirled a bit in the mirror. *This is definitely you.*

Pandora sighed. *Oh, sweet Jesus, I'm gonna steal the groom. I think you should go with the purple one. It fits your body perfectly, and it's backless but sweet. I'll stick with the hot black dress. Oh, yeah.*

Katie laughed as she took the dress back off and put it on the hanger. *Now what?*

Pandora smacked her lips. *In the words of the great Timothy, girl, we need some shoes.*

The general finished typing his report and sent it. It wasn't exactly charging into battle, but he was proud of the work he had done. Sometimes it felt like all he did these days was type reports, but it had to be done. Before he could move on to the next task, however, his secretary came over the speaker. "General, you have a call from German Chancellor Schroder on line two."

The general took a deep breath and picked up the line. "This is General Brushwood. How can I help you, Chancellor?"

The chancellor cleared his throat. "General, thank you for taking my call. I had a rather interesting lunch earlier today with a lawyer from the World Council. He brought up some very interesting points."

Brushwood frowned. Who the hell was this lawyer, and why was he making his rounds to the different heads of state? He was starting to get suspicious of the fellow. At the same time, paperwork was piling so high on his desk that he could barely see over it. He didn't have time for the antics of some misled lawyer.

He collected himself. "I've heard you weren't the only one. I have no idea who this man is, nor have I gotten word back from the Council about his duties."

"No matter. I know who he is, and that is all that is important. What the lawyer did was bring great clarity to a subject I had neglected to put much thought into. I have some concerns about the mercenary Katie and her demon angel."

The general gritted his teeth. "And what concerns might those be?"

The chancellor thought for a moment. "The first would be a simple question. Who exactly does Katie answer to? You know her well, so does she answer to you? To the

World Council? Does she answer to no one but herself? The information has yet to have been presented to us for review."

The general had had enough. Between Romania's Dragos and now the chancellor, he was losing his patience. "For Christ's sake, leave it up to us humans to question one of the few good pieces of weaponry we have. Leave it to humans to turn their backs on the ones who have helped us repeatedly without asking for anything but money in return. Even the money is negotiable. Katie has saved the world a dozen times just this week!"

The chancellor shifted, a strange rustle in the background. "That wasn't my question. Despite her heroic actions, she still needs to be held accountable for anything she might do wrong. She still needs to answer to someone. This isn't some rogue mercenary. She works alongside your men in our countries. She also has a target on her back. The demons know that planning an attack will bring her out in the open. She is, essentially, causing them to attack."

Brushwood narrowed his eyes. "This is not going to turn out well for you, Schroder. You know that."

The chancellor sat back in his office chair with his feet propped up on an ottoman. "I am shocked and appalled that you would speak to me this way, General."

The general growled. "And I am shocked and appalled that you would question Katie. Aside from the fact that she has saved countless lives this week alone, she is an

American. As such, she is subject to American laws. On top of that, she is both a demon and an angel, which makes her one hell of a tool in the war against the demons."

Schroder looked at his fingernails. "Not all tools are safe without proper management. This would be one of those circumstances. I say she should have to answer to the Council if she is to continue to work in multiple countries."

"Chancellor, you are overstepping. If this is such a concern, you need to file it with the Council, and the appropriate people can take it up with me. I don't know who has been whispering in your ear, but whoever it is, you should tell them to find some other game to play. Katie is the best hope we have for a future on this planet."

"Very well. I will file my complaint. I will see you at the next Council meeting."

The general was beyond livid. "What the hell is going on here? I want the name and number of the lawyer you are speaking to. I was not made aware of anything like this."

Schroder laughed loudly. "You can call the Council. I'm sure they will give you the information."

Brushwood hung up without saying another word.

Schroder sat there stroking his chin, smirking to himself. He knew the general would not take the bait; he was too loyal to Katie. That was exactly what needed to happen. The Council would be approached, just as the lawyer instructed, and the general would be put on the spot.

Schroder chuckled and shook his head.

"What's so funny?" a woman's voice whined from across the room.

His head shot up. "Quiet, you bad dog."

The girl giggled. She was down on all fours with a full dog costume on. The girl next to her had a full-body cat costume on, and the third a bird costume. The chancellor walked over, grabbed the leash from the floor, and tugged on the dog-woman's collar. "Come. I have treats for you, my pretty puppy."

The woman dressed as a cat waved her paw in the air and hissed. He leaned down and patted her on the head. "Shh, nice kitty. You know I save the best for last."

General Brushwood slammed his phone down on the hook several times until it latched. His secretary came over the speaker. "General, are you all right?"

The general put his head in his hands. "Fine. Thank you. Hold my calls for a while, please. I need some time to think."

"Yes sir," she replied, clicking off the intercom.

Putting his fist in his mouth, the general yelled from the back of his throat. He rarely did that, but it always relieved his stress; a man in his position had to do something. Then he dropped his hand and sighed. "It's always fucking something."

He pressed the intercom button. "I need my interns, my deputy, and my assistant right away."

"Right away, sir."

A few minutes later, six staff members walked into his

office and stood in front of his desk. The general tried to breathe deeply to calm his nerves. "Some lawyer is saying he works for the World Council. He has so far visited at least the Romanian president and the Chancellor of Germany. I need you to figure out who this lawyer is, and if he is actually part of the World Council. Then I want you to dig and determine exactly why this man is building a case against Katie. Update me twice a day and when any large developments are found."

The staff nodded and began to head out of the room. The general stood, clearing his throat. They stopped in unison. "And folks, consider this Top-Secret. Speak to no one. I have a feeling that we really don't know who we can trust anymore."

Running below the Romanian villages was an old sewer system. It dated back to medieval times and had been repaired and rebuilt countless times. It was still in use. The water was putrid and brown, and the stone walls dripped condensation. Along the cement edges rats scurried, squeaking and screeching as they foraged for food. Waves moved along the shit-soiled sludge as Sasha crawled through, pushing herself along with her eight legs. A streak of blood trailed behind her.

The smell of sulfur and shit filled her nose, and with every stuttering step, she growled a little louder. She made sure to keep her mouth shut in case any of the water splashed on her face. She might like to suck demons dry, but shit and sewage were not things she enjoyed. Her legs could move her, but she was too weak to stand.

Finding a dry place to lean against the wall, she let out a deep breath. She still held the handle of Brock's sword tightly. The blade was buried deep in her stomach. With great effort, she slowly pulled the longsword from her stomach, screeching wildly as it left her purple flesh. She let out a deep breath and dropped the sword. Warm blood spilled from the open wound, and she pressed her claws against it and whimpered. She was unable to remember the last time she'd felt pain of that magnitude.

Narrowing her eyes, she inspected the sword. The blade had a strange sheen that swirled and waved in front of her. It was not ordinary steel. It was some kind of special metal. That made sense. It was a weapon for killing demons, and Sasha was fat with demonic souls. She was vulnerable to the metal's power, as vulnerable as any demon would be. Her wound felt sharp at the entry point and a dull pain radiated out like a wave, affecting her entire body. She tilted her head back, the yellow in her eyes pulsating. Her limbs flinched and spasmed. She knew if she didn't do something fast, she would bleed out in the sewers. She had no intention of dying yet.

"You will not get the best of me, bitch," she whispered under her breath. With all her might, she pulled herself out of the water and onto the ledge. Beneath her a pool of blood collected on the ledge, then ran down her legs into the sewage like a trickling stream.

Sasha was frustrated, angry, and alone. She leaned her head back and screamed until her throat was raw.

Her screams echoed through the empty tunnels of the

sewer system, and reached the ears of the demons hiding below. They were low-level scavengers, and they were starving. Between her screams and the smell of her blood, she had their complete attention. They crept to the edge of the tunnel and peered at her. Their red eyes flashed, but they refused to come any closer. They knew she wasn't human, and not just because she had purple skin and eight legs. They could sense that she was dangerous, and they could smell the remnants of departed demons radiating from her.

Sasha's eyes softened, then she grunted and her body morphed back into her human form. She clutched her stomach with one delicate hand and smiled at a small demon who had ventured into the tunnel. "Come here, little demon. I will not hurt you. I serve your master, and I need your help."

Her voice's sweet tones were melodic and entrancing to the demons. She had a power in her voice that attracted them, a survival mechanism she rarely needed to use. Then again, she rarely found herself covered in sewage with a giant hole in her belly. The demon inched closer and Sasha smiled sweetly. She extended a bloody hand toward him.

The beast pulled his claws in, wary, but he edged closer to sniff her fingers. He pulled back again, not convinced. She poured on the charm. "Oh, don't fear me, small evil one. I am your friend."

The melody of her voice washed over the demon and his fears were calmed. The beast stepped just in reach of Sasha and instantly she had his arms in an iron grip. The demon shrieked as she morphed back to her purple spider form. She wrapped her legs around him and pulled him into a deadly embrace. Sasha breathed in deeply, inhaling the demonic energy. As she exhaled, her moans shook the very stone of the sewer tunnels around them. The other demons scurried off; they had seen the death that awaited them.

She breathed in again and the demon's energy left his body like a mist, flowing upward into her nostrils. With every pull the demon wheezed, his body shriveling into a gray husk. With one final breath, the husk burst into dust in her arms. She let out a last deep moan and dropped her arms. She relaxed her huge body against the wall, where it twisted and morphed back into her human shape. She lifted her shirt, examining her stomach.

All remnants of the wound were gone. Even the blood had dried. She burped and giggled, slowly lowering herself back into the water below. She put one hand out and held on to the wall as she stumbled. She was still weak. One demon wasn't enough to fully heal her. She could still feel pain deep within her body.

"I need more," she snarled as she turned the corner.

A low growl came from Sasha's chest. The other demons scrambled away from her, hurrying down the tunnel. She stood up straight and put all of her arms out. "Come out, come out, wherever you are," she sang. "Momma's gonna get herself some revenge."

13

"Are we even going to be able to get into this club?" Angie asked. She tugged down on the bottom of her short red bodycon dress.

Timothy swatted her hand and sashayed down the Las Vegas strip. "Uh, duh. Of course, we are."

Katie eyed Angie's rear. "Your cheeks are hanging out, they should let you in and buy you a drink."

Sofia was dressed in a calf-length white pencil skirt that clung tightly to her curves. Her white top had a plunging neckline that revealed her formidable cleavage. She walked confidently in her six-inch platform heels, her small veil fluttering behind her. "Are you sure? It's the most prestigious women's strip club in the city."

Stephanie and Katie looked at each other with an evil smirk. Stephanie walked a bit faster, latching arms with Sofia. She had on wide-leg palazzo dress pants, black and white strappy heels, and a tight V-neck top. "Timothy is a fabulous gay man who happens to be a mercenary. He can get in just about anywhere."

Timothy swished his gray cashmere scarf over one shoulder of his perfectly pressed pinstriped Armani suit and patted down his blue ascot. "Girl, *yes*. They know me here."

Katie chuckled. She felt good in her short black dress. There were laces up the front, stopping just below her tits. Pandora sniffed for several moments. *You look fabulous tonight. I am jealous I can't come out and play.*

Katie glanced at the people parting for them as they strutted down the sidewalk. *Everyone knows who we are. I'm pretty sure some of them would freak out if you were in the flesh.*

Pandora sighed. *Fine, I'll just enjoy the man show through your eyes. You're welcome by the way.*

Katie wrinkled her forehead. *For what?*

For loaning you my curves.

Katie looked down. Her breasts were straining the laces, and her skirt was riding up her thighs. *Good Lord, I'm going to* see *strippers, not become one.*

Hey, you'd make mad cash.

Katie chuckled. *I don't think that's allowed for angels. I might get stripped of my wings.*

They followed Timothy past the long line to the club and up to the door. Before he even reached the entrance, the doorman stepped to one side and opened the door. Timothy blew him a kiss and shoved a few hundred-dollar bills into his front pocket. As they entered, they were ushered to a VIP table in the corner. Several bottles of liquor were lined up on the table, and several strippers were lined up waiting to dance for them.

As everyone sat down, Katie handed out rolls of one-dollar bills tied with white ribbons. "Have fun, ladies."

Stephanie began to pour shots. She handed one to Sofia, who waved her hand. "Oh, none for me."

Stephanie's mouth dropped open. "But it's your bachelorette party. That's sacrilege."

Sofia laughed nervously. "I want to be at my best tomorrow."

Katie narrowed her eyes at Sofia but let it go. It was her night, after all, and she thought it was pretty smart to keep her wits about her. Timothy got the party started, pulling Stephanie up to the stage. He began to fan himself with his money. "Do you hear that?"

Stephanie shook her head. "What?"

"Nothing. I'm gawking at man-flesh, and there's no voice in my head. It's heavenly."

Angie rolled her eyes and went after them, not all that enthused about the show. Katie chuckled and sat down next to Sofia, sipping a glass of champagne.

Katie had never been a big fan of the whole banana hammock thing, but she was there to make sure they had a good time. Looking at Sofia, though, her mind was on a bit more than flying dicks. "You okay, girl?"

Stephanie looked back at them, and Katie caught her eye. She nonchalantly motioned for Stephanie to join her. Stephanie told Timothy she'd be back and skipped over, sitting to Sofia's other side. Stephanie gave her a look. "What's wrong, girl? You're at a strip club!"

Sofia smiled sweetly. "I know, and I *will* loosen up. I guess I'm just a bit nervous about the wedding."

Stephanie stuck out her bottom lip and wrapped her arms around Sofia. "Aww, baby girl. There is nothing to be nervous about. You already know you want to be with this man. You already know that even if you hadn't gotten engaged, you would still be together. Marriage is just another step. You're just telling each other that there's real commitment there. You will grow stronger and closer with Calvin by being his wife. It's really amazing how it happens. You share everything. There will always be arguments, weird ones you can't even imagine, but over time you become one with that person."

Sofia took Stephanie's hand and grinned. "I hope you are right. I love Calvin very much, and I am ready to start a life with him. I really am. I guess the pre-wedding jitters are setting in."

Stephanie squeezed her hand. "Don't let them. You are at your bachelorette party! You need to be free and have fun. Don't think about this as the last night of your single life. Think about it as it is, a celebration of you. A celebration of this strong and beautiful woman who is moving from one amazing place in her life to the next."

Sofia took Katie's hand too. "Thank you so much for welcoming me into the fold and being there for me. Not just for me, but for Calvin too. I don't think it's the fighting he is scared to leave. I think it's his family."

Pandora cleared Katie's throat and pushed forward. "This is Pandora. As a previously married woman, I thought I would weigh in."

Katie sighed. "Go ahead, Pandora."

Pandora was proud. "Be excited—you are officially a one-wang woman from now on! Even if it is Calvin's."

Katie pushed Pandora back. "I think that's about enough from the gallery. Don't listen to her."

Pandora struggled back out. "Calvin may have lost his demon energy, but he's got that big-dick energy in spades."

Sofia giggled but shook her head. "It is kind of true. I am a one-dick gal from now on, not that I haven't been this entire time. That doesn't scare me in the least. Calvin and I have an intense attraction to one another."

Stephanie nodded. "Nor *should* it scare you. Getting married doesn't mean your sex life is over. It's actually quite the contrary, or can be. The two of you will be able to really open up and take care of each other. You will be surprised what kind of shenanigans you can get into once you feel completely comfortable with one another. Some of the best sex of my life has been since I tied the knot with Korbin. We have no reservations."

Timothy walked up and began fanning himself again as Stephanie talked. Both Sofia and Katie stared at her with raised eyebrows. Timothy let out a whistle. "Well, if no one else will say it, I will. What in God's name are you two kids getting into late at night?"

Stephanie smirked. "Who says it's late at night?"

"Ooh, girl!" Timothy cooed, feigning a faint.

Stephanie giggled and shook her head. "Some things are better left between the two of us."

Sofia giggled. "Looks like Angie has loosened up."

Everyone looked at Angie, who was putting several bills into a stripper's G-string. Timothy clapped his hands. "I gots to get in on some of that chocolate action."

The girls laughed as Timothy threw up his hands and ran over, slapping a stack of dollar bills on the dance floor. "Dance, baby, dance. Yes! Shake that booty."

Stephanie's eyes went wide. "I think by getting rid of his demon, we might have released the demon."

Sofia pursed her lips. "Mmmhmm. That boy is *sexo-enloquecido*. Sex-crazed."

Stephanie turned back to Sofia. "Do you feel better now? I want you to shake those nerves out and enjoy yourself. You are almost there, almost to that life that the two of you desperately want to have. Why not enjoy the last bit of your night before donning the gown?"

Sofia nodded and hugged Stephanie, turning to Katie. "Do you think Calvin is all right? I mean, he is still recovering, so I don't want him to go too wild."

Katie laughed and nodded as Angie walked up. "What's up?"

"Sofia asked if we thought Calvin would be all right. Because he is still recovering."

Angie barked out laughter. "Oh, girl, trust me—the boys are having their own fun. Do not worry about him. They're going to take care of him. You need to stop focusing on that and focus on the crazy polka dot banana hammock on stage. Who knew you could swirl that thing like helicopter blades."

All the girls looked over as a dancer started to swing it around again. Simultaneously they all tilted their heads to the right, getting a much better view.

The music pumped wildly as Juntto pushed through the crowded club. He had chosen the look of some male model he'd seen in one of Angie's magazines but was starting to regret the decision. Girls were trailing him like ducklings when all he wanted to do was hang out with the guys and celebrate Calvin. They had gotten a VIP private room in the back of the club so they could chill. They could dance if they wanted, but they still had their own space. It was definitely working out well, and they were having a blast.

Juntto stood at the bar and nodded at the bartender. "Seven shots of Patron, please. No limes necessary."

The bartender nodded and poured the shots. Juntto handed him a hundred. "Keep the change."

He gathered the shots up in his big hands and held them high, weaving back through the crowd. "Excuse me. Coming through. Alcohol call for the bachelor!"

Finally, he made it back to the VIP room and stopped in his tracks. It was a massacre. The men were spread out in the booth and across the big table. Brock, his three teammates, Korbin, and Calvin had passed out and were drooling on themselves. Calvin was clutching his crutches to his chest and twitching slightly in his sleep.

Juntto sighed and set the shots down. He thought about waking them up, but they were done for. No sense in letting good alcohol go to waste. He downed the shots himself, one at a time. He toasted Calvin with each shot.

After the last one, he slammed the shot glass on the table upside-down. He sighed at his unconscious friends. "Humans cannot hold their liquor."

The girls cheered loudly. They were lined up on either side of Timothy, who seemed to know his way around a strip club. He put the dollar in his teeth and the stripper chuckled, hopping down and sitting on the edge of the stage. He put his arms out, and everyone followed along. They each tucked a bill in their teeth and used their mouths to tuck it into his G-string. Even Katie got in on the action, laughing through it.

Timothy looked at Katie with surprise. "This is the first time I have ever seen this sister going wild. It's definitely a good look on you."

Katie shrugged. "Everybody's gotta let loose sometimes, right? Otherwise, I would be boring as hell."

Everyone cheered and Sofia laughed. "You guys are amazing. Best bachelorette party ever."

Katie took a shot. "Oh, girl, this shit is just getting started!"

Pandora cleared her throat. *Can I please take over your body?*

You were going to watch through me for your own good.

Just for a little while? Pleeeeaaassse?

Katie groaned. *I don't know. Can I trust you not to make a scene or get us thrown out?*

Pandora began to get excited. *Yes. Yes. Yes. I promise. Angel's honor.*

Katie wasn't convinced, but she figured Pandora couldn't possibly get them in that much trouble. *Okay, but only for a little while!*

Pandora cheered. *Yay! Here I come!*

Katie glanced at Stephanie. "Pandora is taking over. Just giving everybody warning."

Stephanie clapped her hands. "Oh, yay!"

Katie pointed at a passing stripper. "That warning goes double for you."

"Huh?"

Katie shut her eyes as Pandora pushed to the front. She had changed Katie's body to hers at the beginning of the night, so outwardly you couldn't tell that much of a difference, especially in the club lights. She looked down at the stack of money in her hands and gave Stephanie an evil smile. "Oh, girl, this is going to be fun."

Pandora waved one of the strippers over to her, and he danced across the stage. She looked at the others and waved them over too. She reached up with the bills and began putting them in the dancers' G-strings. "You get a dollar, and you get a dollar. And you. You get two dollars, sweet cheeks." She slapped the dancer's ass playfully.

The stripper wagged a finger at her. "Naughty girl. Settle down there."

As the night wore on, Pandora got wilder. A few of the dancers were afraid to dance for her. Finally, Timothy had to drag her back to the table. "You can't be so handsy. They are about to throw you out."

"For one little squeeze?" Pandora scoffed drunkenly. "They are no fun."

Timothy giggled and wrapped his arm around Pandora. "That is for damn sure, girl. Oh Lord, they made a mistake letting us unruly assholes up in here tonight."

Pandora pointed at Stephanie and Angie, who were leaning against Sofia. "It looks like everyone but Sofia is pretty much wasted. Lightweights. I guess we should get these bitches out of here before they pass out and embarrass me."

Timothy rolled his eyes and groaned as he pulled himself from the booth. "You are right. I believe this party has reached its peak. The only one still standing is the lovely bride."

"Can I bring one home?"

"Sorry, girl. No picking up strays tonight. Katie would never forgive me."

Sofia giggled as she scooted out of the booth. "The limo should be parked about a block down. You think we can get these testy bitches back to it?"

Timothy lifted Angie and put his hand around her waist. "We better, 'cause I ain't sleeping in no strip club. Girl, bye with that dirty nonsense."

Sofia went to reach for Stephanie, but Pandora shook her head. "Please, allow me." She pulled the drunk woman to her feet.

Sofia followed them out of the strip club, laughing as they zigzagged into the street. They took a few steps, and Stephanie stumbled against a wall. "Okay. Okay. Let me catch my feet."

"You caught them, but they've been drinking, too."

She giggled, leaning against the wall for a deep breath of fresh air. Everyone stopped and stood there a moment to regain their composure.

"Well, look at what we have here. A bunch of bitches just standing around doing nothing. That's really cute." Three guys walked up wearing leather jackets, jeans, and calf-high boots.

Pandora waved them away drunkenly. "Get the hell out of here. We don't need your shit tonight."

The guy with the mustache snarled. "Mouthy bitch. I'll do whatever the fuck I damn well please, how about that?"

Another guy stepped up. "I second that motion."

All three men pulled out guns, and the women froze. Pandora raised her hands, and the others followed suit. "Very good. You know your place. I want all of you to empty your wallets and hand over all that very fine jewelry you are wearing."

One of the guys ran his finger across Sofia's cheek and she pulled away, her hands still in the air. No one moved to take off their jewelry. The mustachioed man looked at them like they were crazy. "Did you not fucking hear what I just said? Money and jewelry, now!"

Timothy slapped his hands to his cheeks and began to scream at the top of his lungs. The high-pitched noise startled the thieves. They backed up a bit, unsure what to do. Nobody else was on the street. The mustachioed thief shoved his gun in Timothy's face once again. Timothy immediately shut his mouth, letting a smirk cross his lips. The robber moved forward, pressing the butt of the gun to his cheek.

The thief looked at him with furious eyes. "Shut. The. Fuck. Up. You do that shit again, and I can promise you at least one of you is going home in a body bag. I think I would pick that beauty right there."

The robber stared at Sofia, his smile nasty and jagged. "Give the girl something special before she makes her groom a widower, right?"

The women looked at one another. Angie looked scared. Stephanie was shocked. Pandora was gone, and in her place, Katie was expressionless.

Sofia spat in his face and let loose a stream of Spanish. "*Usted sucio pedazo de basura del pantano. No tienes idea de quiénes somos. Estas señoras te arrancarán las pelotas y las empujarán por el culo.*"

The thief wrinkled his nose. He had no idea what she was saying. Timothy started screaming again. The thief put his hands to his ears. "Enough!"

Timothy laughed loudly. "I'm just fucking with you."

Angie's scared face fell away, and she yanked a gun from her bag. Stephanie, Katie, and Sofia stepped forward.

Timothy sighed, looking at his nails. He glanced at the robbers. "I almost feel bad for you guys."

Together the women rushed the poor, stupid thieves.

Morning light cascaded over the desert. A cold breeze blew through, waking the workers of the fall carnival from their slumber. All across the carnival's camp, you could hear the sounds of the animals waking in their cages. Carnies loading up trucks and flatbeds filled the air. They were headed for their next performance and woke with the sun to get a move on.

There were carnies of all types, everyone pulling down tents and getting ready for a big move. There were ride operators, a strongman, a bearded lady, and about three dozen more freaks of nature, or curiosities, in the caravan. They had to work year-round to make ends meet. Now they were traveling south to Phoenix for the winter. They would set up shop there and enjoy the warmth.

As the workers packed their trunks into the trucks,

Beelzebub ripped open a portal in the center of the Ferris wheel. He stepped out onto the metal platform and looked down at all the unsuspecting carnies below. A flood of demons rushed through behind him, the beasts snarling and growling as they climbed down the wheel and ran into the camp.

Beelzebub grabbed one of the demons by the neck. "Remember, no killing. I mean, not at first. You get it."

He let the creature go, and it howled as it ran toward the humans.

14

Katie groaned as she rolled over in the bed. After a few failed attempts, her waving hand hit the alarm. Her head was pounding, and the room was still spinning. *Hey, bitch. Why are you not saving me from this horrible hangover?*

Pandora growled. *Because the hangover has gone deep, my friend. I feel it, and I don't even have a body. Lucifer's balls, I must have drunk more than Juntto's body weight last night.*

Katie pulled herself to the edge of the bed and sat up. The world tilted, and her head throbbed. She grabbed a receipt from the nightstand and read the tab the bachelorette party had managed to accrue. The numbers didn't help her hangover. *I assume you drank the whole bar. This tab is thousands of dollars.*

Pandora yawned. *Hey, we party like rock stars.*

Katie crumpled the paper. *And now we meet Calvin in the dining room for breakfast like hungover college freshmen.*

That's not fair. If we're acting like college freshmen, there should at least be a dumb, cute boy to kick out of bed.

Katie pulled on a pair of sweatpants and a t-shirt and shuffled down to the dining room. Calvin was trying to open two boxes of donuts as he leaned on his crutches. He looked just as hungover as Katie. Katie snorted and fell into the chair. "You look as bad as me, and I'm nursing two people's hangovers."

Calvin chuckled and sat down. "I don't think I've ever been that drunk in my life. Juntto is an animal."

Katie scoffed. "As soon as Pandora stops spinning, hopefully she'll take care of my hangover for me."

Calvin went silent. He took a donut from the box and stared at it rather than eating it. Katie took one too but set it down. She grabbed a cup of coffee first, sipped the deep, dark brew, and let out a deep breath. She could see Calvin was lost in his thoughts. "What's up with you?"

Calvin shrugged. "Honestly? I miss Marty. Not so much the company, but what the demon did for me. I was indestructible. A hangover was something to laugh at, but now I feel like I got hit by one truck and backed over by another."

Katie patted his hand. "I'm sure that feeling will go away in time."

Calvin looked at Katie. "Will it? I don't think it will. God, Katie, I have mulled this over and over and still haven't come to a conclusion. Everything in me wants to ask you to grab another demon for me. To put me back together like I was before. I don't know how to live like a normal human being. What do I do with myself when all the excitement wears down and there is just quiet? Read a book? I don't know how to do it."

Katie was shocked. She hadn't expected Calvin to feel that way about his demon. She figured he would be happy to live as a normal human for the first time in over a decade, but at that moment, he looked beat down, worn out, and desperate. There had been a time when they'd talked about having a normal life every day. That was something all Damned thought about at one time or another, but when given the choice, they almost felt powerless. They couldn't imagine life without their demons.

Pandora cleared her throat and spoke very carefully for the first time in her life. *Look at him, Katie. He is desperate to be himself again. He has had a demon so long that he doesn't know who he is without one.*

Katie sighed. *Yeah, but he will figure it out. When you first become Damned, you don't know how to live your life* with *a demon, but it comes to you. You learn. This is all fresh and new to him.*

Pandora didn't agree. *Some men are made for this. Calvin is a badass, and he could be of use in the fight against demons. This war needs a man like Calvin.*

Calvin could tell Katie was thinking. He put down his donut and leaned forward. "Look, you can do it, I know you can. I've seen you do it. You did it for Stephanie and Korbin when they decided they wanted to rejoin the fight, and you did it for Brock a few days ago. Granted, that was to save his life, but it shouldn't be any different for me. I feel like I need to save my life."

Calvin sat back. Katie looked at him for a few long moments, thinking about what he was asking her to do. She was torn. It was ultimately his decision, but she knew that he would regret it if it affected his relationship with Sofia.

Katie wiped her hands and let out a deep breath. "Calvin, this is a big decision. You were given a second chance at having a normal life. I know it's hard to think about living the rest of your life without a demon, but that will fade. You will be able to do it and be happy in it. That being said, if you are sure it's something you really want, I will do it for you."

Calvin let out a sigh of relief. "Thank you, Katie."

Katie shook her head. "Don't thank me. I'm not done yet."

Calvin looked at her sheepishly. "I should have seen that coming."

Katie chuckled. "If you really want to go back to the fight, then yes, you need a demon. But is this really about the fight? Is it about the battle between humans and demons or is it about the battle with yourself? Are you uncomfortable because you are left with just your thoughts? If that's the case, then you need to think about this some more. Life doesn't give you second chances very often. You know as well as I do that when we become Damned, we assume that it will be until death do us part. For many of us that came sooner rather than later. It's a big choice if you haven't figured that out yet."

Calvin's hands dropped to the table. Katie picked up a donut and began to eat it while he mulled the decision. After a few moments, he slumped his shoulders and shook his head. "I want it, Katie. I do. I want to fight to save the world. I want to kill demons. I want to get rid of that silence in my head. I want all of that. But…"

Katie was relieved to hear a "but." Calvin nodded, taking a sip of his coffee. "I want a life with Sofia more, and I don't know if I can have both. Having a family and a marriage while battling demons? What's that life like? Always being in danger, never being able to settle? That's not the life I want to give her. She deserves so much more than that, so I guess I choose Sofia."

Katie smiled and winked at Calvin. "That's the right choice, Daddy."

Calvin assumed it was Pandora speaking. "Thanks, Pandora."

Pandora came forward to reply. "No problem, Big Papa."

Calvin wrinkled his forehead. "Okay, that's quite enough creepy sexual daddy references. It's starting to make me feel like a weirdo."

Pandora cackled out loud. "You better get used to it. Pops."

Calvin faked a laugh but stopped. His eyes slowly rose to meet Katie's. "Wait…"

"You're going to hear that a lot," Katie added and her eyes sparkled.

Calvin dropped his donut. "Do you mean…"

Sofia walked up behind the chair and leaned over to place her lips at his ear. "That's right. You made the right choice. You're going to be a father."

Calvin's expression went wide, and he struggled to his feet and hugged Sofia tightly. "I'm gonna be a dad. That's fucking amazing."

Timothy came stumbling into the room, red-eyed and

groggy. He rubbed his forehead and held the iPad tightly in his hands.

Sofia laid her head on Calvin's shoulder and winked at Katie. "I want you to be happy, I do. And if being Damned will do that, I won't stand in your way. But I ask that first you think about us, and you think about this baby. You are being given the opportunity to be a father. How amazing is that?"

Calvin kissed Sofia's forehead. "I would never go against that. I have wanted to be a father my entire life. I cannot turn my back on that. Being Damned with a family would be far too dangerous. I am going to be your husband very soon, and that is a huge responsibility. I am supposed to protect you and my children from any harm, and as a Damned I cannot promise that."

Sofia put her hands on his face. "I love you. You are going to be the most amazing father ever. You don't need a demon in you to be whole again. We are here to fill that space in your life. We don't need a hero; you're already one. We need you—just you."

Calvin looked at Timothy and put his hands in the air. "I'm going to be a dad!"

Timothy lifted an eyebrow. "Wow. There is a lot of information rolling in right now."

"I know, I can barely believe it myself."

"Not that. I mean, that's great, but there's a lot of activity, is what I mean."

Katie looked at the screen of the iPad and saw a blinking warning sign. "Timothy, what's going on?"

Timothy looked down at the screen and jumped. "Oh,

yeah. There has been an incursion close to the base. It's out near an old highway about fifteen miles from here."

Pandora pushed her way to the front. She slapped Timothy hard on the back. "Duty calls, drunk bitch."

She sank back into Katie and went to work on her hangover. Katie whirled and stared at Calvin for a second. They didn't have to speak. He put his arm around Sofia and smiled at Katie, giving her a nod. Katie grinned and turned, happy that Calvin had chosen to stay human. He was going to be a father, and that trumped the fight in all of their eyes. The Damned didn't have that option, or at least the women didn't.

Katie looked at Timothy, feeling relief as Pandora eased her hangover. "Are you getting any readings on the number of demons?"

Timothy pressed some buttons on his screen. "No. Actually, it looks like this happened a couple of hours ago, at least the first portal signature reading. But there are no heat waves. Then again, I'm not sure what the area looks like at this moment. The satellites are busy this morning. There could be a building, a covering, or any number of things keeping the satellites from reading the heat index. I would go prepared. If you don't find anything, that's even better."

Katie nodded. "I want Joshua and the girls to be on high alert just in case. We know they know where we are. If this is a diversion, I don't want you guys to be caught with your pants down. Alert the front security guards, and wake up Korbin and the rest. I don't care how hungover they are. We need to be on our toes. Demons don't just pop up for no reason."

Timothy's fingers danced over his tablet as he sent Joshua an alert. The lights in the building flickered as they always did when Timothy started the alert system.

Katie took off out of the room and down the hall, heading for her room. *Time to gear up. Shit is going down.*

Katie burst out of the doors of the barracks and covered her eyes. The sun shone brightly. She pulled out her glasses and slid them on as her wings spread wide. She sprang up and flapped them hard, which sent her racing through the sky. The guards watched her pass, dirt swirling around on the ground around them.

Katie spun and made her way as fast as she could to the incursion site. She told the others to remain on standby until they knew what they were facing. Until then, she was scouting. There was something in the distance. Katie circled the campsite, which had been torn to hell. Several carnival rides lay in pieces. The Ferris wheel was the only large ride still intact. It was swaying in the wind, still mounted on the back of a flatbed truck.

She slowed her wings, searching for any sign of demons. *What the hell is this?*

Pandora sniffed. *Ugh, carnies. I had a run-in with some two lives ago. Not the nicest people to hang out with. They cheat at cards. But still, I don't smell any demons, at least not any who are still there.*

Katie lowered herself to the ground in the center of the site. *Strange. Their animals are all still here, but there isn't a soul around.*

She walked up to a board full of ads for different attractions. Katie frowned at the pictures of clowns and old sketches of a bearded lady. *I don't like this at all.*

No shit. It's creepy enough to warrant burning it to the ground.

Katie shivered. *For once I agree with you. There are no demons, no bodies, and no workers. It's just an abandoned carnival.*

Katie and Pandora took a tour around the place, checking out the different tents. There were belongings, empty beds, and full suitcases, but no carnies. Katie stepped out of the tent and put her hands on her hips. *Nothing. So fucking weird.*

Pandora groaned. *God help us if there are demon carnies rolling around. I'll shit my pants if I have to fight a demonized clown.*

Katie chuckled, glancing down at her phone. "Oh, shit! We're going to be late for the wedding!"

She pulled her phone out and dialed Korbin's number. He answered in a raspy voice, "What does it look like?"

Katie glanced around. "Like something out of a creepy horror flick, but there are no bodies. No people either. Nothing. There might have been a portal here, but whatever came out is not here now. They either took the carnies with them or they are hiding somewhere. Pandora can't smell them."

Korbin let out a deep breath. "Okay. If there is nothing there, then there is nothing for you to do. Might as well come back and enjoy the festivities."

Katie looked around again, lifting an eyebrow. Her instincts told her to track them down, but her best friend was about to get married. She wouldn't miss that for anything. "On my way, after we call someone to come get the animals."

Katie hung up and spread her wings wide. "Let's hope they're just hiding."

Timothy took a bracelet from a velvet box. Sofia held out her arm. He carefully wrapped the diamond jewelry around her wrist and closed the clasp. Stephanie walked behind her and fluffed her train, smoothing the fabric. They were helping her get ready for her big day, and they were on high alert. Between Sofia getting married and the incursion that morning, nothing felt as peaceful as it should have. That was the merc life, though, and Sofia knew that.

Timothy held up two dangling diamond earrings. "Something old. Diamond earrings from your grandmother."

Sofia put them in her ears. "I feel like a princess."

Timothy nodded, looking at her. "You should since you look like one. Now you have something new—your dress."

Sofia smoothed her hands down the tight fabric. "Yep. The dress of my dreams."

Stephanie touched the clip in her hair. "Something borrowed, thanks to Timothy."

He waved his hands, giggling. "I can't let my girl go down the aisle without a piece of me. You know I'll always find a way to make it about me."

The girls laughed. Stephanie put her hand to her cheek. "What about something blue?"

Sofia grinned. "I have a blue garter on underneath this."

Stephanie clapped her hands. "Perfect. Now, what about your family? I know you come from a big family. Weddings are big deals."

Sofia sighed, looking at herself in the mirror. Her dress was exactly what she wanted, plain white, strapless and tight like a mermaid down to her knees, where it burst out in layers of tulle. Her necklace hung across her chest with long shards of sparkling metal dangling from it. "They may be upset. They weren't invited, but all of this was so last minute. I'm not too worried. They love Calvin, and this just means we'll have to go to Mexico and have a big family wedding with everyone later on."

Timothy jumped with joy. "A second wedding, omigawd. You have to let me help decorate that one. I will brush up on my Spanish, and we can make it both traditional and chic."

Sofia laughed. "I think my mother would love that. She always hated planning big events. It is part of the culture, though, so she has become accustomed to it. I personally love small and intimate gatherings like today. This has become everything I ever wanted it to be. Not overblown, but elegant enough for my personality."

Timothy brushed a strand of hair from her cheek and looked at her reflection in the mirror. "My little Calvin is all grown up. He's gonna marry this voluptuous queen and have a happily ever after. It's the most fabulous thing I've done in a very long time. Girl, and this dress. *Valentino*. I'm dying over here."

Stephanie laughed. "Don't die. I need you for this."
"The fabulousness will kill me. Ugh."
"Hold it together, jerk."

15

Katie stood in front of the mirror and admired her lavender gown. It cascaded over her curves and lay gently on the floor. Spaghetti straps held it up in the front, and wisps of sequins peppered the thing all the way to the hem. She approved of the back of the dress, or lack thereof. It scooped low, curving right below the dip in her back. Her hair was pulled back and carefully pinned in luscious curls off her neck.

Around her neck was a slender silver chain with a single diamond hanging from it. She pulled on her strappy silver heels. Just then Pandora walked around the corner wearing a tight black halter dress that went straight down to the top of her pointy platform heels. Her black hair fell around her shoulders in lush ringlets.

Pandora took a deep breath and put out her arms. "Tell me, do you think I should go in my human skin or my demon skin?"

She flashed her demon scales, her body a red so deep it

was almost black. Her eyes flashed red. "I think this may be a bit too much, but at the same time I feel like my human skin is a bit douchey, you know?"

Katie lifted her eyebrows. "Human, definitely. You look like a block with your scales and black dress. Besides, Sofia isn't Damned, and we don't want to freak her out with a demon standing behind her."

Pandora flashed back to her human skin. "Good thinking. You look fucking radiant, by the way. Good Lord, Brock is going to piss himself."

Just then there was a knock on the door, and Pandora smiled. "Speak of the devil."

Katie walked to the door. "I hope you don't mean the actual devil."

She opened the door to find Brock standing in the hall, one hand in his tuxedo pocket. Her jaw dropped. He looked suave as hell. His new demon had done the trick; he didn't have a scratch on him. She waved him in, and he chuckled as he walked past her into the room. Katie admired him. "You are good as new."

Brock put out his hands. "And you are a vision. Fucking beautiful."

Katie blushed slightly, and Pandora held back a snicker. "How is your demon?"

Brock laughed. "Like a thirteen-year-old boy ready to go."

Katie shook her head. "How in the world did you heal so fast?"

Brock shrugged. "I gave him a little incentive to get a move on."

Katie wrinkled her forehead. "What was the incentive?"

Brock reached out and grabbed Katie by the waist, pulling her hard into him. He ran his lips across her neck before pulling back with a grin.

Katie's breath caught in her throat and she giggled, putting her hand on his chest. "Hold on there, buddy. We've got a wedding to get to."

Pandora stepped forward with a snicker. "But after the wedding? Look out."

Calvin pulled his coat over his shoulders and buttoned the front, then looked at himself in the mirror. He lifted his chin and straightened his bowtie just a smidge.

Korbin walked up next to him, and Calvin laughed. Korbin held his hands out and looked at his jacket. "What? What did I do?"

"In all of the years I've known you, Korbin, I don't think I've ever seen you in a tux. You look like an actual human being in that thing. I can now see why Stephanie has a thing for you."

Korbin slanted him a look and shook his head. "I know, surprise, surprise, Korbin is more than just an evil dictator endlessly harassing his mercenaries."

"I never thought of you as an evil dictator." Calvin was laughing just the same. "Maybe just a bossy-ass demon-slayer."

Korbin opened his hand, showing Calvin a set of gold and blue cufflinks with his initials on them. "These are for you. They were my grandfather's. He had the same initials as you. He was a lucky man, and hopefully some of that will rub off on you and Sofia."

Calvin took the cufflinks and shook his head. Suddenly he hugged Korbin tightly. "Thanks, man. That's really awesome."

Juntto cleared his throat, and the guys looked at him. He was staring down at his untied bowtie. "How do you tie one of these things?"

Korbin shook his head. "Don't look at me. Stephanie tied mine."

Calvin chuckled and put the cufflinks on. He walked over to Juntto, who had his Channing Tatum look on again. It made Calvin laugh. "This whole Channing Tatum thing is interesting. Just don't start Magic Miking it during the wedding."

Juntto grunted. "I may have his face, but my moves are much smoother."

Calvin laughed, tying Juntto's bowtie. "Have you ever been in a wedding before?"

Juntto shook his head. "No, things are a bit different on my planet, ceremony-wise. There are no flowers or anything like that. We take a dip in the teal pond below the ancient shrines of our gods. It is the everlasting pond, full even through the drought that crippled our planet. The parents are there to exchange the money."

Calvin lifted an eyebrow as Juntto continued, "Yes, money. How much did you pay for your wife? She is very beautiful and very intelligent. She would have raised a lot of currency for her hand on my planet."

Calvin finished tying the bowtie and glanced at Korbin. "We really have no idea what you are talking about. We decided we loved each other and we wanted to get married. In fact, *she* asked *me* because I was dragging the line on that one. You pay for your wives? Do they have a say?"

Juntto nodded. "Like your culture, we pick our wife, or wives, depending on our stature. When you choose a bride, you must present goods to the woman's family. You offer a sum of money to the father. The poorer folk offer food, the pick of the harvest or a number of beasts for slaughter."

Calvin shook his head. "Beasts?"

"Or a harvest. Like corn?" Korbin was interested now.

Juntto nodded. "Oh, yes. A woman like Stephanie, for example, would be worth quite a bit. If not money, she would be worth at least five beasts and three full spring harvests."

Korbin chuckled under his breath. "My wife would be worth five beasts? I'm sure she would be happy to hear that."

Juntto nodded seriously. "Oh, yes, that's a very fair price for a woman like her. Sofia is worth at least a dozen tribbles."

"What is a tribble?" Calvin asked cautiously.

Juntto waved his hand toward the window. "They are like your goats."

Calvin nodded slowly. "And what is the goat-to-beast ratio here? Are we saying Sofia isn't worth as much as Stephanie, or is she worth the same? I need a cheat sheet for this."

Korbin thought about it for a moment. "When you have a son, you have to have enough goods for your own family and enough to pay for a bride?"

Juntto nodded. "Many farmers have become poor when their sons married up in society. They were not prepared for that. It is a slap in the face to offer less than what a woman is known to be worth."

Korbin opened his mouth to speak but thought better of it. Calvin frowned. "So, wait. You're telling me you judge the worth of your women based on beasts, goats, and vegetables? I don't think most Earth women would be very happy about that."

Juntto shook his head. "Not her worth as a person. Women are regarded very highly on my world. The tribbles and the harvest, these are simply signs of what the man is willing to give up to have her as his wife. What sacrifices he and his family will make to ensure her family is taken care of."

Calvin let out a deep sigh. "I don't get it. Seems wasteful."

Juntto waved his hands at them. "If you don't understand, I cannot explain it to you."

Calvin turned to Korbin with a smirk on his face. "I wonder what Timothy will pay one day for a husband?"

Korbin chuckled. "Knowing him, nothing less than fourteen tribbles, three beasts, and a handful of corn on the cob."

They all started to laugh, including Juntto. "No, two men do not pay the fee. They just marry."

Calvin nodded. "I like it. Your planet seems progressive

in that way, but a little old-school when it comes to women marrying men."

Juntto made his way out of the room. "We grow our babies, so we don't care who marries who."

Calvin and Korbin both stopped. Calvin mumbled, "Well, that's convenient."

Korbin shrugged. "Makes sense. You'd have to be one hell of a woman to carry a behemoth like Juntto."

A row of black town cars kicked up dust as they drove down the road toward a historic Spanish chapel near the base. Timothy had directed a team of emergency decorators to do some restorations on it before the wedding. A few new pews, an intense cleaning, and a few flowers went a long way to bringing it back to its former glory. The stained glass window in the front shimmered in the warm sun, reflecting a rainbow onto the dusty path in front of the chapel. The first car came to a stop and Calvin and Korbin got out, walking quickly inside, or as quickly as Calvin could walk with his cane.

Katie and Pandora rode together in the next car. The driver opened their door and helped them both out. They went to the front and positioned themselves to wait for the guests to arrive. It was a small wedding, with Katie serving as maid of honor, Korbin as best man, and Pandora presiding over the service. Timothy took his seat in the pews with Stephanie. She had to hold his hand. He was already crying.

Brock walked in behind several of the military service

men and women who were stationed on the base and winked at Katie as he took a seat next to Juntto and Angie. Katie cleared her throat and looked away. He did look damn good.

She glanced at Pandora, who nodded at her knowingly. Katie rolled her eyes and stood up straight. She held a small bouquet of flowers in front of her. Normally she would walk down the aisle, but the place was so small it didn't make much sense to do so.

Doctor Ozu, Doctor Thorough, and Alice all walked in, waving to Katie and Calvin and taking seats in the audience. The rest of Brock's team were still too banged-up to get out of bed, so they sent their good wishes from the barracks and stayed behind with the nurses. Timothy stood up and kissed Stephanie on the cheek. He walked quickly out of the church. Joshua and several of the girls tiptoed into the church and filled the back row.

Pandora reached behind her and pressed the Play button on the iPad hidden on the pew and the sound of playfully chirping violins echoed through the old adobe church. Flowers hung from the ceiling and were draped over the wooden benches, and a white runner led up the main aisle. It was beautiful, and exactly what Sofia wanted —elegant, floral, and intimate.

Calvin was holding onto his cane with one hand at the front.

Pandora leaned over and whispered to Katie, "I still think we should have worn matching dresses."

Katie sighed and shook her head. "The person presiding over the wedding and the maid of honor wearing matching dresses? That would have looked weird as hell, and we would have looked like freaking twins."

"No fun. You are no fun."

The music switched, and everyone quieted down. The crowd in the pews stood as Sofia appeared in the doorway. Her jewels sparkled wildly, and her face glowed as she clutched Timothy's arm as he led her toward her groom. Calvin smiled sweetly, a tear filling his eye. Sofia reached the front of the chapel and Timothy giggled as he handed her to Calvin.

He pulled her veil back and grinned. "Oh, hey, there."

"Hey, yourself."

"Ready for this?"

"I was born ready."

They grinned at one another.

The crowd sat back down, and Pandora cleared her throat. "Well, hell, we made it, didn't we?"

Everyone laughed. Pandora looked down at a cheat sheet Sofia had written for her and started the service. "Ladies and gentlemen, Damned and innocent, we are gathered here today to celebrate one damn good show. Today we will witness the joining of two of the most kickass people I have ever known, Calvin and Sofia. They let me choose a reading, and as much as I wanted to go with some of my own words of wisdom, Katie thought I should stick to something more Earth-bound."

Sofia smiled and looked back at Katie, mouthing, "Thank you."

Pandora cleared her throat. "I chose a prayer instead. Lord, we thank you for giving Calvin and Sofia the blessing to become one today. We thank you for kicking

Marty the hell out of Calvin since he didn't do well with the tacos."

Everyone chuckled.

"Lord, we ask that you allow these two to live together as a family with peace and love in their lives. You of all people know that Calvin is one of the most deserving of your soldiers. He has defeated more demons in his life as a Damned than almost anyone else. Give him the strength to protect his home now and forever, even as a measly human. Amen."

Pandora nodded at Sofia. "Now the vows." She looked at the crowd. "They wrote their own vows. I tried to help. I always say, there should be at least three positions explicitly stated in your wedding vows, so you know what your partner is into. Not including missionary, which is a baseline basic-bitch type of…"

Katie shook her head wildly, and Pandora shut up. "Okay. Sorry. The vows, please."

Sofia turned to Calvin and breathed deeply. "I will make this short and sweet. I promise to walk with you in life, follow you in death, and honor our family every step of the way. I promise to help mend your broken bones, and I promise to love you for the rest of my days."

Calvin beamed at her. "Sofia, my sweet. I never imagined a life outside of training, dungeons, and bloodbaths. But then there you were, waiting for me to save you. In the end, you saved me. You have given me the ability to see past who I was and look forward to who I will become. I promise to love and cherish you all of our days. To walk beside you in life, and to always, always, put my dishes in the dishwasher."

Sofia giggled and wiped a tear from her cheek. Calvin kissed her hands. "Here is to forever with you."

A ways down the dusty trail, Gabriel stood and listened to the service. His white and silver robes fluttered around him, and his silver hair whipped around his head like a halo. He smiled as Calvin kissed Sofia's hands, then wiped a tear from his eye.

He lowered his head and raised his hands in prayer. "May Calvin, Sofia, and their unborn child find the light of God and the protection of all the angels. Amen."

Gabriel raised his head sharply, and the smile dropped from his lips. He tilted his head to the side and listened intently.

His brow furrowed. With a swish of his hand he disappeared from sight, sparkles of sunlight blinking where his hair had just been.

A shimmer pulled Pandora's attention to the open door, but there was nothing there. She narrowed her eyes. Under the flowers and Calvin's joy, she could sense an angel's fleeting presence. Under her breath, she whispered, "Gabriel, you asshole. What now?"

Outside the chapel a cloud of dust began to swirl, obscuring the horizon. Katie looked at Pandora and followed her eyes outside. The two stepped forward without speaking. They walked past Calvin and Sofia, waiting with bated breath as something approached. Katie squinted into the dust. "What is it?"

"Doesn't your angel know?" Pandora closed her eyes and took a deep breath. When she opened them again, they were glistening bright blue. "Demons."

As the words left her lips, the infected carnies came stomping over the hill. In front was the strongman, ruby-eyed and pounding his fist in his palm. Next to him was the bearded lady, her eyes bright red, twirling her finger through the long beard on her chin. They led the rest of the carnival workers, men and women who were performers and Ferris wheel mechanics and everything in between. They all had bright red eyes. They stopped on the dirt road and stared at the small church.

Pandora wrinkled her nose at the bearded lady. "Oh, honey. We are going to need to get you to the salon, *stat*. They are gonna have to use a whole bucket of wax on that shit."

Calvin joined them and peered at the strange group. "What the hell do we have here?"

A little person wearing brown corduroy pants, a white Henley, and suspenders pushed through to the front of the crowd. Pandora smiled. "Aww, look at the little person. He's so adorable."

The little person growled, showing spiked teeth. He ran to the front of the church and began hissing and snarling at Pandora. She tilted her head to the side. "Hmm, you are not quite as cute as I thought."

Katie picked up the front of her dress and turned to the congregation. "Those who can fight, get into position.

Those who can't, stay in the church. This is holy ground, so you should be safe. Calvin, that means you."

Calvin gritted his teeth, then looked at Sofia and nodded at Katie. "Be careful out there."

Pandora smirked, reaching down and ripping the bottom of her dress off up to her thighs.

Timothy gasped.

Pandora winked at him. "Be right back. Momma's got to deal with some wedding crashers."

16

The soldiers took off their dress jackets and filed out of the church in shirts and ties. The carnies were gathering down the road as if waiting for something. That was fine with the soldiers. They popped the trunks of their cars in unison and pulled out cases of weapons.

In the church, Sofia smirked at Calvin. "Really? Your friends brought guns to the wedding?"

Calvin shrugged helplessly. "When they party, they party hard."

The soldiers slapped on body armor and slammed magazines into rifles. They had come prepared and were ready for a fight. They knew full well there was always a possibility of an attack, especially when they weren't expecting one. They were just glad it wasn't on the base since there was too much there to lose.

Katie waved her hand to direct the soldiers. "Form up! Front line, I want you to mow down the smaller guys. Flanks, push out as many as you can. We want to cut this pack down to size."

The soldiers hustled down the dirt road toward the carnies, then took their positions and waited. The circus people screamed a battle cry and charged the soldiers, who let loose a brutal barrage. The wave of carnies crashed into them, and shrieking and screams echoed across the entire valley. Soldiers blasted their guns into the crowd, dropping several of the infected. Some of the larger infected fought back with hellish strength, making a dent in the soldier's line.

Korbin and Stephanie pulled on their vests and grabbed their weapons. Stephanie pulled a pair of pants out of the trunk and dropped her dress, then changed into something more suited to battle. Korbin looked down at the small gun strapped to her leg.

"For the wedding? Just in case?"

Stephanie shrugged. She dropped the small hold-out gun in favor of twin pistols. "*You* never go anywhere unprepared."

Korbin smiled and kissed her on the top of the head. "I fucking love you, woman. You think of everything."

Stephanie pulled Korbin's favorite gun out of the bag and handed it to him. "Sure as hell do."

Juntto pulled off his clothes and handed them to Angie. He kissed her on the cheek and roared as he turned toward the rampaging carnies. He grew tall, blue, and ferocious—his frost giant form. Without hesitation, he charged at the strongman. Before the strongman knew what was happening, Juntto had wrapped his arms around him and was wrestling him to the ground. The strongman lived up to his name, but Juntto was, well...Juntto. The frost giant grabbed him by the neck and lifted him into the air with both hands before slamming him hard into the ground. The ground shook beneath them as he pounded his fists into the man's chest.

Stephanie ran into the fight and leveled her pistols at the bearded lady. "Look, I know beards are in style right now, but I think you might have gone a bit too far."

The woman snarled with rage. Her eyes flashed red and long talons grew from her fingertips. Stephanie shot at her but she dodged, moving with demonic speed. The woman's beard fluttered as she lunged at Stephanie. At the last moment, Stephanie flipped sideways in a cartwheel and landed on her feet. She whirled and pulled the trigger, striking the bearded woman in the left arm. The woman wailed in pain but charged Stephanie again, unwilling to give up.

Korbin circled around the crowd and charged the large group of Damned fighting the soldiers in the back. As he ran his foot hooked on something and he fell, rolling across the ground. Korbin cursed himself. That had been an amateur move. Before he could get up the little person pounced on him, stomping his chest. The little person then snarled and fell toward his face. Korbin grabbed him around the waist and held him high as he struggled to his feet.

He stood there with the snarling, slashing guy hanging from his hands, unsure what to do next. Juntto walked up and tapped him on the shoulder. "Hey. Do you mind?"

Korbin handed him over. Juntto reared back and punted the little person across the field. Juntto chuckled. "I figured out that I'm pretty good at football." Korbin shook his head as another carnie tackled Juntto's legs. They slid past Korbin and rolled in the dirt. Juntto pounded the carnie into the dust.

Korbin shook his head. Shit had gotten just plain weird in recent months. He was fighting carnies and little people. It was definitely not like the old days with demons and poltergeists.

A loud roar brought Korbin's attention back to the fight. An extremely tall, thin man with red eyes charged him. Korbin brought his gun up and fired.

Calvin hobbled to the doorway and leaned on his cane, watching the fight rage across the desert. His team was pummeling through demons, but all he could do was stand there and stare. He slammed the tip of his cane against the ground in frustration. "I should be out there fighting these bastards. Instead I am in here with this damn cane!"

Calvin threw his cane across the church, where it slammed into the wall. He put his hands over his face. Anger and frustration flooded into him. He knew there was nothing he could do about it. He was about to apologize to the others when a force plowed into him and sent him flying into the pews. He struggled to stand until Sofia's screams brought him to his feet.

At the altar was one body with two heads. It was the conjoined twins. Their heads were mostly bald, except for a small sprout of a ponytail popping from the top of each. They advanced on Sofia, who had backed herself into the crucifix. Calvin looked around for a weapon. Just outside the door was a small gun and holster set—Stephanie's holdout piece. He grabbed the tiny thing and checked the ammo. Fully loaded.

He limped as fast as he could back into the church, where the twins were grabbing at Sofia. Her diamond bracelet unlatched and fell to the ground, breaking into shimmering pieces on the floor. Calvin growled and limped down the aisle. "Get the fuck away from my bride, bitches."

He pulled the trigger twice. One bullet slammed into one head, then the other. They dropped to the ground and turned to dust right in front of Sofia. She looked absolutely terrified and ran to Calvin, wrapping her arms around him.

She wiped the tears from her eyes and turned to the piles of ash. "They were infected, but they were people, too."

Calvin nodded, putting the gun in the back of his pants. "That's the life of a Damned."

Belphegor pulled at the collar of his white button-down shirt. He stopped at the edge of the palace and pulled the skin on his face into place. The heat in Ghana was helping to shrink his human skin against his demon body. It was no longer sagging, but it still wasn't fitting quite right, either. The skin was starting to look a little worse for wear after all of the places he had been. He was there to speak to Ghana's head of state about Katie. He hoped they would join the rest of the World Council in condemning her.

Inside the palace, he sat with the leaders of government

and gave them the same spiel he had given the others. Ghana had yet to be targeted by the demons, but that made the threat of a future attack even more worrisome. The country was largely impoverished, so they would never recover from any substantial attack.

The president took a deep breath. "If she is that dangerous, then we do not want her here."

Belphegor smiled and nodded. "Good. Then you will sign?"

The president looked at the others. "I am not sure. I would like to hear more from the Council on this."

Belphegor snickered, looking around. "Why hear from them if you can *be* one of them?"

The president raised an eyebrow. "What do you mean?"

Belphegor swallowed hard. "If you sign this condemnation for Katie, I will make sure you have a seat on the World Council. Not just any seat, but one of the leadership positions. Take Ghana off the sidelines and find your rightful place in this world."

He thought about it for a moment. With a small smile, the president reached out and shook Belphegor's sweaty hand. "We will be in touch."

Belphegor was shown out of the palace. He walked quickly back into the village, ducking into an alley. He wiped the sweat from his forehead and opened a portal to hell, then stepped through and sighed. Home again. Before he could say anything to Baal, the big demon rushed toward him.

Belphegor put up his hands to stop the demon. Baal was livid and he snarled, "What are you doing out there? I hired you to do a job, but I have seen nothing from you. In the meantime, I have Beelzebub knocking down my door and pointing fingers."

Belphegor groaned. "Relax. I am working on it. I have a plan, but in order for it to work, I have to have unanimous consent from the World Council. We need to turn every single one of them against Katie. They have to fully trust me, rely on me. I have this all worked out. By the end of this we will have our angels. You can count on it."

Baal found a wayward Chihuahua and snapped its head off. "You better be right."

Katie pushed the straps of her dress off her shoulders and let the dress fall in a pile at her feet. Underneath she was wearing a tight black corset and black stretch pants. She leaned down and took off her heels, throwing her clothes into the car. She grabbed her boots and slipped them on, lacing them up quickly.

Pandora rolled her eyes. *Why didn't I think about that? Oh well, the world's gonna see what Pandora has under her dress today.*

Katie shook her head and straightened, rolling her shoulders. She used her energy to summon her angel powers and stood there as the light burst above her. Her golden armor covered her chest and shoulders, her shield hung from one arm, and her sword was sheathed on her back. She grabbed her holster from the car seat and strapped it around her waist, patting Tom and Harry.

A bolt of lightning shimmered across the sky and

Pandora's angel armor appeared, black and silver with a long sword to match.

Katie was impressed. "No robes or crown of thorns today?"

"Let's fuck these bitches up."

Pandora stepped forward, but Katie put her hand out and stopped her. "Wait."

"*Wait*? They're attacking us."

"These people were just changed. We should be able to pull the demons out of a bunch of them. What do you think? We've already got the wings, so why not do a little angel work today?"

Pandora shrugged. "Hell, why not? Might as well be a force for good." She winked at Katie. "Just this once."

Katie smiled, and the two charged onto the field. They moved in tandem, reaching at the same time to grab demons by the neck. Pandora sank her claws into the infected human and pulled out a snarling demon, holding it up in the air. It screamed and clawed at her. Pandora's eyes went so blue they burned, and the demon exploded.

Katie slammed her target on the ground and rammed her hand into his chest. The human groaned, and she yanked out the demon. The human mechanic slumped, passing out, while his former demon raged in Katie's hands. Katie tossed it in the air and watched with blue eyes as it hissed and burst. Katie dusted off her hands and nodded at Pandora.

"Not too shabby."

Pandora snickered. "Two down, twenty more to go."

They went to work. They moved as a team through the carnies, grabbing infected and exorcising their demons.

Stephanie and Korbin understood. They began catching infected and holding them until Katie or Pandora could exorcise them.

Juntto had no interest in mercy. He slashed through the carnies looking for the strongman. The big carnie was nursing his wounds at the back of the crowd, where he stood over the bodies of two soldiers. His eyes blazed red when he saw the big blue frost giant.

Juntto stomped over to him and drew his fist back, landing a huge right hook on the strongman. The man stumbled but righted himself. He growled and launched himself at Juntto. Juntto let him come. He wrestled the strongman to the ground, then grabbed him by the head, leaned back, and pulled as hard as he could. The skin on the strongman's neck began to rip, and with a wet crunch, his head popped off. It slipped out of Juntto's hands and went flying.

Juntto looked at the bodies of the fallen soldiers and nodded to them. He dusted his hands.

Stephanie was battling the bearded lady, dancing and weaving to avoid her claws. Just as she was about to slash at Stephanie again a flying head slammed into the carnie, knocking her down. Stephanie frowned. It was the strongman's head. Stephanie scanned the battlefield. Juntto stood yards away. He grinned and waved at her. She laughed and waved back. She aimed her gun at the woman's head for several moments before sighing and putting it back in its holster.

She grabbed the woman's arms and dragged the half-conscious creature toward Pandora. "I'm getting fucking soft." Stephanie dropped the woman in front of her. "Can you pull out her demon?"

Pandora smirked. "Aww, look at you, getting all angelic. That's sweet."

Pandora reached into the bearded lady's chest and pulled out the demon. The creature spat and fought to crawl back into the woman, and Pandora pulled the demon's face to hers. It froze, recognizing her. Pandora glared at it with her blue eyes, and the demon let go of the body. It floated upward. The bearded lady slumped, unconscious, as the demon exploded.

After the last body had hit the ground, Katie tilted her head back. Only the soldiers were left standing. Katie caught her breath. "Well, if that wasn't a kickass reception, I don't know what is."

Pandora snickered. "This was definitely my kind of party."

The soldiers immediately began collecting the passed-out carnies and loading them into their cars to take them back to the base. Katie and Pandora walked up the steps of the church and found Sofia and Calvin standing in the back. Pandora took Sofia's hands in hers. "Sorry we ruined your wedding. We thought we had enough time."

Sofia sniffled, looking down at the pile of ash. "I knew what I was getting into when I proposed to Calvin. I didn't know at that time if he would continue to be a merc. Either way, I was prepared."

Sofia hugged Pandora, then Katie. Calvin handed his gun to Katie and limped over to retrieve his cane. "That was definitely creepy as hell, but hey, I didn't see any clowns."

Pandora rolled her eyes. "I would kick one of those bitches right in his fucking red nose."

Sofia laughed. Korbin, Juntto, Stephanie, and Angie joined them. Stephanie grinned. "Did we forget to tell you we hired a circus for your wedding? Bet you didn't see that one coming."

Sofia shrugged. "Maybe not a demon-infested carnie show, but I am not the least bit surprised it was something freaky."

Pandora laughed. "*We* are the freaks, honey."

They started to leave the church when Katie grabbed Calvin and Sofia. She cleared her throat. Pandora gave her a quizzical look. Katie nodded to the couple. "Forgetting something?"

Pandora slapped her forehead. "Oh. Duh." She raised her hands over the couple. "I now pronounce you Hunk of Man-meat and Hot Momma." She wiggled her eyebrows at Sofia. "Honey, if you don't kiss him, I will."

Sofia laughed, grabbed Calvin, and kissed the hell out of him.

17

Katie tapped her foot as she waited for the sugar to melt in the pan. It was the same pan she'd had at the original base, stained and burned from the copious amounts of sugar popcorn she had made over the years. As the sugar swirled around, she put several drops of food coloring in and stirred that in, too. She poured the mixture into the container of popcorn and put on the lid. She shook the container, doing a private little dance as she coated that popcorn in dyed sugar. She tossed the pan into the sink and ran hot water over it. She had learned her lesson about leaving the sugar residue in the pan. If she left it, by morning it had turned into a brick.

Pandora sniffed the air. *Mmm, this is a treat. What's the special occasion? Besides my obvious awesomeness, of course.*

You don't remember the wedding?

You know what I mean.

Katie poured the coated popcorn into two large bowls. *We are all together. We have no calls. Tonight we're taking a* quiet evening to enjoy our soaps. Figured it would be a good opportunity for family time, especially now that the guys can be out of the med wing whenever they want.

Pandora groaned. *Always so mushy.*

Popcorn, though.

This is very mushy, so I get a lot of popcorn.

Fair enough.

Katie grabbed the bowls. Pandora might be complaining, but deep down she knew her demon really enjoyed being part of their little family. She walked around the corner into the living room and smiled when she saw everyone there. She hadn't seen the whole group in one warm place in a very long time. Pandora was too busy trying to reach out of her and grab popcorn to enjoy the moment, but that was all right.

Katie put a bowl down on each of the small tables. She smacked Pandora's hand and laughed when she yanked it back inside. Katie tossed some popcorn into her mouth and walked to the television, appropriating the remote. She cleared her throat and addressed the crowd. "Welcome, everyone, to our not-often-enough *Days of Long Since Past* binge-watch. Some of you have already seen many of these episodes, but you are going to have to just deal. We all need to get caught up. I would appreciate a lack of spoilers as we watch."

Juntto put up his hand, looking like a big blue third-grader. "Why do they call it a soap opera?"

Timothy shot his hand into the air and shook it wildly. "Oh, oh, I know this. Because in the 1930s when they started making serials, soap manufacturers were the first sponsors."

The whole crowd murmured. Katie nodded, impressed. "Thank you, Timothy. I didn't know that."

Timothy bowed to them. "I am a beautiful capsule of useless information."

Katie turned to the television and pointed the remote. "Are we ready?"

There were a couple of groans, a cheer, and some grumbles. Katie shrugged. "Good enough. Here we go."

She turned on the episode and jumped on the couch with Brock and looked around the room. Everyone was lounging all over everyone else. It was a comfy and homey scene, something they desperately needed. Hopefully, it would scrub the battle from their minds. Katie was happy to be back with the whole team for a little bit.

Timothy was sitting in the big armchair, dressed in satin pajamas with his initials embroidered on the pocket and filing his fingernails. Eddie, Sean, and Turner were in a row to the right. They were no longer confined to their beds, but they were all in wheelchairs. They looked like they were getting back to normal. Turner was texting on his phone, Eddie was poking at him, and Sean was rolling his eyes. They were definitely acting like their old selves, even if they couldn't run around. Katie was situated at the far end of a long moon-shaped couch with pillows everywhere. It was new and incredibly comfortable.

Although they seemed relaxed and comfortable, reminders of their battles were all around them. Calvin sat at the opposite end of the couch with a cane propped up against it. His eyes seemed to wander away from the television from time to time as if he were lost in his own thoughts. Sofia was curled up in the crook of his arm, munching on popcorn. Next to them, Korbin had his arms stretched out on the back of the couch. Stephanie was curled up like a cat against him.

Juntto crossed his legs in front of him. He had morphed to look like one of the characters on the show. As the story progressed, Juntto stared at the screen, completely confused. "Those two douchebags are demon-killers?"

Angie nodded. "Yeah, they started hunting demons when the portals were opening."

Juntto chewed his mouthful of popcorn. "They know Tomas is an infected, and he's not a good guy. Why don't they just kill him? Or even get that weird bourbon-drinking priest to exorcise him? They just kind of let him run around like an evil wizard."

"Money. Power. All those things we crave as humans," Timothy answered.

Angie rolled her eyes. "Timothy has this absurd theory that the demon hunters are being paid off to leave him alone."

"But you don't believe that?" Juntto asked.

Angie scoffed. "No. I think it's a low-budget soap opera and there are plot holes—like we haven't seen them in this show before."

Juntto shook his finger at the television. "But wait. Who is this person now?"

The guys threw pieces of popcorn at Juntto, shushing him. Angie laughed and patted his leg. "Just watch, baby. I can explain things later."

Katie chuckled and ate another piece of sugar corn. She put her hand down on top of Brock's. Instead of pulling away, she squeezed his hand and glanced at him. Brock looked her deep in the eyes and smiled. Katie got butterflies in her chest. She smiled and leaned her head on his shoulder.

Pandora laughed. *Uh oh. Looks like sexy time is only a matter of hours from going down. That's right, girl. Get it!*

Quiet down. We're having a sweet moment.

Sweet and salty, girl. As with everything in life, you need a balance.

The bright desert sunlight crept between the cracks of the blinds on Katie's bedroom window, slashing across the floor and over Katie's face. She wrinkled her nose, her eyes shut tightly, and turned onto her stomach. Her hand slipped beneath the sheets and encountered warm skin next to her. She opened her eyes—it was Brock. She smiled and snuggled into the pillow, watching him sleep.

Pandora yawned. *Isn't it a bit early to be thinking deeply about Brock? For fuck's sake, he just plowed you like six hours ago. The man is still in your bed.*

Katie let out a slow, quiet breath. *I know. I just was thinking about everything and how so much is going to change. I know Brock thinks he is going to roll back into fights like nothing is different, but I don't know if I can let him do that. I don't know if I can have him on the main team. We do the most dangerous jobs, and his demon is just not up to par. I would be worried about him during the entire fight.*

Pandora sighed. *Yeah, but he's not going to be terrible. He's just going to have to compensate for the loss.*

Katie rolled over on her back and put her hands on her

belly. *You know I love being a merc; it's like my thing. My calling.*

Pandora was suspicious. *Yeah.*

Katie watched the blades of the fan spin above her. *At the same time, things have changed. Seeing Calvin and Sofia making choices for their future makes me wonder if I shouldn't consider the same thing.*

Pandora scoffed. *And do what? You and Brock run off into the sunset and get a farmhouse in the hills? Hide from everyone? I don't think you could do it. I think no matter how much you care about Brock, you will always be drawn to this fight. For fuck's sake, Katie, you are made for it with your angel blood.*

And there's nothing else I want to do, believe me. I don't even know what Brock wants.

You seemed to have a pretty good idea last night.

Katie smiled to herself. *You're not wrong there. But with Calvin getting married and leaving the team, it just makes me think.*

Pandora grumbled. She was hungry, but she also knew the conversation had to be finished before she would get food. *Look, they are going on their honeymoon. He might not have a demon anymore, but he isn't completely abandoning the family. He hasn't even decided what he's going to do. And Korbin and Stephanie are married, but they have chosen a life of fighting.*

Katie looked at the time and slowly worked her way out of the bed. *Maybe you're right. Either way, we have to go out and see Calvin and Sofia off. I had the jet chartered so they wouldn't have to fly commercial.*

Pandora giggled. *Uh oh, you're gonna have Long Dong Calvin giving it to his new bride all over your new jet.*

Katie grimaced. *I'm just going to imagine them sleeping on the flight. I don't even know where they are going. Calvin wanted to keep it a secret for security purposes.*

You mean, so he could have private time with his lady.

Whatever. I let him work all that out with the pilot.

Katie pulled on a pair of black stretch pants and her black halter top. She grabbed a cardigan and pushed her arms through the sleeves. She looked at herself in the mirror and twisted her bulky hair into a messy bun on the top of her head. She pulled the covers back over Brock and kissed his forehead.

She poked her head into the dining room but it was empty, so she made her way outside to the landing strip.

Sofia stood near the plane with the cool desert wind blowing around her. She looked beautiful in a peach-colored satin dress and a warm faux fur wrap around her shoulders. Calvin put the last piece of luggage into the storage area beneath the plane and hobbled back to them.

Sofia took Katie by the hands. "Thank you so much. For everything."

Katie hugged her tightly. "You are more than welcome. Only the best for my BFF and his new girl. Where are you guys jetting off to?"

Sofia reached out to straighten the front of Calvin's sports coat. "He won't tell me. The only hint he has given is that it is someplace warm and tropical."

"That sounds amazing. I'm pretty sure there is snow in New York City right now. Not looking forward to the cold-as-hell winter fight coming up."

Sofia looked at the two of them and kissed Calvin on the cheek. "I'm gonna go on up."

Calvin nodded. "I'll be right there."

They watched Sofia board the plane, and Katie turned back to Calvin. "Long Dong Silver has finally tied the knot."

Calvin narrowed his eyes. "Katie or Pandora?"

Katie laughed. "I'm not letting Pandora out right now. She is being feisty. Have you given any thought to what you are going to do when you get back?"

"No, not really. I'm sure Sofia and I will talk about it. We have a baby to plan for and a future to figure out."

Katie nodded. "Yeah. No need to think about it all right now. Just enjoy your honeymoon. Please don't get caught up in any strange drug-cartel deals while you are gone."

Calvin laughed, turning to board the plane. "I can't promise you a damn thing."

Eddie stuck his tongue out and closed one eye like he was sighting a rifle. He pointed between two buildings. "So, down the straightaway, then loop around that barracks, across the back of Joshua's building, and back here. No shortcuts through the mess hall, no bullshit. First one back gets to claim that foxy nurse Tina as their own."

Sean raised an eyebrow. "Does Tina get a say?"

"Sure, but how could she resist?"

Turner tilted his head to the side. "We're not supposed to be exerting ourselves."

That was true. They were all still in wheelchairs. Both Eddie and Sean stared at him. Usually, Turner was the one who had zero self-control. He looked at them for a second, then broke into a smile, wagging his finger at them. "Psych. Ha! I am going to cream you assholes."

They lined their wheelchairs up, still talking shit. Eddie raised his hand and started the countdown. "Five, four, three, two, *go!*"

They took off across the dusty ground, pumping their arms quickly. Their wheelchairs rattled and shook as they sped across the base, moving at speeds the chairs definitely were not built for. As they passed the midway point, Katie stepped into their path. All of them raised their hands and tried to slow down. Sean and Turner managed to come to a safe stop, but Eddie barreled forward. He pulled his brakes at the last minute and skidded across the ground. Katie stood there calmly as he came to a stop just inches from her legs.

Eddie gave her a grin. "Hey there, Katie."

She returned the grin. "I thought you boys weren't supposed to be exerting yourselves? If you manage to hurt yourselves, it means that much more time before you can move out of the med wing."

Turner threw his head back. "But just sitting around is so boring."

"You can't think of it as boring. You have to think of it as relaxing. Just imagine you're sitting on the beach instead of being in the hospital."

Turner just blinked at her. Katie shook her head. "Whatever. You need to take it easy, but that's not why I found you guys. I had a question for you."

Eddie smiled. "Yes, we will go to war with you in our wheelchairs."

"We need a cool name," Sean mused.

"Rolling Roughnecks?"

"Wheelie Warriors?"

"Oh, I like that one."

Katie smirked. "Thanks for the offer, but that's not quite it. I wanted to find out if you guys would like demons again. You aren't healing very fast, but that's how humans work. And when you *do* heal, what will you do? Will you go back to regular military duty? You may be discharged, or you may be put back into battle without a demon."

Turner sighed. "I really haven't given it a lot of thought. Personally, I don't know if I want to be Damned again. It was cool, but now I have a chance for something else."

Eddie and Sean nodded. Eddie pointed at Sean. "You sure you don't want your demon back?"

"I don't know, man. I've seen some shit. Spiderwomen, towns covered in lava. I don't mind being a soldier, but being Damned was something else."

"But your demon gave you abilities," Eddie pointed out.

"Yeah, like healing." Sean looked down at his legs. "I'm all messed up."

Eddie thought for a moment. "And reading, too."

"What are you talking about?"

"Your demon could read. You know." Eddie cracked a wry smile.

Sean frowned. "I can read."

"Come on, we all know you were illiterate before you became Damned."

"I can read!" Sean's face grew red.

Eddie looked at Katie. "Poor boy. Can't read a stop sign. Another child left behind."

Sean rammed his wheelchair into Eddie's. "I can read, dingleberry! I'll read all day! I'll read right now."

Katie cracked up and shook her head. "Okay. I can see I'm not going to get anywhere today. Not a problem. I just figured I would put it out there. You don't have to decide anytime soon. Take your time."

"In the meantime, you need to be resting," Brock put in. He walked up behind them with Korbin.

Turner growled. "Look who's talking. You just got back too. Where the hell are you going? If you get to fight and the Wheelie Warriors are stuck here, I am protesting."

Korbin chuckled. "Relax. No one is fighting."

Katie looked at Korbin, slightly confused. "Where are you guys going?"

Korbin glanced at Brock, realizing he hadn't had a chance to talk to Katie. "Brock isn't going anywhere. He is staying here to get back in shape. I have business elsewhere for the general. I will bring you up to speed on the details later, but I have to get a move on. Timothy will be accompanying me for now, but if he is needed back here at any point I'll put him on a plane right away."

Brock led the guys back to the med unit, kicking at their wheelchairs to keep them in line. Katie crossed her arms on her chest. "And Timothy will be safe without a demon?"

Korbin nodded. "We are going into territories that need to be reinforced. Fortified, just like we've done here. The general wants me to oversee the construction of battlements. These are places that have already been attacked or are in danger of being attacked. Prime targets. It's for the general, so we'll have military support. The incursions have always been bad, but they're getting worse. You can't be everywhere at once. We need to give people around the world a place to stand and fight."

Katie nodded. "Right. Good. I don't mean to question your thought process."

Korbin chuckled and put his arm around Katie. "It's a good thing. This is your team, and you are keeping everyone safe. I'm assuming you're going to head back to New York?"

"Eventually."

"Stephanie is in charge of the base, then. She knows the ins and outs better than anyone. Brock is staying on. I spoke with the general, and if he wants the job, he's my new head of security here. He knows tactics and demon fighting better than most of the people left here."

"It'll be good for him to get back to the grind without being thrown out into the field right away. The guys already know Brock, and they respect him."

Korbin shook his head. "Those were my thoughts exactly. As far as the Special Forces guys, Turner, Sean, and Eddie? They have been given the okay to stay here if that is what they want. Once they are healed, the general will talk to them about what's next. General Brushwood was very adamant about them having choices. They've been crucial to the war effort so far."

Katie looked back at the guys. They had teamed up against Brock and were knocking his shins with their wheelchairs. He was trying to fend them off. "Good. I'm glad they'll be here, where I know they are comfortable.

I'm not sure what my plan is right now, but I will help wherever I can."

"Good." Korbin squeezed her shoulder. "Because you are a true leader. You and Pandora both."

Pandora sniffled. *Oh, get off it, old man. Get out of here.*

18

Timothy leaned back in his chair and sighed. He put his feet up on the desk and swayed in his office chair, his mind stuck in the events of the night before. He had finally managed to hook up with one of the soldiers who had been flirting with him for over a year. He was tall, dark, and handsome—just how Timothy liked his men. It had been a very long time since he had gotten down and dirty, and he was feeling renewed.

He reached over and grabbed a handful of grapes from a bag by his computer, then tossed one up in the air and caught it. He rolled it to the front of his mouth and held in between his front teeth. Suddenly an alarm began to sound, and his feet crashed to the floor. He chomped the grape while typing feverishly on the computer. The screen flickered a bit, and a bright red box appeared in front of him. An incursion had come out of nowhere.

Timothy scribbled down the coordinates and lifted an eyebrow. "Who attacks Canada? They are like the baby sister of the world."

The bright red box was right over Toronto. It was a bit stronger than the one he had seen a few days earlier, the one that had brought a wave of infected carnies. He grabbed his phone and dialed Katie. She yawned as she answered. "I was just talking with Korbin about your little trip."

Timothy nodded. "Yeah, we can talk about that later. Right now you have an incursion to deal with."

"Well, hot damn, I was wondering how long it would be until another hit," Katie replied.

Timothy read through the scrolling information on the screen. "Looks like a decent-sized one, too. Right over Toronto."

Katie wrinkled her nose. "Why would anyone, demon or not, attack Canada?"

Timothy slapped his knee. "That's what I'm saying! Anyway, they haven't participated in the demon training too much, so they are going to need some backup. I'm not even sure they have a protocol in place to handle a demon incursion. Here, let me send your phone a few images."

Katie sighed. "Okay, I'll head down and get ready. Do me a favor and let everyone know. I will take this one alone, though. Stephanie needs to stay here. Besides, from the images you just sent to my phone, it looks like I've got it. Handled bigger ones on my own before."

Timothy hated when she went out alone, but she was the boss. "Will do. I'll get the information to the general as well."

"Perfect," Katie replied before hanging up.

Timothy looked at the incursion site and shook his

head. "Looks like we got some hockey-playing demons this time around."

Katie hurried down the stairs to the training area. Pandora stepped out of her and rolled her shoulders. Katie glanced over and rolled her eyes. "Why are you never wearing clothes?"

Pandora looked down at her naked body. "Because I live inside of you."

"You live inside of me naked? Gross."

"Plenty of people, men and women, would pay to have me naked inside them."

"But…"

"You heard me. Besides, it's not quite what you're thinking, asshole. And I'm usually given a bit more notice. It's an emergency, so my cooch is out. A thousand fucking apologies, okay? Don't worry, I got clothes in the locker over here."

Katie took her boots from the locker and pulled them on, lacing them up the front. "I would bring a coat since we're going to Toronto in the winter. It's going to be cold as fuck."

Juntto walked through the door, glanced at Pandora, and looked away. "Jesus, put some clothes on. I don't walk around with big Juntto hanging out."

Pandora snorted. "You don't walk around naked anymore. It's not like it's the first time you've seen these tatas."

Juntto walked to Katie and sat down on the bench. "Hope it's the last, though."

Katie chuckled. "What are you doing?"

Juntto cracked his knuckles. "The general called me. I'm taking side jobs with him."

Angie hurried into the room carrying an armful of gear. She dumped it next to Juntto. "Here. You would forget your head if it weren't attached."

Juntto kissed Angie on the cheek. "The true angel."

Pandora zipped up the front of her spandex suit and pulled a holster around her waist. "So Big Boy Leviathan is working with Brushwood. How did that happen?"

Juntto shrugged, taking his clothes off. "He needed help, and all the good soldiers are down. He is making me Juntto-sized weapons."

Pandora snarled her lip. "What does that even mean?"

Joshua came rushing through the door, rolling a cart with a large black case on it. "It means a whole lot of metal, a huge cast, and working as fast as we could. Juntto, this is the first of many."

Juntto morphed into his frost giant form and lumbered over to Joshua, his head close to the ceiling. "What do you have, weapons man?"

"I'm working on some things for you, but I have a friend who put together a prototype in New York. It's actually a modified anti-aircraft gun from a battleship. Anyway, we're going to airlift it to you in Toronto. But in the meantime?"

Juntto helped Joshua pull the case off the cart and unlatch the large catches holding it shut. He opened the lid, and Juntto gave an appreciative grunt. Joshua put his hands on his hips proudly. "This is a giant war-spear completely constructed out of special metal. I wouldn't accidentally brush it against Katie or Pandora since it would hurt like a bitch."

Pandora walked up next to Joshua and put her arm on his shoulder. "Look at you, getting all badass with your weapon making. Good job, Joshua. Now all we have to do is get you a woman, and you'll be the bee's knees."

Joshua chuckled nervously. "I'm good, thanks."

Pandora shrugged. "Suit yourself. All right, gang, you ready?"

Katie slammed Tom into his holster. Juntto kissed Angie again, this time nearly knocking her over. "Be safe. Kick ass."

Juntto gave her a big blue thumbs-up.

Pandora slashed her hands and opened a large portal. Katie flinched as the heat hit her like a punch. Pandora waved them through. "In and out, no lingering in hell."

Juntto snorted as he stepped through and found himself next to a lava mountain. "Yes, because I long for a hot, hellish vacation."

Pandora jumped back into Katie, which allowed her body to tolerate the heat of hell. Katie raised her hand, and it became Pandora's as she opened a portal—only nothing happened.

Uh, Pandora?

Shut up, I'm concentrating. Pandora waved her hand again, and a tiny portal opened.

Juntto frowned at it. "My left nut wouldn't fit through that."

Tell the blue popsicle to piss up a rope, Pandora growled

and slashed her hand down, ripping the portal open wide. *There we go. Sorry.*

You okay?

I'm great! Let's get the fuck out of here, how about that?

This time instead of intense heat hitting them, frigid cold air blasted their faces. Katie and Juntto stepped through and the portal snapped closed behind them.

Pandora came forward just to chatter Katie's teeth. "Santa's nutsack, it's fucking cold here."

Steam rose off Juntto's body. He breathed the cold air in through his nose and let it out with a sigh. "I miss cold, snowy weather. Fantastic." He roared and shook his spear in the air. "The cold makes us strong!"

Katie rolled her eyes.

Down the street was the hockey stadium the Toronto Maple Leafs called home. Shrieks and screams echoed from inside. Juntto raised his eyebrows. "Hope you brought your pads, because it looks like this incursion is on ice."

Katie turned her head toward Juntto. "Great. Not just demons but angry hockey demons. I feel like that could be more dangerous than Moloch was."

Pandora sniffed. *They're definitely in there. Come on, let's get this over with so I can defrost. My nipples could cut diamond right now.*

They made their way to the stadium and broke in through the service entrance, then climbed into the stands and looked out over the rink. Below was a mixture of strange demons, crazy demon creatures, and infected hockey players. Half the demons were scrambling around on the ice, falling down and sliding into walls. The hockey players were faring a bit better. They held their sticks firmly as they circled the rink. Their eyes were blood-red. The thud of Juntto pounding his spear on the floor echoed through the stands. The creatures turned to him and snarled, then clattered over and scratched at the glass partition furiously.

Katie shook her head. "Calm down, assholes. You won't have to wait long for me to kick your asses."

She closed her eyes and summoned her angelic armor. The gold armor shone as it appeared. Katie's eyes flashed blue as she reached back and pulled the sword from its sheath. She nodded to Juntto, and the frost giant grabbed Katie and tossed her up and over the partition. She spread her wings and floated to the ice, flapping them as she landed. They helped her get traction.

Pandora snarled and growled. *I hate fucking hockey. Fuck this. I want to fight.*

Katie didn't have a chance to say a word before Pandora leaped from her body in a skin-tight bodysuit and skates, tackling one of the hockey players and yanking the demon from his chest. She pushed his body out of the way and jumped back to her feet. "Time to kick some ass. Hoo, boy. This is gonna be fun."

Katie rolled her eyes. She spun around and slammed an approaching demon in the chin with her fist. She swung her sword brutally and sliced the demon's head off its shoulders. Another demon was already charging her, lowering its shoulder to hit her hard in the chest. She grunted but gripped the demon's head. His massive strength pushed her across the ice into the glass partition. She struggled to raise her sword, then jammed it into his gut. The demon squealed loudly and turned to dust, freeing her weapon.

Across the rink, Pandora hummed a light tune as she sped along, turning and twisting like a professional skater. She picked up speed and jumped, spinning three times with one blade extended. It slashed the throats of the demons surrounding her. They hit the ice and turned to dust before she even landed. She came to a stop and took a bow. "Triple axel, bitches. Gold medal."

A demon snapped at her from one side, and she frowned and grabbed it by the throat. With a grunt, she ripped its head off its shoulders. "Don't rain on my parade, you fucking piece of shit."

Juntto slipped wildly on the ice and groaned, knowing he was going down. Several demons screamed as his huge form connected with them, imprinting their bodies into the rink floor. His huge spear clattered across the ice.

Pandora cackled. "Isn't ice your element, you big blue bitch?"

Juntto roared, "My time with the humans has made me weak! Don't worry, I got this."

Juntto shook it off and jumped up. Ice skates formed on the soles of his feet, and he sped around the rink throwing Damned into the walls. He picked one up and looked at Pandora.

Pandora grinned and squatted, putting her hands out like a catcher. He tossed the Damned hockey player at her and she leaped up, grabbed him, and shoved her claw into his chest. She ripped the demon from his body and threw it toward the ceiling. It writhed and screamed before exploding. Pandora's eyes flashed blue as she lowered the unconscious hockey player. She put him in the penalty box for safekeeping, then ran back into the crowd of demons.

Juntto found his spear and threw it through the crowd. It impaled at least seven demons before it stuck in the wall on the other side of the rink.

Juntto nodded. "Juntto-sized weapons will get you every time. I am so much more productive!"

He raced over on his skates, the ice cracking below him from his massive weight. He yanked out his spear, backhanding a snarling demon while he was at it. The demon flew and Pandora caught it, ripping the snarling beast's head off. "Yeah, teamwork, bitches!"

Juntto threw his spear again, this time taking down three demons and two hockey players. Katie pointed her sword at the demon shish kabob. "Juntto-sized weapons. I get it now."

She turned back around to fight just as one of the Damned slugged her in the face. She fell back but quickly regained her balance. Her eyes flashed blue and her wings spread wide, lifting her just off the ice. The hockey player snarled and dove at her, slamming into her armor. The hit knocked the air out of her lungs, and the sword fell from her hand. Her wings folded over the two of them as they tumbled across the ice and into a wall.

The Damned straddled her, snarling and drooling, and pulled back to slash her with his new claws. As he leaned back, Katie thrust her arm into his chest. She growled and pulled the demon out of him, and the hockey player's eyes went wide. His whole body froze for a moment, then he shuddered and passed out, falling to the ice.

Katie stood and tossed the demon in the air, where it

burst. Katie caught her breath. She was feeling the strain of the fight. Without Pandora inside her she wasn't healing quite as fast as she normally did. Still, she had to keep going. It was going to take all three of them to clean up this demonic mess. She sheathed her sword and pulled out Tom and Harry. Katie ran forward and her wings unfolded, lifting her gently from the ice. She glided along inches from the ice, blasting at the oncoming demons. Bullets whizzed through the crowd, finding targets and turning them to ash. She came to a soft landing on the other side of the rink, quickly reloaded, and blasted another Damned in the head.

The guy flew back, his skin pulling on his bones as the demon scratched and writhed to get out. His mouth fell open, and a deafening scream echoed from his throat. Katie winced, putting the heels of her hands to her ears. She watched as something attempted to claw its way out of the hockey player's body, stretching his skin like taffy, then fell still. Katie carefully walked up to the demon, pointing Harry at his head. As her shoulders began to relax, the hockey player's eyes opened wide and he bared his teeth. The dead man leaped up.

Katie jumped, then pulled the trigger and turned him to dust. "Fuck, dude. You can't fucking roll at people like that! Shit!"

Katie put her guns back in their holsters, ready to pull her sword again. As she reached up, a demon grabbed her from behind and threw her. She slammed into the glass partition and groaned as she fell to the ice. Breathing heavily, she scratched her fingers into the ice, her eyes flashing a bright blue. Her entire body began to tremble as she rose.

As she spread her wings, a blue glow emanated from her body and she screamed. Her hair blew back, and a wave of energy burst from her entire being. The blue flame slashed the demons in its path, and they squealed and turned to ash. She had a moment to breathe.

Pandora saw the blue fire come from Katie and dove into the penalty box. Juntto frowned as the blue wave passed through him, but he barely felt it.

Pandora peeked from the box. "What the fuck was that?"

Katie chuckled. "Sorry. I was getting my ass kicked."

A demon popped up next to Pandora. It was in the penalty box with her. That made her jump and she screamed, grabbed the demon by the face, and ripped half of it off. The demon stumbled and ran out onto the ice. Pandora stood up and followed the wounded creature onto the ice. She wagged a finger at Katie. "Hey, would you try not to eviscerate me? Some of us demons are on the side of the angels."

Katie waved her hands. "Yeah, my bad."

Pandora did a double-take at the demon running around with half its jaw missing. She sighed and grabbed it by the top of its head. "At least you're fucking quiet."

She twisted the demon's head off with ease and tossed it behind her. Black blood splattered the ice beneath her feet. The sound of choppers overhead caught their attention. Through the glass tiles in the dome, they could see several Army choppers hovering. Pandora called to Juntto, "Bro, I think they're here for you."

Juntto shook his head. He jumped up, smashing into the ceiling with one huge fist. Chunks of glass and concrete and steel fell around him, plummeting to the ice. "Watch out, they're dropping weapons."

Pandora lifted an eyebrow. "Why would we have to watch out? It's just going to be a few crates of rifles."

A case the size of an SUV dropped from one of the choppers. The huge thing slammed into the ice, which flew everywhere. Demons scattered in all directions. Juntto slid his spear into a sheath on his back. He ripped open the case and lifted a launcher that looked like it should have been mounted to the deck of a battleship. "Juntto-sized weapons."

Pandora pursed her lips. "Right. Didn't think that one through. Go to town, buddy. Just don't shoot Katie or me!"

Katie peered at the thing. "Is that a rail gun?"

Juntto nodded enthusiastically. "Prototype. Badass."

He pointed the huge barrel at the center of the rink and Katie's eyes grew wide. "Uh oh."

She flew out of the rink and hovered up in the stands. Pandora gave her a look. Katie dropped down and grabbed Pandora from the ice just as Juntto pressed the trigger. A rocket shot out of the barrel and slammed into the center of the rink. Ice and demons exploded into tiny bits, and debris flew everywhere. Pandora rolled her eyes.

Katie dropped her back on the ice. "Don't you have wings?"

"Sorry. It's been so long since I used them that I forgot."

Katie flapped over to Juntto. "I think maybe that one is best used outdoors."

Juntto nodded feverishly. "I'll use the other."

He picked up another gun that looked like a tommy gun for giants. Or frost giants. He spun and pulled the trigger, spraying special bullets around the rink. The gun was pretty accurate for something so big. At least a dozen demons turned to dust. Pandora was impressed. "That's what I'm talking about."

Korbin handed a box of ammo to one of the soldiers helping him load the plane. He looked at the side of the airstrip, where Timothy was hugging Stephanie tightly. He let go and jogged toward the plane. Korbin nodded as he passed. "I'll be there in a few. Get comfortable. I think there is lunch on board."

Timothy pursed his lips. "Uh, duh. 'Cause I ordered it, silly. Go give smooches so we can hit the road, Jack."

Korbin took a deep breath. "It's going to be a long few months."

When he reached Stephanie, she smiled and slid her arms around his neck. Standing on her tiptoes, she kissed his lips gently. "I can't believe you are going to be gone so long. We aren't usually apart like this."

Korbin groaned. "I know. It's the hardest part about the whole thing. But when we're done, hopefully, I will be here more. These fortifications should cut down on the number of fights the mercs are needed for, not to mention the hundreds or thousands of lives they will save."

"I'm so proud of you. Always looking out for everyone else. You are my hero."

Korbin snorted, lifting Stephanie from the ground. "I just want to keep you safe, warm, and in my bed."

Stephanie smirked. "Mmm, I'll be waiting for you to return."

Korbin kissed her again and set her down. "Hold the fort, and try not to worry about me. I'll have my phone, and Timothy will have his. You can also communicate through the program with Timothy. Unless we are sleeping, there will always be a way to get hold of us. Besides, we are not going to be in combat. This is a building and security mission, that's it. It's not public knowledge yet."

Stephanie raised an eyebrow. "That's positive thinking at its best. Just don't let your guard down. You know the moment you do, some snarling bastard of a demon will come at you. And keep Timothy safe, please. He doesn't have a demon anymore so he won't have the strength or healing powers he did before. That could be a death sentence for him."

Korbin squeezed her hand. "I promise to watch after Twinkle Toes. Not sure if I'll survive this, though. I might end up feeding him to the wild animals out there."

Stephanie giggled. "Oh, stop it. He brightens up every situation. Use his positivity."

The plane's engines hummed behind him, and Korbin kissed Stephanie one last time. "I gotta get out of here. I'll call you when we land in Romania. I love you."

Stephanie blew him a kiss as he boarded the plane. "Please be safe out there."

The flight attendant smiled as Korbin climbed into the plane. "We are ready for takeoff." She secured the door before slipping off to the back. Korbin took a seat and buckled his belt, letting out a deep breath. He waved at Stephanie, who looked more worried than he had anticipated. Korbin didn't blame her, though. He was nervous about leaving her on her own, too.

When the plane had taken off and reached cruising altitude, Timothy turned on his iPad. "I figured this would be a good time to talk about intel. That way we can just enjoy the peace and quiet of the flight afterward."

Korbin nodded. "Sounds like a perfect idea."

Timothy showed Korbin the screen. "Okay, so this is the same town we pulled Brock and the team from—a small Romanian village surrounded by lush forests and flanked by an extensive mountainous arena. There is lava filling every single street, and many of the buildings burned down during the last incursion. From what I've been told, the fires are all out."

Korbin accepted a soda from the attendant. "Good. I've had enough fire for one lifetime."

"The thing is, when I've monitored this Romanian town, it looks like it is a place of constant incursion. Despite the military's reports that all portals have been closed, it looks on the map like there is one open. I can't seem to figure out what these readings mean. From the pictures, I expected to walk into a crowd of demons thicker than a Cher concert during Pride Week, but that's not the case. When I talk to the boots on the ground, they say that the area is clear."

Korbin furrowed his brow. "How can that be? That's strange. When I talked to Katie, she said it was a ghost town. Besides that church in the middle of town, there were no bodies. All the demons had been killed. Anyone who *could* get away did. Anyone who hadn't disappeared into the lava or was ripped apart by demons."

Timothy pulled up a split screen and brought up two different maps. "This one on the right was what Incursion Day looked like, or would have looked like. The one on the left is that town in Romania. It's showing a deeper and stronger concentration of energy than we had on Incursion Day. That's bad news bears, but not a whisper of any demons or even Damned running around."

Korbin took the iPad from Timothy and squinted at the screen. "And it's been like this the whole time?"

Timothy nodded. "Yep. Ever since the incursion. Do you think maybe it's the lava because it came from hell? Maybe it's made up of some detectable heat sources they didn't tell us about?"

Korbin stared at the screen. "I'll be honest, I have no idea. But you better believe I'm going to find out."

Baal pounded his fist on the round wooden door to Beelzebub's cave dwelling. The door slowly creaked open on its own, and Baal marched in. He wasn't going to allow himself to fear Beelzebub or his stinky cave. He entered the dimly lit living room and looked around. "Come on out. I know you're here."

Beelzebub stepped out from the shadows, swallowing the tail end of a baby black bear. "What can I do for my dear friend Baal?"

Baal snarled. "There is something really sneaky going on, and it has your name written all over it. I want to know what exactly you are doing to Earth and the meatsack inhabitants."

Beelzebub smirked. He wanted to toy with the other demon, but he knew that he had to tell Baal what was going on. He had been too active. Baal would find out sooner or later. The last thing he wanted was for Baal to go to Lucifer before he had a chance to take care of the situation. He picked up a glass of Scotch and swirled it, then took a sip.

Baal crossed his arms. "Well? Start talking."

"Oh, my dear Baal, it's really very simple. I was the one who opened the lava over that small Romanian town."

Baal whirled his hand. "Yes, yes, we know that. But why?"

Beelzebub walked to his fireplace and looked down at the dying flame. "Because now that the molten hell is all over the town, I can create an outpost with it."

Baal lifted an eyebrow. "An outpost? Excuse me? It sounds to me like you are trying to station some sort of demon army there, but that would be ridiculous, right? Because you have no control over the demon armies."

"You can make an army out of anyone, Baal. I just needed the little rogue idiots to follow me. I've been sending droves of demons there. A small batch at a time, of course. They are hiding in the town, avoiding the soldiers. Once the military is gone, they will be able to take over."

Baal didn't understand. "Yes, but why are you doing all this?"

Beelzebub smiled at Baal. "Why, to have a little bit of hell on Earth. Wouldn't it be nice? I want to claim my section of the planet, and I think this is the best time for it. Once I have raised my demon army, I will spread them across Europe. I will own a vast amount of Earth. Don't worry, there will still be room for you."

Baal narrowed his eyes. "If you think you will succeed, you're insane."

"I have a vision. I have ambition, and the means to achieve my goals."

"If Lucifer finds out, your vision won't last long. He'll rip your eyes out."

Beelzebub shook his head. "He'll reward me for doing what Moloch could not."

"And Lilith?"

"In time. I'm keeping her busy while I build my army."

"That sounds to me like you don't have a plan for her. I promise you, if you don't take care of Lilith first, any plan you have will be absolutely and undeniably fucked."

19

Katie landed on the ice next to Pandora. It was cracked and covered with ash. Pandora put her hands on her hips. "Well, that wasn't so hard, was it?"

The ground shook, and a loud clap echoed through the stadium. A portal flashed open, melting the ice beneath their feet. In no time they were up to their calves in water. Katie pulled out her guns, aiming at the portal.

Pandora sniffed the air and began to back up as well. "Oh, balls."

A stream of the strangest demons Katie had ever seen came galloping out of the portal. The first looked like a black-scaled rhino with seven horns and jagged red streaks running down its black hide. Its eyes were beet-red, and fire shot from its nostrils as it charged Katie. "Holy fucking hell, what is that?"

Pandora called down her angelic armor and was suddenly encased in black and silver. She spread her wings. "Jump, bitch!"

Katie and Pandora leaped just as the rhino plowed

through where they had been and slammed into the wall behind her. It slashed its many horns and made a low wailing sound. Strange sounds came from the portal and a shaggy beast slowly emerged. Its long black fur shimmered under the flickering lights, and its teeth dripped black ooze. Its long fur-covered claws dragged in the water as it roared three times as loud as a lion. Glass broke all over the stadium. Katie rose to Juntto's eye level.

Pandora flew up to join them. "Well, who said this was supposed to be easy? I'll take the right, Pandora the left, and Juntto, you blast everything you can. Just watch your shots."

Juntto nodded and pulled his gun around as the two flew off. The demonic rhino slammed into him, and Juntto groaned as the gun slipped from his hand. The rhino turned quickly and charged again. His solid hooves smashed the weapon to pieces. Juntto howled with rage and pulled the spear from his back. "No one smashes my Juntto-sized weapons!"

He pulled his arm back and launched the spear, and it flew through the air and slammed into the rhino, the point bursting through the rhino's other flank. The beast thrashed for a moment before falling into the water. Juntto reached down and yanked the spear out. "I hate zoos, especially the ones in hell."

The rhino tried to pick its head up, but it fell back down, wailing. It finally collapsed and turned to dust. The demonic lion snarled and charged toward Juntto. Juntto snarled back. "Come and get some, pussy."

Juntto ran at the beast. The whole stadium shook as his massive feet hit the floor, and the two monsters slammed together in the middle of the rink. Juntto grabbed the lion by its mane and held it off the ground, dodging the swipes of the demon's long, sharp claws. He grabbed the great beast's head with both hands and twisted, breaking its neck. The lion went limp and burst into a cloud of dust and fur.

Pandora raised her sword and sneered at a scaly three-headed gorilla. Its fangs were sharp, and each head's features were twisted with rage as the monstrosity beat its chest. It charged, and she reared back and kicked it in the chest hard. It flew back and slid through the water. She waved her sword at the thing and crouched, ready for action. "Come on, King Kong. Let's get some of this."

The beast growled and charged again. Pandora waited patiently, and when the beast was close, she spun in a circle, the blade of her angelic sword cutting off all three heads. The creatures behind it backed up, then squealed and ran off, preferring to leap back through the portal rather than face the vicious red-scaled angel in front of them. Pandora chuckled and straightened up. "That's right. You mess with the bull…"

"Fuck!" Katie screamed as a flying demon slashed at her with razor-sharp claws.

As she chopped off one of its legs, a larger demon with a bright red mohawk slammed its foot into her chest. She flew back and hit the glass partition, the air leaving her lungs. She was covered in cuts and bruises. Katie was getting beat to hell and didn't have Pandora to heal her.

Pandora watched Katie struggle to stand. "Aw, goddamn it. Fuck this shit."

She sheathed her sword and shook off the enchanted

angelic armor. The black and silver armor slipped off her body and dissolved. Pandora ran at full speed and dove back into Katie. *Hold on,* chica, *I'll get you back up. Just keep swinging!*

Katie growled, forcing herself back up on her wobbly knees. The shimmer of her armor was slowly fading with every blow she took. She gripped her sword tightly and swung wide, killing the mohawked demon with a brutal slash to the chest. Above her, Juntto's great spear skewered the flying demon. She jumped out of the way as it slammed into the ground and burst into dust. Juntto stomped over and picked up the spear.

Katie nodded her thanks. "Thanks. I'm struggling."

"I will finish these. You close the portal."

Katie pulled a special metal grenade from her bag and stumbled toward the portal behind Juntto. He slashed and stabbed with his spear, clearing the way. She pulled the pin of the grenade and held down the lever, narrowing her eyes at the gateway to hell. "I think you forgot who you were fucking with."

She threw the grenade hard, but at the last second a jabbering demon jumped up and knocked it to the ground.

Pandora gasped. *That knob-gobbler blocked the grenade! Fuck that.*

Katie took off. She leaped over the demon and kicked the grenade. As it passed through the edges of the portal, it exploded. The debris went inward, but the shock wave of the blast blew Katie off her feet.

She slammed into the wall and slid down. Her eyes were a faded red. The rest of the demons made a run for the portal. Juntto slashed at those he could reach but finally gave up as the last of them flew back into the portal, and it snapped shut behind them. Juntto stomped over to Katie, scooped her out of the water, and carried her into the stands. He carefully set her down on a bench.

Katie's eyes were shut, but she could hear Juntto's gentle, deep voice. "Katie. Are you all right?"

She groaned, and her eyes fluttered. "I think so. Pandora is on it."

Juntto shrank down to human size and sat next to her.

Her cheek was black and blue, and her lip was busted. Blood trickled down her chin. Her face was covered in soot, and there were several slashes across her back. Her angelic armor faded and she let out a deep breath, putting her hand to her stomach. *How bad is it?*

Pandora sniffed. *Not terrible. You'll feel better in no time. I think Juntto will carry you back.*

Katie nodded. *For now, I'll just sit here.*

Juntto and Katie sat quietly as Pandora worked her magic, healing anything that might be deadly to Katie in the long run. When she was done, she stepped out of Katie and gave Juntto a high five. "Good work, big man."

Juntto nodded, but he was concerned for Katie.

Katie winced as she sat up. "Not having a demon fucking sucks."

Pandora snorted. "*Being* a demon is pretty fucking cool."

"It looks as if things are changing," a voice said from their left.

Gabriel ambled toward them, his robes trailing behind him. Pandora rolled her eyes. "Oh, great, *this* cock-holster. You sure do have good timing. You couldn't have stepped in, oh, I don't know, fifteen minutes ago when the deadly fucking rhino was trying to kill us?"

Gabriel smiled kindly. "You know how things are, Pandora." He inclined his head toward Katie. "It will heal. Even without Pandora's demon powers, the angelic ones will take care of your wounds."

Pandora snorted. "Yeah, at a fucking glacial pace. It's like angel powers are 1980 Atari, while demon powers are the newest Xbox."

Juntto nodded. "Yes."

Pandora laughed. "I figured you would understand that analogy. Juntto, have you met this shitbag? This is Gabriel, God's greatest warrior. The guy who likes riddles and never helps with anything."

Juntto studied Gabriel, who gazed back at him with bright blue eyes. Flashes of wars of the past ran through Juntto's mind. He remembered a time those eyes had stared at him from the other end of a sword. "We've met, but it was a very long time ago. Not sure we parted on great terms."

The chopper picked Calvin and Sofia up from the airport and carried them on a forty-minute trip over the ocean. It landed on the wide, empty beach and Sofia and Calvin grabbed their things. Calvin nodded at the pilot, who handed him a card. "You need anything, give me a call. Only a flight away. Katie said it's all on her."

Calvin gave the guy a mini-salute and stepped out of the chopper. They ducked as they hurried away from the blades and covered their eyes as the sand whipped around them wildly. The chopper lifted off, leaving them alone on the private beach. Sofia set her bags down and walked across the white sands, her long pink bathing suit cover-up flapping in the breeze. Up on the hill was a beach house, and just visible from the beach was a shimmering blue infinity pool.

Calvin had some trouble in the sand with his cane, but he walked up beside Sofia and kissed her shoulder. "Alone at last. What a beautiful place."

Sofia took off her sunglasses and turned to Calvin. "Could have been the slums of New York as long as I'm with you. I do have to admit, though, this is much better."

Calvin chuckled and kissed his bride. He pulled back, and the two looked out over the ocean as the sun began to move toward the horizon. Sofia put her head on Calvin's shoulder and sighed. "I wonder how everyone is doing?"

Calvin shrugged. "Probably fine." Together they stared at the vibrant colors in the sky. "But let's not think about that for a while."

Gabriel walked toward Pandora with his hands clasped in front of him. "I have not seen this before. Your angelic abilities are conflicting with your demonic powers. You are changing. Certain abilities will develop over time, but you will need to adapt."

Pandora raised an eyebrow. "What exactly does that mean, O Great One?"

"Your demonic energies are fading." Gabriel shrugged. "I'm not sure what that means, to be honest."

"Of course, you aren't. That would be too convenient. What's going to happen to me, you pompous jerk?"

Gabriel smiled and turned away. "Only time will tell, Pandora."

Pandora, Juntto, and Katie looked at one another for a moment. Katie turned to speak to the angel, but he was gone.

She looked around, but Gabriel had disappeared once again. Pandora slapped her hands on her legs. "Seriously, I think the guy was just hired by the Big Man to play Jedi mind tricks on people. It's like he gets a kick out of fucking with us."

Katie smirked. "He probably *does* get a kick out of fucking with *you*. If I were him, I definitely would take advantage of that whole right-hand-of-God thing."

Pandora opened her mouth, but Juntto raised a hand to silence her. "I have thoughts."

Pandora tried to stifle a laugh. "Can we help you? Does it hurt?"

Juntto ignored Pandora's snide comment. "All this talk about demonic energy and powers got me thinking about Brock and the guys. The biggest question has been how they were stripped of their demons, right? And how they were drained of all their energy? They were found on the brink of death."

Katie nodded. "Yeah, that's exactly it. That purple bitch had something to do with it."

"Yeah, she sucked me dry, and it wasn't as fun as it sounds."

Juntto morphed into Channing Tatum. "I have seen something like this before, or at least I saw the victims and heard the stories. It is very much like the vampire queen. She sucks the energy out of living creatures. She mostly feeds on demonic energy, but she will take any life she can."

Katie's mouth dropped open. "Wait, you mean to tell me there are vampires too? I thought demons were just demons."

Juntto tilted his head. "Yes and no. She does not live off blood. She lives off energy. The more emotional you feel, the stronger your energy. Demons are always angry, which is why she prefers them. She holds on tightly in the heat of the kill to absorb that emotion. She feels the ecstasy of your emotional energy."

Katie furrowed her brow. "She is a demon, though?"

Juntto shook his head. "No, she is the enemy of the demons. She is the enemy of all. If I am right about this, this spiderwoman sounds very much like the Leviathan Teyollucuani. Her stories are old, and she has not been seen in centuries. Even in my prime, she was a legend. It was thought that she had been killed. Others say she retreated to a cocoon of her own making and took a long sleep."

Katie nodded. "Like you."

Juntto shook his head. "No, I was forced into the snows, and my body went into hibernation to survive. She chose this. She had enough energy to sleep for a millennium."

Pandora was listening quietly to the side, her arms folded across her chest.

Katie glanced at her, noticing that she was focused on this information. "Do you think this Leviathan was awakened to cause problems? I just don't know why demons would bring her back, especially if her food of choice is, well, *them*."

Juntto shrugged. "She is one of the last beings the demons would summon. It would have to be a real emergency."

Pandora tapped her foot and shook her head. "She told me she was Teyollucuani, but I thought she was some hot vampire bitch, so I ignored her. You know, the kind with big tits, perfect skin, and only two arms and two legs?"

Juntto shook his head. "She's a Leviathan. Her blood is actually energy. That's how she feeds."

Pandora took a deep breath and began to pace. "I didn't expect a purple eight-legged spider thing, but then again I didn't know what to expect. I suppose I never put a lot of thought into it because she wasn't there in front of me. I know a little bit about her, though."

Katie sat up excited. "You do? Like what? Anything that can help the guys heal faster?"

Pandora pursed her lips. "Not really. I know that she can feed off humans, angels, and even Leviathan. However, her favorite food is the sweet, sweet demon energy nectar. She craves it and looks for it. It consumes her at every pass. Her hunger is insatiable, which explains the mounds and mounds of bodies in the church. She got what she could from the humans until the demons started to show up. She built up her energy to be unstoppable."

Katie narrowed her eyes. "But who woke her?"

Juntto sat back down. "I don't think even Lucifer would do such a thing. Ruthless or not, there isn't a demon out there who would want Teyollucuani free. She doesn't make deals, and if she does, they are never honored. She might help a demon, but in the end, she would feed on him. Like Pandora said, her hunger is insatiable. When feeding, she is uncontrollable."

Katie suggested, "Maybe a demon got too close to her cocoon and woke her up?"

Pandora chuckled but shook her head. "I don't think so. The war between Earth and hell has only intensified over the last couple of years. There are more demons on Earth now than ever before. Demonic energy is flowing freely across the entire world. I think she could sense that even in her hibernation."

Katie nodded. "And that woke the monster from her dream state. The demons aren't going to want her here any more than we do. She is an enemy to all." Katie frowned. "Common ground with the demons; that is very strange."

Pandora barked laughter. "I wouldn't read too much into that. You could have a twin who is a demon and they would rarely find common ground with a human, much less an angel. It just means they are going to try to use her against us if they haven't already. I smelled a very familiar scent when that portal opened, one I thought had been banned to the outer reaches of hell. If I'm right, things are going to get even worse very soon."

Juntto shook his head. "I think you have bigger problems than that. Once the Leviathans start waking up on their own, the shit is going to hit the fucking roof."

Katie took a deep breath. "All we can hope for is that we were right and Teyollucuani was mortally wounded."

Pandora shrugged. "You know what they say: hope in one hand and shit in the other…"

20

General Brushwood finished reading his emails and turned off his computer. He was ready to call it a night. He had been there late at night every night for three months straight. With the incursion in Toronto wrapped up, he felt the need to spend some time at home. He straightened the papers on his desk and stood up, gathering his coat and hat.

As he was about to walk out of his office, his secretary spoke over the intercom. "General, a few of your aides are here to speak with you about their findings."

The general put one hand on the desk and grumbled to himself. Of course, they were. "Sure, send them in."

He clicked off the intercom and tossed his hat and coat on the chair. Three of the aides came through the door with files in their hands. The general waved them in. "Close the door behind you."

The staff members walked up to the desk, and the senior aide stepped forward and set a file in front of Brushwood. "We thought it would be better if just the senior aides came. We figured too many people would make it confusing, sir."

The general nodded. "Good thinking. So, what did you find out?"

The woman swallowed hard and took a deep breath. "Well, it seems that a lawyer has been talking to the members of the World Council. He's contacted all but the major leaders. He is telling them he has been appointed by the Council, but we could find no record of his employment. These members and the attorney have been gathering findings and information against Katie. There is some sort of charter or agreement being signed, although we couldn't get our hands on the specific document."

"What? You mean to tell me they are building a case against the one person out there saving their asses?"

"Yes, sir. Reports claim that Katie is doing more harm than good. We've heard the agreement might even claim she is working with the demons, although we can't confirm that."

"Good grief. Are we talking a lot of World Council members or just a few of the shadier ones?"

The senior aide leaned forward, flipping open the file. "It seems that it started with one or two, but the agreement has quickly spread to the other leaders listed here over the last couple of days."

He closed his eyes. "Thank you, ladies. If you find out anything further, let me know."

The staff nodded and quickly left the office. The general put his knuckles down on the desk and stood there for several moments with his eyes shut, trying to breathe. He thought about a big, comfy chair at home and a nice bottle of wine he had tucked away. He even had a Cuban cigar he'd been saving. Not tonight. He slashed at his desk and sent his pens flying. "Goddamn it!"

He pulled out his phone and dialed Katie. She sounded tired. "Katie, it's Brushwood. I need to speak to you about something I'm sure you don't want to hear."

Katie sighed. "Great, more sunshine and happiness. What have you got?"

Brushwood flipped open the file to a blurry snapshot of Belphegor in his skin suit. "It seems some lawyer has been posing as a World Council legal team member and has rustled up a very big following. They are collecting information about you that leads me to believe they are trying to take you down."

Katie growled. "Are you fucking kidding me? I am on a plane, flying back from saving thousands of people from a demon attack in Toronto!"

"I know, I know. I'm going to get to the bottom of this. Until then, keep your ears open."

Katie was irritated. "I will. I just am not in the mood for these assholes to be Monday-morning-quarterbacking my life."

The Romanian town was quiet. The lava covering the town had long since cooled. The military detachment was focused on clean-up and load-in. There was no real reason for so many of them to be there. They still had two sectors of the town to search, but that wouldn't take more than one platoon. In the center of the town, the heat index began to rise.

The ice that had formed on the roofs and sidewalks of the village began to drip, quickly forming puddles. A portal tore open, rattling the remains of the nearby buildings. Beelzebub stepped through and to one side, and several dozen demons scurried onto the streets. He smiled at them like a doting parent. "Remember, do not leave the confines of the city until I tell you to."

The demons began to run around the city, hungry and looking for prey. The place was deserted. All of the humans who had lived there were either dead or gone. The searching demons did not find any human scent, so they turned back to Beelzebub and awaited orders.

"This is your home now, at least for a little while."

Several of the demons hissed, letting Beelzebub know they weren't happy with that. He put his hands up, quieting the crowd. "One of the first duties in your new playground is to make this place home." He pointed at the tall steeple a few blocks away. "I will not have any churches on my unholy ground. Tear it down, burn it, blow it up—I don't care. Just get rid of it."

The demons headed toward the church, and Beelzebub quickly stepped back through the portal. He smiled and shut the portal behind him, leaving them to it.

The demons ran through the shadows of the lava-filled streets. They hissed and cackled as they swung from signs and smashed windows out of storefronts. When they reached the lawn of the church, they stopped and snarled at it. They were intent on tearing it down brick by brick.

Normally the demons had no inclination to follow

orders, but they were both terrified of Beelzebub and hungry to destroy things. The smell of rotting human carcasses from inside was like an aphrodisiac for them. The demons ran forward, clawing at the walls of the church and screeching loudly. They tore at the large wooden doors until they opened and hurried inside. The ash and dust from their dead brothers floated up around them as they ran into the sanctuary. The demons in the front came to a screeching halt.

They sniffed the air like wild dogs. All around them were rotting piles of flesh, and along the sides of the church leading to the pulpit were gray, dripping cocoons. One of the demons snarled and scratched at the cocoon, spilling the ooze on the ground. He snarled and ripped through the webbing, trying to get to whatever was inside.

A demon dropped from the cocoon. It was weathered, wrinkled, and gray. The first demon jumped back, hissing at the half-dead one. It snarled at the others for confirmation. Several of the demons got close, sniffing the dying demon and wailing loudly. They flung the goo from their claws and began to get rowdy yet again.

The sound of soft sniffling drew the attention of the crowd, and a hush fell over the entire sanctuary.

Slowly the demons crept up the aisle. They looked cautiously at the cocoons still hanging above them. Some were torn open and empty, while others housed demons too weak to scratch their way free. Standing beneath the leaning crucifix was a scared human woman.

It was Sasha in her human form. She feigned fear, putting her hands to her lips and crying, "Oh please, not me."

The demons growled and snarled, scratching at the ancient wooden floors. They went wild over what they thought was fresh meat. Suddenly a demon leaped from the pack and charged Sasha. The rest quickly followed behind, running across walls and leaping over pews.

Sasha dropped her hands. "Bad move, fucktards."

She roared as her skin turned purple. The skin on her body seemed to tear from the bones as she grew into an eight-legged creature that had been waiting patiently for more victims. The demons squealed in surprise, but it was too late—their momentum carried them forward. Beelzebub's army grew smaller by the second. They never even had a chance to tear down the steeple.

Romanian President Dragos pulled the fur collar of his coat up. Timothy and Korbin walked beside him. They were surveying the small Romanian village from the hills above town. Timothy shivered, wishing he had worn more than just a statement piece as a coat. Maybe even some long johns.

Dragos let out a deep sigh and looked at the lava-filled town. "Such a shame. So many dead."

Korbin agreed with him. "It *is* a shame. Our condolences go out to your entire country. But it is time to move forward, to start thinking about how to prevent these kinds of tragedies from happening again. This town was the victim of a terrible tragedy, but together we can rebuild it."

Dragos nodded. "We need to make sure nothing like

this happens again. We also need to make this village secure so people can return to their homes and livelihoods."

Korbin clasped his binder to his chest. "Absolutely. I believe the best move would be to focus both on defenses and tech installations simultaneously."

"Very good." Dragos grunted. "As long as this does not include Katie."

Korbin was slightly taken back. "I'm sorry?"

President Dragos pointed to the tall steeple in the center of town. "Katie went to that church, and inside she rescued her people from evil. Never in history has evil pierced those doors until she came around. That church has stood for centuries. It was the first building to be built in this village. It was blessed by the Holy Roman Empire and is one of the holiest places on Earth. Or at least it was."

Korbin wrinkled his forehead. "I hope you aren't insinuating that Katie had anything to do with that."

Dragos snapped his head toward Korbin. "She somehow got inside with her filthy demon. Why should I believe she is innocent?"

Korbin tilted his head. "Well, for starters, Katie is not just infected. She is also an angel, as is her demon. They are blessed by the hand of God. You can't get much holier than that. I have known Katie since the moment she was infected, and she would never do anything to put innocent people's lives in danger. I give you my word on that."

Dragos was about to respond angrily when Timothy grabbed Korbin's arm and pointed to the streets. "Look. Demons."

Korbin and Dragos peered down, not believing it.

Korbin muttered, "All the demons in this village were destroyed."

Sure enough, there they were. Demons ran down the streets, screeching and hollering. A small squad of soldiers stood their ground in the middle of the street and blasted them full of bullets. The demons burst into ash and blew away with the cold winds. President Dragos narrowed his eyes and looked at Korbin. "Where did they come from?"

Korbin shook his head, getting closer to the edge of the embankment. "I have no idea, Mr. President. This is the first sighting of a demon down there in days. Something fishy is going on around here."

21

Katie lay in her bed attempting to read a book. The wall shook slightly, and the sound of Angie's moans echoed through the condo. Katie sighed and dropped her book in her lap. *Seriously? How are they still going? It's been freaking hours.*

Pandora snickered. *All day fuckathon. Ahh, how I miss those. Maybe you should be taking notes? I'll start. First, stay hydrated.*

No, thanks.

Really. It's important. Second, make sure you have all your toys, ropes, costumes, and cuffs handy. Like, in a backpack. A sex kit! That's what you need.

Katie rolled her eyes and reached into her side table's drawer, pulling out an iPod and headphones. She put the buds in her ears and pressed Play. She waited a moment, then smiled. If there was still moaning, her music covered the sound. She crossed one leg over the other and picked her book up, going back to reading. A few moments later her wall shook again. The picture of her mother over her dresser dropped off the wall and crashed to the floor. Katie narrowed her eyes and pulled the buds out of her ears.

She put a pillow over her face, screaming into it. The sounds coming from Angie's room, which was all the way across the condo, permeated the thick down stuffing of the pillow. *I can't take it. I mean, good for them, but fuck! It sounds like a porno studio in here.*

Pandora snorted. *No, those are actually a lot more technical than you would think, and they have soundproofing.*

I don't even want to know how you know that.

Hey, I told you I wasn't a saint. I may be an angel again, but I was not a good girl in between.

Katie got up from the bed and pulled her dresser open. She grabbed her normal spandex outfit and changed, and quickly laced her boots up. If she couldn't relax, she was determined to get as far away from the condo as she could.

Pandora looked at Katie's reflection in the mirror. *Do we have a gig?*

Katie pulled her hair back in a ponytail. *Nope, but I can't sit around here any longer. So, I guess we are going to go fight crime.*

Pandora gasped. *Are you serious? Oh boy, oh boy, oh boy. More adventures of Slut Girl on the way!*

Katie finished getting ready and hurried out the balcony door. She jumped, spread her wings wide, and began gliding upward. She flapped her wings a couple of times and climbed above the buildings. She liked it better up there. There was no one to notice her. She let out a deep breath, listening to the heavy traffic and sirens in the city below. It was definitely better than the sound of Angie having an orgasm every ten minutes.

Katie shivered in the cold air, but it made her feel alive and awake. *So, apparently General Brushwood is under some serious pressure from the World Council. They are trying to take us down.*

Pandora scoffed. *I'd like to see them try. Don't they get it yet? We are unstoppable.*

Katie took a right, flying between two of the taller buildings. *I think a room full of fat old men think they can do anything they want.*

Yeah, well, they have another think coming. We cannot be under anyone's thumb right now.

Katie looked down at the people below. *As much as I hate to admit it, you're right. I can't worry about people dying in battle with me. That includes Brock. And I can't sit around constantly worrying about people like the World Council second-guessing my every move.*

Pandora agreed wholeheartedly. *You need to be in control of this. That was the whole reason we maneuvered the team the way we did. You didn't want to be governed by anyone but yourself. The general understands that, but it seems these douche canoes don't know what game they are playing.*

Katie chuckled. *Damn right they don't. I know it shouldn't bother me, but it really pisses me the fuck off. I do all this work, lose my men, save many others, and they want to take me out of the picture? If I left, they would be taken down in a heartbeat.*

Katie felt a familiar tug in her chest, and her eyes went blue. Pandora sniffed. *Got one. Two blocks down, some jackwads are causing problems.*

Katie pushed thoughts of the general and the Council out of her mind and focused her angel abilities on the problem, listening to two young kids telling someone to leave them alone. Katie flew faster. There were kids in trouble. She pulled her wings back and pointed her feet down, falling toward the two asshats below.

The two grade-school kids had backed themselves into an alley. The two older guys were attempting something Katie didn't even want to think about. She landed softly behind the two guys and put her fingers to her lips so the kids wouldn't say anything.

One of the guys snickered. "Why don't you just give in and get in the van, kid? You are going in there, one way or another."

Kate thrust both hands out and grabbed the guys by the backs of their necks, then slammed their heads together and threw them to the ground. She glanced at the kids. "Go on, guys, go home. I'll take care of these two asswipes."

The kids ran and left Katie alone with the two men. A shadow fell over their faces as she spread her wings wide. "You want to fuck with little kids, huh? Well, you're going to answer to me for that."

Both of the guys put their arms up and screamed as Katie's fists flew toward their faces.

Korbin stood at the edge of the town, talking with the sergeant. After the demons had been seen in the town, President Dragos had quickly scurried off. Korbin found it odd but brushed it off. He figured fear had gotten to him, as it had so many others. The man's negative attitude toward Katie bothered him. That too would have to be handled another day, though.

"You want us to put up anti-aircraft guns around the village?" the sergeant asked.

Korbin nodded, looking around the perimeter. "For now, yes. Ultimately I want a solid perimeter wall around the village, just like a medieval castle. I also want dozens of these guns pointed outward to ward off any incoming attack. In between will be missile launchers with a 360-degree firing range. The missiles can be fired at the portals, forcing them to close. The guns can take care of any riffraff coming from the open portal."

The sergeant nodded, taking notes. "Okay, but what's priority right now?"

"For now, I want the guns up and pointed at the town."

The sergeant was taken aback. "I thought the point was to get people back into the village?"

Korbin nodded. "It is, but right now you still have a demon problem. Those guns can fire at them from a distance. I don't know where they are coming from, but I will be looking into that."

Timothy typed into his iPad, clicking through the different tests he wanted to perform on the village. It wasn't often that he was at an incursion site and able to study it. He glanced at the Romanian soldier standing guard next to him. He was tall and handsome, with arms the size of Timothy's head.

Timothy cleared his throat. "If demons come, I'm going to need you to protect me. You see, I am no longer a Damned. See the beautiful blue in my eyes?"

The soldier looked at him and tilted his head. "*Nu inteleg. Vorbesc romaneste.*"

Timothy covered his mouth and giggled. "Aren't you

just the cutest thing ever? You don't understand a damn thing coming out of my mouth. Why do I feel like you're just a big dumb sexy man?"

Timothy went back to his work, but his eyes went wide. He typed a few more things and let out a deep sigh. He waved Korbin over. "I need to show you this."

Korbin excused himself and walked over to Timothy. "What's going on?"

Timothy shook his head. "I wish I knew. The whole town is reading like there is an actual incursion happening right here and right now, but when you look out there, there is nothing. I thought maybe it was the system, but it doesn't show that way anywhere else in the world right now. Even the Toronto incursion site is just specks of red now. This incursion ended weeks ago, but it's still red-hot."

Korbin scratched his head and looked around. There was something not right about the place. Something was missing, but he couldn't put his finger on it. "This makes no sense whatsoever. I've never seen a town like this. By now things should be back to normal, but there are still demons running around. Just two days ago they claimed that not a single demon still existed."

Timothy let out a sigh. "It is obvious they were way wrong, or somehow a portal is still open in this place."

Korbin waved to Timothy. "Come here, I want to show you something."

Timothy put his laptop down and followed Korbin to the edge of the hill. He pointed down to where the church was. "We spotted them shortly after getting back. I can see them, you can see them, the whole damn recon division can see them. But that's not the problem."

Timothy took a step closer and furrowed his brow. "They look like gargoyles."

Korbin nodded. "Yes! They look like tiny statues standing in the street. They don't move, growl, snarl—nothing. We have held the troops back. It looks like a trap, doesn't it? Or worse, it looks like they are literally holding territory. We do this all the time in war. Of course, we tend to move around a bit more, but you get what I'm saying. They are using tactics. They are protecting something or someone down there. I think that is the reason for your readings."

The sergeant walked up next to Korbin and Timothy. "Are they still down there?"

Korbin glanced at him. "They are, Sergeant, and they haven't moved a muscle. We even threw in a canister of tear gas, but they stayed at their posts. I've never seen demons act that way."

The sergeant frowned at the strange demons. "I know. The creatures that come out of those portals tend to be dumb as hell, that's for sure. Why don't I lead a strike team down there and just waste them? If they are protecting something, they will fight back."

Korbin shook his head. "I don't think that's a very good idea. We don't know what's wrong with them, who put them there, or what they are keeping us from. Like I said before, it could easily be a trap. I think we should hold out and try to get more information about that area. I've got my guy working on that part of it."

Timothy waved. "That's me. The system is capturing real-time footage. Let's see if we can get any heat signatures. If anything moves, we will know it."

The three of them stared at the strangely still demons. Korbin squinted at them. "I don't like this one fucking bit."

The two would-be kidnappers screamed and yelled as Katie held them by their shirt collars and flew them over downtown New York. "You might want to stop moving. I don't really have a great grip on you. If one of you falls, I'm just letting the other one go, too. Too much paperwork otherwise."

The guys attempted to keep perfectly still at her words. They were trying not to look down or cry. Both of them were pretty roughed up. Bruises covered their faces, their shirts were ripped, and blood trickled from their noses. The larger of the two looked at Katie. "Where you taking us?"

Katie smirked. "I figured I'd open a portal to hell and toss you in. You are going there anyway, so you might as well get started on your life sentence."

The kidnappers whimpered as Pandora cackled. *I'm pretty sure the one on the right just pissed his pants. It's golden showers for whoever is below.*

Katie giggled as she spiraled toward the ground. She folded her wings behind her and walked toward the police station, dragging the crooks. A cop at the station opened the door for her. "Thank you."

She walked inside and nodded at the cop behind the desk. He chuckled and walked to the office door. "Good to see you. Been a while."

Katie smiled. "I know, right?"

As soon as she walked into the precinct, Travers and Schultz were on their way to her. Schultz looked at the two guys and waited on an explanation. Katie shrugged. "They are two very clumsy guys. Both of them tripped at the same time and fell right into my fists. Craziest thing. Anyway, before that, these two idiots were trying to kidnap two grade-school kids in Brooklyn."

Schultz whistled to one of the desk cops and waved him over. "Book these two for attempted kidnapping. Throw them into holding. I'll take care of them when I get a chance."

Both of the kidnappers were more than happy to get away from Katie, even if it meant they were going to jail for a really long time. Travers put out a hand and shook Katie's. "Been a while, kid. We've been following the craziness on the news. Good job on those monsters in Toronto. That shit looked wild."

Katie chuckled. "Yeah, there was a fucking three-headed gorilla in there somewhere. Things get weirder every time a portal opens."

Schultz scoffed. "You're telling me. We field calls constantly, and we're seeing some of the craziest shit out there. People are really losing it. Luckily, we had this nice young lady give us some pretty good training."

Katie laughed. "I hope it's working."

Katie's phone rang, and she fished it out of the top of her shirt. "I gotta take this, but it was good seeing you. I'll stop by soon."

Travers put his hand up as she walked from the office. "What about the paperwork? Dammit! She *always* does that."

Katie gave the cop at the front desk a thumbs-up as she put the phone to her ear. "Korbin, what's going on? You in Romania yet?"

Korbin sighed. "Yeah. Things are a little strange out here, and they get stranger by the second. I need you to pack up and get out here ASAP. I am going to need your help with this. I've honestly never seen anything like it. Timothy's readings are off the charts."

Katie stepped to the side of the building. "What's going on?"

Korbin craned his neck at the sky. A massive portal shimmered above the town. "Well, besides statue-like demons just standing there like they're guarding something invisible, there is a giant portal sitting open over the town."

Katie was surprised. "What? Is there anything coming out of it?"

Korbin chuckled nervously. "No, not a thing. Even the heat doesn't seem to be as bad as normal. It just doesn't make any sense."

Katie clicked her tongue. "What is the mood like there?"

"Weird. I mean, everything is absolutely silent. There is no more breeze, and the birds are gone. Seriously, it feels like a kettle ready to boil over. The pressure in this place is just building and building, and I don't know if any of us want to be here when it finally explodes."

"I spent a lot of time there looking in every nook and cranny of that place when I was searching for Brock. I know the village pretty well at this point. I'll come and take a look. I want you to call me as soon as anything changes.

Like, I mean, if a cockroach runs across the street or a demon picks his ass, I want you to call me."

Korbin chuckled. "Will do. Are you leaving soon?"

Katie looked at the sky. "Yeah, I just have one thing to take care of, and I'll be on my way. Be safe, and until I get there, don't go poking around. Okay?"

Korbin laughed. "Yes, boss. Just be safe getting here."

Katie hung up and stared at the ground for a moment. *What the fuck is going on?*

Pandora shrugged. *I don't know, but I bet we'll find old spider-legs somewhere in this fucked-up situation. Why can't we seem to get away from that fucking village?*

22

The general hung up and cleared his throat, then started flipping through his schedule. A sound outside his office made him pause. He narrowed his eyes as he heard his secretary try to tell someone they couldn't just walk in. Suddenly the door flew open, and Katie marched into his office.

His secretary huffed. "I'm sorry, General, she didn't understand that she needed an appointment with you. And she is still armed. Would you like me to call Security?"

He put his hand up. "That won't be necessary. Thank you."

The secretary glared at Katie and walked out of the room. Katie chuckled and pointed at the door. "That woman has some serious balls. We need more people like her on our side. She gave zero fucks about shutting me down. I have two guns, four knives, and a sword on me. A *sword*, for fuck's sake."

The general chuckled and leaned back in his seat. Katie sat down across from him. "It's really good to see you,

Katie. I was hoping we would get to visit with each other soon."

Katie took a deep breath. "As much as I would like to say I'm here for a friendly chat, I'm not. I've thought about the whole Council thing. I'm already worrying about everyone else during fights, and I've started taking orders when not too long ago I said I was done with that. When it all comes down, it's simple. I need to be in charge."

Brushwood looked shocked and opened his mouth, but Katie stopped him. "You know I am dedicated to this war. You know I am dedicated to protecting the innocent, killing demons, and figuring out a way to put an end to this war. I will fight to my last breath, but I won't be beholden to any government's authority. It is getting in the way of progress. For me, that equals one big fat distraction. We both know what happens to mercs when they become distracted."

"Sadly, I know exactly what happens to you when you become distracted during battle. I have laid to rest far too many soldiers in this war. Katie, I made a promise to you the moment you struck a deal with us. I am not your boss. You have every right to fight the way that you see fit. I am not changing my mind on that because some World Council formed two seconds ago wants to stick their noses in. I fully support you in this."

Katie looked surprised. "Oh. Well, thank you. I was really hoping you would feel that way. I know that the World Council is tricky to navigate and you are taking all kinds of flack for me. I'm sorry I cause these problems."

He waved it off. "It was my choice to back you, and it is my choice to continue to protect you. I'll honor the deal we made. I will sit down and speak to the Council. I know that outside influence has caused them to grow wary of you, but that is all because of one man's rhetoric."

Katie looked around the office. "One thing I've noticed is that when one of them latches on, they all do. They will stand for something they know is blatantly wrong because they don't want their egos bruised."

The general chuckled. "And we both know that they won't win against you. If they lose, they are going to have to face these demons on their own. None of them wants that. They'll back down before things go too far. Nobody wants to see their cities burn to the ground. Trust me, if rhetoric can sway them one way, it can sway them back. You will have your chance to say your piece."

Katie smirked. "They might not like that too much."

The general laughed. "No, but it might be what they need."

Katie breathed deeply and relaxed her shoulders. "General, I want to fight. Not just for the USA, but for the whole world. This isn't one country's fight. This is a war for all humanity. There are no politics in what these demons have set out to do. I've put my life on the line for years to help the entire world. I've watched friends die, and I've faced death. I guess I am having a hard time swallowing the fact that the world might not want my help."

Brushwood leaned toward her and spoke passionately. "No matter what those fools say, deep down they *do* want your help. They just might not realize it until they are face to face with pure evil. I have been told you are going to go help Korbin in Romania. I will try to smooth things over with President Dragos. You go get on that plane."

"I think I'll take a shortcut."

"Oh, yeah?"

"Yeah. Things are progressing quickly." Katie walked with the general to his office door. "Thank you. I'm sorry I rolled in here like a bat out of hell. I've been a bit high-strung recently. Actually, I have been a bit high-strung for a while now."

He smiled and gave her a hug. "Things will get better. We just have to have that faith."

Katie nodded and walked out of his office.

As the general shut his door, his smile faded. Unfortunately, things might not be as simple as he'd made them sound. It was going to be tough to change the Council members' minds. Still, he was going to do his best. The first order was to call Dragos. He hoped he could get him to soften his tone toward Katie.

Belphegor sat in his small cottage in hell watching his screen. President Dragos doing paperwork. Belphegor tried to keep tabs on all his contacts to make sure nobody needed a push in the right direction. He popped two deep-fried mice into his mouth and chewed. His human skin was hanging from a hook on the door. His scaled body was finally free. He was trying to dry out. An immense amount of sweat accumulated in that damn thing.

President Dragos's phone rang. Belphegor narrowed his beady red eyes and turned up the volume as the president answered. "This is President Dragos."

"President, this is General Brushwood. I was hoping to get a moment of your time."

Dragos sat down heavily in his chair. "Just a moment, yes. I have meetings."

The general maintained a light, even tone. "It's about Katie. I know that people like Katie can be intimidating, but you have nothing to fear from her. I promise that the lies you are being told are just that—falsehoods. Just this afternoon, in the middle of saving two young people from a kidnapping, Katie took a call from Korbin. There is some serious stuff going on in that Romanian village. Do you know what Katie said?"

Dragos was interested. "What?"

"That she would be there as soon as she could."

Dragos rubbed his chin. "To help us figure this out?"

The general cleared his throat. "Yes, President, and to make sure you are all safe. That's the kind of person she is. Half-angel, half-human, with an angel/demon inside of her. That's a hell of a lot to deal with, in my opinion, but she's still trying to help us all."

Dragos grunted. "Yes, it's looking that way."

"All I am asking is that you reconsider this document you signed. Look at the good she is doing for you and this world. She cares about everyone, not just those in her own country. She is a true citizen of the world. She has told me time and time again that she is here to protect the world from the demons. That includes you, even though she knows World Council members are trying to bring a charge against her. Even with that type of negativity aimed at her, she does not hesitate to come to your aid."

Dragos nodded. "Okay, I will consider this. Thank you for your call."

Belphegor could see he was starting to change his mind. He donned his human suit and opened a portal, appearing at Dragos's door. Dragos was not surprised to see him. He had figured that there was more to Belphegor than sagging skin.

Dragos pursed his lips. "General Brushwood wishes me to reconsider."

Belphegor scoffed. "The general is unreliable at best. He is caught in Katie's and her demon's spell. Besides, it's not like he is the supreme leader of the world or anything. He can easily be disposed of. There are other ways to get things done."

"Are there?"

"Of course. And the world is always looking for strong new leaders."

President Dragos chuckled and gave an evil smirk. "I like how you think."

Katie took a deep breath and knocked on Juntto's door. She hoped beyond hope that he was clothed. The door swung open, and Angie smiled at her. *She* was clothed, thank goodness. "Hey! Where you been? We came to see if you wanted lunch, but you were gone. We're over here playing video games."

Katie blinked. "I couldn't relax, so I went searching for criminals."

Angie chuckled. "Uh oh, Slut Girl is back at it."

Pandora scoffed. *Like she has any room to talk. Bet she can barely sit down right now.*

Katie nodded toward the condo. "Juntto in here?"

Angie laughed and stepped to the side. "Sorry I'm guarding the door like a security officer. Come on in."

Katie walked inside and tripped. "Ouch."

Angie closed the door and pointed at two large cases. "Oh, yeah. Those were delivered to Juntto earlier today from Joshua in Las Vegas."

Juntto came into the living room wearing a pair of jeans but no shirt or shoes. This time he looked like Khal Drogo from Game of Thrones. He had wavy hair down to his shoulders and a long braided beard. "Those are more Juntto-sized weapons! My other guns were destroyed by asshole demons, but now I've got new ones! He is hooking me up."

"Good, and you are going to need them. I have to go to Romania. Some crazy shit is about to go down, and I'm pretty sure we are going to need you."

Juntto clapped his hands. "Yes. I can try my new guns. I'll get dressed."

He skipped down the hall to the bedroom. Katie chuckled as he knocked his head on the door frame and yelled. Angie laughed nervously. "He is a bit of a klutz. Good thing the condo upstairs is empty right now. So, you guys are fighting?"

Katie shrugged. "I don't know yet. Something crazy might be about to fall from the sky."

Juntto came back out dressed in half-unlaced black boots, a black Henley, and jeans. He grabbed the two cases.

Angie kissed him on the cheek and stepped back. A worried look crossed her face.

Pandora opened a portal and made a sound like she was lifting something heavy.

Everything okay?

Yeah. It's just tougher than I thought it would be. Let's move quickly, okay?

Katie caught Angie's eyes. "Don't worry, everything will be fine." Katie jumped through the portal with Juntto.

The portal shut behind her and the two found themselves in hell. Pandora grunted again. *Shit. Maybe my demon powers are changing like that buttmunch Gabrielle said.*

Let's not linger, okay?

Pandora opened another portal. Katie was surprised when she wasn't hit with a blast of cold air. Juntto ducked through with his guns and his spear on his back. Katie followed. They were on the hill overlooking the town. The temperature was at least eighty degrees, and the snow was melting.

Well, this is pretty nice.

It's not a Romanian winter, though.

Juntto looked at Katie, confused. "Are we in the right place?"

"You are." Korbin walked up from the camp and gave Katie a hug. "Thanks for coming, guys. I was just about to call you."

Katie lifted an eyebrow. "Uh oh. That doesn't sound good."

Korbin sighed. "Well, good or bad we have yet to determine. Come with me. We can see the entire village from over here."

Katie and Juntto followed Korbin to the edge of the hill that looked out over the village. Korbin pointed at the church. "The town has been absolutely silent. The demons guarding it like statues have all disappeared. We haven't seen or heard a peep out of any of them. The portal also shrank. It was over the whole town, but now it's just lingering over the church."

Katie groaned. "What is it with that fucking church? That is where I found Brock and the others. That's where the spider bitch was hanging out. I have a feeling this has something to do with her."

Juntto put down his cases. "Have you sent anyone down there?"

Korbin shook his head. "No, we were waiting for you guys. We figured with limited intel it would be stupid to send in regular military."

Katie nodded. "That was a good call. I can tell you right now, if it *is* that bitch, they would have been taken down in two seconds. That, or wrapped in one of her creepy-ass cocoons. Not sure which one would be worse."

Katie watched the portal swirl wildly over the church. The streets were empty, and the sound of helicopters echoed through the lava streets. This village had been abandoned, bled dry by the previous fight, yet there was still a portal to hell overhead. Maybe the Leviathan was not working alone. It would take a demon to open that portal. Whether Sasha knew it or not, she had an ally, at least for the moment.

Juntto morphed to his frost giant form, then opened his cases and pulled out his new Juntto-sized weapons. "I say we head down there. Things are changing. It looks calm now, but who knows where things will stand in an hour?"

Katie agreed. "Korbin, can you give us some support?

"I've got perimeter guns set up. My men will service those. If any demons come out, I'll shoot them on the spot.

"If it's this Leviathan, we will have our hands full." Katie looked thoughtful. "I learned my lesson last time. I do not want a single soldier getting in the way of that thing. Pandora, and I? We could barely handle her. She killed a handful of soldiers last time without wasting a breath. I won't have that on my conscience."

Korbin nodded and waved to the men waiting for his instruction. Katie situated her guns on her hips and called for her angelic armor. In a moment she was encased in gold. Pandora sniffed. *Should I step out?*

Katie shook her head. *No. I am going to need you inside me to keep me going. If you're outside, who knows what could happen? We know how much she enjoys your personal brand of energy. Even if it's not the Leviathan, I'll still need you to heal me.*

Pandora didn't fight her. *I'm ready. Remember, if it's her, don't get too close to her legs. When she has you, it's almost impossible to get out of her grasp. Aim for her chest, her head, or her stomach. Having to regenerate her limbs slows her down but not by much.*

Katie caught Juntto's eye, and the two of them made their way down the hill. Korbin and his soldiers followed them. They paused at the guns and prepared them for firing. Korbin stopped Katie. "Be careful in there. This fucking freak has already done her share of damage to our team."

Katie patted his shoulder. "I got this, Pops. This bitch is going to get a beat-down. If not, I'm going to take my frustration out on whoever is dumb enough to be in that town. Either way, we are going to solve this once and for all." They left Korbin to organize his men.

Juntto and Katie walked carefully through the village, but it was dead silent. As they approached the church, they looked at the open portal overhead. "Not as much heat coming from that thing."

Pandora growled. *Must be open from the outer rings. I smell Beelzebub all over this one.*

Katie shook her head. *How many fucking high-level demons are there? They all seem to want to hop on this train. Don't they notice when I chop the others' heads off?*

Pandora chuckled. *Demons don't learn their lessons very well. They all think they are invincible.*

Please allow me to instruct them otherwise.

Katie surveyed the area with her hand on her gun. "All right, this part of town looks clear. Right below the portal, but there aren't any demons. That doesn't seem like a good sign this time."

Juntto took a deep breath. "Not if it's Teyollucuani. Tell Pandora she is going to have to be the one to shut that portal. I didn't bring the missile launcher."

Pandora perked up. *You got it. I'll close the portal, and you two neutralize the threat. Hopefully, I can take care of it without leaving your body.*

Katie breathed deeply. *Make that a priority, please. I'd like to survive this.*

As they went to step forward, the doors of the church swung wide open. Katie pulled out her gun and Juntto lifted his, ready to fire. Standing in the doorway in her purple spiderwoman form was Sasha. She was huge and bloated. Behind her, Katie could see numerous cocoons and many piles of ash on the floor.

She was the reason there were no demons. She had killed them all.

Pandora grimaced. *Damn, girl, you've put on some weight. Look at how big she is.*

I have a feeling that equates to her being even more deadly than before.

Sasha smirked evilly and tapped her many legs on the floor. She put her top two arms out and moaned, throwing her head back. "You came. I've been waiting for you."

23

Juntto raised his gun to Sasha. "And we came prepared, bitch."

He unloaded on her. The tommy gun shot massive bullets and sounded like thunder. Round after round smashing into the doorway, the floors, and Sasha's body. A huge dust cloud billowed up and chunks of the church came tumbling down. Juntto stopped shooting and they stood there silently, waiting for the dust to clear.

Juntto took one step forward, but Katie put her hand out. "Wait."

One of Sasha's long legs swirled out from the smoke and knocked the massive gun from his hand. He stumbled back and grabbed it before it hit the ground. Sasha stepped through the dust and ash, her body pulsing with energy. There wasn't a single bullet hole in her. Katie and Juntto looked at her in shock and awe. Sasha breathed heavily, balling her hands into fists. With each breath, she grew just a little bigger. She was enormous, rivaled only by Juntto's bulk.

Sasha opened her mouth and let out a high-pitched squeal. Her feet began to move. With every step forward, Juntto and Katie took a step back. Her legs flailed wildly, punching holes in the stone columns.

Katie sighed. "Well, I think we just pissed her off."

Juntto gritted his teeth and fired again, but stopped as soon as he realized it was no use. Her purple hide was impenetrable. The energy pulsing from her was knocking the bullets away before they could touch her. She grabbed Juntto around the waist. Katie reached for him, but Sasha was too quick. She yanked him close to her body.

As her legs wrapped around him, squeezing the air from his lungs, Sasha smiled. "Hello, big guy. Normally I prefer demon energy, but Leviathan will do just fine."

Juntto growled. "Over my dead body."

Sasha laughed. "As you wish."

She took a deep breath, sucking the energy from his chest. He howled, trying to resist her. Using everything he had, he pulled one arm free and punched her in the side of the head. It stunned her long enough for him to break free of her grasp. He fell to the floor and she snarled, venom dripping from her teeth. Her hand darted out and grabbed his foot, and she flipped him over and dragged him back to her. As he was pulled along the ground he flailed, his hands finally finding an old iron street lamp.

He roared and yanked the thing from the ground, then flipped over and wailed on her with the streetlamp. She let go and he pummeled her, knocking her to the ground. Her eyes rolled back for a moment and she swayed, obviously trying to collect herself. Juntto backed up next to Katie, throwing the bent streetlamp aside.

As Sasha sat there dazed and distracted, demons began to fall from the portal above. Katie cursed and pulled out Tom and Harry. "You get her, I'll take care of them."

Juntto nodded.

Katie ran toward the demons as they landed, blasting away with her guns. One after another they went down hard, their bodies bursting into ash. Using one of the falling demons as a step, she pushed herself into the air, crossing her arms in front of her as she turned. She pumped the triggers, sending bullets in every direction. She landed on one knee, snarling, out of bullets.

Get it, girl.

Katie reloaded quickly and flung Tom out, firing into a charging demon's skull. The beast shrieked and fell to the ground, bursting into dust. Katie breathed heavily as she stood up. A demon was suddenly right beside her. With a quick motion she holstered Tom, grabbed a dagger from her waist, and slashed another demon across the throat. Black blood sprayed across her face, but she barely noticed.

Pandora was shocked by how badass Katie was. *Girl, see? I told you. Get laid, and you become an even better version of yourself. I'm telling you now, you better keep that hunk of meat in your fucking bed.*

Katie chuckled as she grabbed a demon by the throat and jammed the dagger into its heart. She turned the knife, carving a large hole in the demon's chest. She yanked the knife out and rammed her fist into its chest, pulling out the demon's still-beating heart. She stared the demon in the face as she crushed his heart in her hands.

Pandora cheered. *What the fuck was that? Do it again. Never stop doing that.*

Just showing you how much of a bitch I can really be when it comes to matters of the heart.

If you did that every time we went out, I would never hound you about sex. Okay, that's a lie, but it would definitely decrease.

Katie laughed. *Yeah, right.*

Pandora sighed. *Okay, fine. It wouldn't decrease, but you would be one badass fucking woman. At least even more so than you are now.*

Katie jammed her dagger into the neck of a demon and yanked it back out. She slugged it hard in the face for good measure. It swayed to the side, blood squirting from the wound. It tried to reach up and stop the bleeding, but before it could, it burst into ash. *I think maybe you're right. Sex with Brock makes me killer in the field. It's like a lucky rabbit's foot, only it's a dick and I can't carry it with my keys.*

Pandora sniffed. *Uh oh, I smell trouble. Is Korbin ready for what might come?*

Korbin is always ready.

Behind them, Juntto tackled Sasha, holding down her four arms. She tried to suck his energy, but he slammed a big hand over her mouth. "Sorry, lady. There's only one woman I let suck me, and you are definitely not her."

Sasha yelled as she kicked Juntto into the wall. "Maybe you'll have a change of heart."

Juntto flexed his muscles as he stood up. "I don't like chicks with that many arms. It's fucking nasty."

Sasha's eyes glowed bright yellow as she scurried across the floor toward him. He grabbed a piece of cement from the crumbling church and flung it with all his might, and it hit her in the face. Her upper body bent back, and she paused before straightening up again. A trickle of purple blood spilled out of her nose and she glared at him as she wiped it away.

Sasha did not like getting injured. It unleashed an anger inside of her that Juntto hadn't seen yet. She charged him, her arms grabbing him around the waist and slamming him to the ground. He slapped away her arms, breaking them as they tried to grapple with him. She screeched loudly, her fangs close to his face. She reared back and shot webbing at his legs, wrapping it around his ankles. She grabbed the webbing like a rope and flung him into the air. Juntto flew over Katie's head and smashed through two buildings next to the church. They crumbled, and dust filled the air.

Katie glanced at the resulting piles of rubble. *Oh, shit. No.*

A massive blue fist punched through the rubble, then Juntto leaped out of one pile and roared an ancient war-cry. He charged Sasha, dodging a spray of sticky webbing as he went. Sasha ran from him, scurrying up the side of the church. Juntto launched himself at her. She hung upside-down and kicked him in the chest, and he went sailing back, landing in the same pile of rubble as before.

Katie took off across the yard and jumped onto the pile. She yanked large pieces of wall off his chest.

The angel slapped him on the cheeks several times until he came to. "Juntto. Are you all right?"

Juntto shook debris from his hair. "Bitch has a strong arm."

Katie looked over her shoulder at the beast. "Oh, yeah? Which one of them is it?"

Juntto chuckled. "Uh, the fourth one?"

Katie smiled and tapped his chest. "Sit this next round out and let me have a go at her."

Juntto grabbed Katie's wrist. "Are you sure? She is one tough Leviathan."

Katie smiled, red flashing in her eyes. "Someone needs to teach this bitch a lesson. Who better to do it than the biggest bitch on the block?"

Pandora cleared her throat. *Don't you mean "bitches?"*

Katie marched toward Sasha. *Hell, yeah, I do.*

Korbin watched from the sidelines as Juntto flew into the building. Katie took off after him, and demons began falling from the portal and scattering all over the town. He turned to his soldiers. "Without shooting our guys, aim those guns at the demons and send them back to hell. Do not shoot the spider, please. We don't need that kind of attention."

Korbin backed up behind the guns and bullets riddled the town. Several of the running demons went down hard, cut to ribbons by the guns before turning to dust. The portal vibrated wildly. Korbin narrowed his eyes, wondering what was next. Five demons fell from the portal and hit the ground running. Their claws dug into the dirt and they headed straight for Korbin and the guns, determined to stop them.

Korbin jumped on the last empty gun and waved his hand in the air. "Send these fuckers back to hell!"

The guns blasted the five demons as four more landed

on the ground. These four were different. They moved fast, dodging the barrage of bullets.

Korbin leaped from his gun and pulled his twin swords from his back. The demons raced toward them on all fours. Their heads were hyena-shaped, and their bodies were long, lean, and cheetah-like. Two of them were caught in a hail of bullets, but the other two dodged the fire.

Korbin backed up, readying himself. The first demon leaped at him. He lashed out with one sword and felt it dig into the beast's body, cutting the thing in half. He ducked as the two halves of the body flew past him. They bounced on the ground and turned to ash.

The second hyena demon roared in a furiously high pitch as it charged Korbin. As it got closer, it swiped at him with a black paw, catching Korbin in the left hand and knocking a sword away. He winced but held tightly to his remaining sword. Blood flowed from his hand. The hyena lunged again, and Korbin stepped around a swinging paw. He jammed the sword into the side of the hyena's head. The creature bucked backward, whining and yelping. When Korbin released the sword, the beast fell to the ground, whimpered, and turned to dust.

Timothy jumped down from a gun and ran to Korbin. "Are you okay?"

Korbin grabbed the handkerchief from Timothy's front pocket and wrapped it around his hand. "I will be now."

Timothy was horrified. "You just used a four-hundred-dollar handkerchief to bandage a wound. Fabulous."

Korbin chuckled and patted him on the shoulder. "Thanks, pal."

Timothy shook his head as Korbin jumped back on the gun turret. "When I had a demon, I was in a control room for every battle. Now that I'm just little ol' me, I'm right in the middle of the shit. If the demons don't kill me, the irony will."

Sasha growled as she pulled herself to her feet. She wiped the blood from her nose and spat on the ground. Snarling, she scurried around the side of the church. A small demon ran past her, not paying any attention to his proximity to the Leviathan. She snatched him and held him close, and the demon howled as she sucked the energy from him. As she exhaled, she dropped his shell to the ground. Her head went back for a moment and her eyes closed. She moaned happily.

The sound of boots hitting the ground snapped Sasha back to attention. Katie was charging toward her. As Katie ran she opened her wings wide, lifting off the ground. She hovered for a moment.

Pandora growled, *Look at that fat fuck.*

She's strong, and getting stronger.

She's feisty, sure. We'll just have to ground and pound this bitch until all the feisty has been beaten out of her.

Katie flipped herself upside-down and rocketed toward the ground. She pushed her shield out in front of her, aiming right at Sasha. The Leviathan raised three of her arms to block the blow as Katie plowed into her. Light exploded from the point of impact, and the force drove Sasha's body a foot into the ground. Katie got to her feet and stumbled away. She shook her head, her ears ringing and her teeth clenched.

As she stepped away, a hand reached out of the ground and grabbed Katie's leg. Katie tried to pull away, but Sasha yanked her closer. Four of her legs reached over the edge of the hole and she moved her bulk out of it, bringing Katie closer all the while. Katie tried to grab the sword from her back, but Sasha was faster. Her many hands closed around Katie's wrists and hips and tugged her close. Sasha took a deep breath of Pandora's energy and her eyes blazed yellow with satisfaction.

Pandora screamed as she felt the intrusion. *You fucking energy-guzzling pile of dog shit. Fucking let go right now, or I'll show you what it feels like to be assaulted.*

Katie was still holding onto her shield. She wrestled her arm away from Sasha, and with a great heave, she slammed the shield into the Leviathan's chest. Sasha snarled and fell back into the hole. Katie backwinged, landing hard on the ground a few yards away. She wiped the webbing from her forehead.

Pandora was panting, and Katie was worried she had been hurt. *Pandora, are you okay?*

Fuck, that bitch is a real fucking asshole. We have to change this up, dude.

It's too dangerous. She'll go right for you.

And I'll tear her tits off. You need to let me come out and fight.

Katie shook her head. She was about to tell her no when something moved in the corner of her eye, and she whipped her head up to see Sasha jump at her. She slammed into Katie and tackled her to the ground. They rolled across the lawn, legs and arms flailing. Katie kicked hard and managed to roll over on top of Sasha, but the spiderwoman lashed out, slamming one of her legs into Katie's head. For a moment Katie's vision blurred, but Pandora quickly corrected it. *This is what I'm saying!*

Katie groaned, pulling her shield up. *Not. The time. To argue.*

Katie attempted to duck behind the shield, but Sasha grabbed her by the cheeks and shoulders. She sucked hard, dragging even more energy out of her.

Pandora groaned. *I'm going to shove those legs so far up your ass you will be walking on your face, you twatwaffle.*

Katie twisted her head away and pulled her shield in front of her face. She struggled with the creature, locking several of Sasha's legs down with her own thighs. Katie banged Sasha's face with her shield, but Sasha just laughed. "You stupid angel. You think you can beat me? I am all-powerful, bitch. Just give in and let me suck you dry."

Pandora cringed. *That's fucking disgusting. Seriously, she needs a new pickup line. Come on, let me out so I can have a go.*

Katie punched Sasha in the face and shook her head. *No. I'm getting the hell beaten out of me, and I need you in there to heal me. If you don't stay where you are, I might not walk away from this.*

Sasha bucked Katie up and flipped her on her back, then loomed over her. Thinking quickly, Katie pulled her knees to her chest. She thrust her feet into Sasha's chest and sent her flying backward into the side of the church. Immediately Katie was on her feet, unfolding her wings. She flew high enough that Sasha couldn't get to her, then put her hands on her waist and breathed heavily.

Pandora gave her a burst of energy. *It seems that she can use any energy, but demon energy is what really gets her going.*

Yeah. She sucked energy out of Juntto, but it didn't do nearly what demon energy does. Maybe you're right. Maybe we need to fight together.

Pandora let out a deep breath. *Yes. We can fight her as angels. In the meantime, she won't keep growing like a fucking tarantula if we can keep the demons away from her.*

Katie's eyes flashed blue. *What we need to do is end this bitch now. She has done enough damage to our bodies and our lives. Get out here. We are going to kick this Leviathan's ass.*

Pandora cheered and pulled herself out of Katie's body. As soon as she was out, she called her angelic armor and hovered next to Katie. Katie could tell Pandora was just as exhausted as she was, but they had to continue. They were the only ones in the world who had any chance of killing the bitch.

Katie nodded at Pandora. "You okay?"

"Besides needing to sleep for the next ten years? Yeah, I'll pull through."

Katie laughed bitterly

Pandora pulled her sword. Her shield shone in the sun. Her armor was silver and black, and her blue eyes were stunning. "Let's finish this twat."

24

Katie hovered on one side of Sasha, with Pandora on the other side. Sasha smirked as her arms and legs moved a mile a minute, fending off their attacks. Katie lashed out with her sword, swiping at Sasha's tangle of legs. With every swipe she knocked off another chunk, but by the time she moved on to the next leg, the first limb was already growing back. Sasha's healing powers were off the charts.

Pandora put her sword away and held her shield up. She dodged the spiderwoman's flailing limbs, but she had to time it perfectly. Every time she saw a hole, she would slam the shield into the Leviathan's body. A small groan came from Sasha each time, but she didn't budge. Pandora dodged to the right and swiped the edge of her shield across Sasha's face, slicing through the skin of her forehead. Blood trickled down her face.

Pandora laughed. "Look who's not so beautiful now, bitch."

Sasha growled and Pandora hit her hard in the face

with her shield, bloodying her lips. Sasha screamed loudly and scurried backward. Webbing shot into the ruins of the church, and Sasha zipped out of sight. Katie put her hands on her knees and looked at Pandora. "This is going well, right?"

Pandora chuckled through her gasps. "Oh, yeah. Sure. At this rate, it will be approximately seven years before we wear this bitch down. Where the fuck did she go? I didn't know we could call breaks."

Sasha suddenly dropped in front of them and snarled as she held Brock's sword up. "A little parting gift from my favorite energy source."

Katie narrowed her eyes. She recognized the carvings on the flat of the sword. "You fucking bitch, that's *Brock's* sword!"

Katie was livid. She charged forward, pulled her sword from her back, and swung it wildly at Sasha. The Leviathan kept a smirk on her face as she met Katie's sword with Brock's. Pandora pulled her own sword from the sheath on her back. She swung hard, trying to catch Sasha off guard, but the spiderwoman was fast. She blocked Pandora's blow before parrying Katie's. Somehow, she was managing to fight them both at the same time.

Pandora screamed, pushing back against the sword. "You think you are such hot shit, but the truth is you're a shriveled-up hag and you'll never be beautiful again once I'm done with you."

Sasha laughed loudly. "I think you have it backward. When I suck the demon energy out of that body, *you'll* be the shriveled-up hag."

Katie lunged forward and slashed the tip of her sword

across Sasha's cheek. Blood ran down and Sasha gasped, putting a hand to the wound. Seeing her chance, Pandora cut off one of her hands and kicked her hard in the stomach. Sasha stumbled back and kept retreating. She scooted across the ground until she had her back pressed against a large pile of rubble, then looked around wildly, realizing that she had managed to back herself into a corner.

She tried to climb, but Pandora flew overhead and punched her with her shield. "You aren't going anywhere, bitch. Sit still while we give you a little lesson on keeping your fucking hands to yourself."

Katie flew over and sneered at the purple Leviathan, then looked at Pandora and nodded. Together they slashed through her gaggle of legs. The two angels cut through limb after limb, but again and again as they regrew. Though Sasha was weak by that point, the assault still wasn't doing enough damage.

Sasha bared her teeth at Pandora and inhaled, trying to drain her demonic energy. Pandora flew to Katie's side. "This isn't enough!"

"What else can we do?"

Pandora went silent for a moment. She thrust out her hand. "Grab it."

Katie glanced down. "What? I really don't think this is the time for a show of friendship!"

Pandora rolled her eyes. "Take my hand. Trust me."

Katie looked at her like she had lost her mind, but she did as Pandora asked—and her head flew back and she gasped. Their individual angelic energies converged. It was warm and overwhelming, and all Katie could do was hold on as tightly as possible. Bright spears of blue light began to shoot out from their hands. Sasha screamed as they sliced through her, pulling at her every fiber. Katie gripped harder as the light increased, growing so bright that it blinded them.

Pandora's voice cut through it all. "We've been fighting her, which means we've been fighting all the demons she's absorbed. We need to exorcise them."

Katie yelled, feeling the intensity of the energy swirling around them. Pandora groaned and vibrated the spears of light, pulling the energy back out of Sasha. "It's working. Keep holding on."

Katie took a deep breath and held tighter, exorcising all the demons. Familiar energy surged around her—Brock's demon. Sasha screamed, her body shrinking to half its previous size. Her many legs curled to her chest and she leaned her head back, her mouth falling open. A beam of light shot from her throat and slammed into Katie and Pandora.

Pandora held tighter to Katie. "Look, she's shrinking. Our energy is pulling hers out. Keep going! We're almost there!"

Katie opened one eye and blinked through the light, seeing Sasha's arms curling into her chest as well as her legs. Several of her limbs fell off and turned to dust beneath her. She was still shrinking when Pandora finally released Katie's hand. Pandora spread her fingers, sending the excess energy into the ground. Katie pulled her sword and slashed at Sasha. "Her arms aren't growing back!"

She sliced off another and another until the Leviathan was only left with two arms and two legs. Katie smirked. "Now we are on a level playing field."

Sasha's head hung low, and her breathing was short and labored. Her body shook wildly as she searched for any remaining energy. She couldn't even lift the sword.

Katie advanced on Sasha. "It's time to finish this."

As Katie stepped forward, Pandora yelled. "Not yet!"

Katie furrowed her brow and turned to Pandora. "Why?"

Her body jolted. Pandora watched as the confused expression melted from Katie's face. Her eyes flickered between blue and red, and a soft gasp came from her throat. Katie looked down at her side. Brock's sword was jutting from a seam in her armor. Sasha yanked the sword out of her flesh, and Katie grabbed the wound. Blood poured out, and she fell to one knee and put a palm on the ground.

Pandora reached for her. "No!"

Sasha reached up and grabbed her by the wing, then flung her to the ground. She was like an injured dog pushed into a corner. She might not have been strong any longer, but she had the survival instinct of a wild animal. Pandora fought to get up, but Sasha laughed loudly and held her down. "I'm going to make you watch your human die before I suck the life right out of you."

Pandora looked at Sasha with bright red eyes and growled. She swiped her hands at the Leviathan's face, but she was held back by unimaginable will. Her eyes moved past Sasha and saw a huge blue monster standing behind her.

Juntto.

He winked at Pandora and lifted his giant war-spear. Pandora began to laugh uncontrollably. She didn't stop laughing when Juntto plunged his spear through Sasha's heart. She dropped Pandora and grabbed the end of the spear jutting through her chest.

Katie struggled to her feet and retrieved her sword from the ground. Steadying herself, she raised the sword over her head and held it there for a moment.

She muttered, "Suck this." The sword fell, slicing through Sasha's neck.

The spiderwoman's head fell to the ground and rolled across the courtyard, rolling ear over nose until it came to a stop in the middle of town.

Pandora stood shakily and took off, flying toward the portal. She extended her hands and closed her eyes, groaning as she used every ounce of her strength to slam the portal shut. When Pandora floated back to the ground, Katie was holding onto Juntto with one arm. Blood trickled from the corner of her mouth, and she winced as she moved. The cut in her side was deep, but that hadn't stopped Katie from removing the Leviathan's head.

Katie and Pandora exchanged smiles as they locked eyes. Pandora grinned. "Oh, come here, you badass bitch."

"I don't know if you want to do that. It was a special metal sword."

Pandora rolled her eyes. "Fuck me. How much do I love you?"

She dove into Katie.

The news reporter looked somber standing next to a video of the Romanian Leviathan slaying. "This footage was taken by soldiers near the fight. You can see Katie was deeply wounded by the beast, but that didn't stop her. She persevered and sliced the creature's head off her shoulders."

Beelzebub and Baal winced as Sasha's head came to a stop right in front of the camera. Beelzebub shook his head. "What a waste. She was a badass Leviathan. Dangerous, but badass."

Baal clicked the television off and stood up. He growled at Beelzebub. "I knew it. I *knew* you were up to something. I mean, fucking *seriously*? You were sending demons to occupy a Romanian village? You really thought that you would be able to make hell on Earth? That is the stupidest thing I have ever heard. There is a reason that the planet cannot sustain our environment. To think you actually thought Katie would let you get away with it. It's laughable, really." He thought for a moment. "Wait. Teyollucuani. Did you dig her up or what?"

"No fucking way. I wanted to make hell on Earth. I just picked a shitty spot. All the demonic energy must have knocked her out of her slumber. What a shitshow." Beelzebub put up his finger. "Hey, it *almost* worked. If that Leviathan hadn't sucked the energy out of every single one of my demons, it would have had a really good chance of working."

Baal scoffed, rolling his eyes. "Please, almost doesn't count, ever. Repeat this sentence: I *almost* kept my balls when Lucifer found out I was a complete fuck-up."

Beelzebub winced. "Okay, good point. He's not the type to give you points for effort. I don't think this will warrant another trip to his office, though. In reality, I didn't do any harm this time around. That was all Teyollucuani."

Baal poured himself a drink and shook his head. "You think Lucifer will give a fuck whose fault it was? No. The truth is, I have come up with something much more interesting. This plan is better than hell on Earth, better than all of Moloch's ploys. I've actually been planning this for a long time, but I didn't know if I would have the chance to use it."

Beelzebub narrowed his eyes. "What are you doing?"

Baal chuckled. "I'm doing something way more evil. I am playing a long game. Basically, I'm playing with politics."

Beelzebub groaned and rubbed his face. "Politics is bullshit. All I have to say is, you better know what you're doing. Your plan could turn around and bite you right in the dick if you aren't careful."

Baal didn't seem worried. He waved his hands at Beelzebub. "It will be fine, I swear. I have been watching the idiots all this time, taking notes, and figuring out the exact right moves. This won't be a repeat of Moloch's fuck-ups, or even yours."

Beelzebub snarled and grabbed the glass out of Baal's hand. "Then I guess this is to you. May you not crash and burn on your epic journey to take over Earth."

He threw back the whiskey and put the glass back in Baal's hand. Baal growled and shook his head. "I haven't failed."

"*Yet.*"

Pandora quickly began healing the wound in Katie's side. Juntto scooped her up in his arms and climbed back up the hill to where Korbin and the others were waiting for them. Juntto laid Katie down in the grass, and Korbin and Timothy rushed to her side. "How bad is it?"

Timothy got really nervous. "Oh, God. I cannot be standing here with no demon watching one of my best friends die."

Katie opened one eye. "If I die, I'm totally haunting you, and I am going to wear cotton sweat pants and a sweatshirt with no hood."

Timothy let out a deep breath. "God. You are okay. And don't you ever threaten me with such an atrocious act ever again."

Katie lifted her shirt to show off the hole in the fabric and a whole lot of blood, but there was no longer a wound. Beneath the surface, Pandora was working overtime. She winced, feeling the aftereffects of being stabbed with a special metal sword. It was minor but still painful. Katie's body had absorbed the brunt of the blow, but it was a really good thing Pandora hadn't been inside. She wasn't sure if she could have survived something like that.

Katie put up her hand, and Korbin helped her sit up. Pandora finished repairing the last of her internal issues and stepped out of Katie's body. She sat next to Katie and took a deep breath. They listened to Korbin and Timothy talk about how badass the three of them were. Timothy smacked his lips. "And you totally did the Hulk smash, Thor hammer, blast off. You pushed that bitch a foot or two into the ground. It was fucking *amazing*."

Korbin shook his head. "And whatever the two of you

did by holding hands, that was badass too. We were all blinded by the light. We couldn't see what happened. How did you know that would work?"

Katie pointed at Pandora, who shrugged. "It was a gut feeling. I don't usually listen to them, but it worked out this time. I knew angels could produce energy. I just took it to the next level. We exorcised the bitch."

Katie looked at Timothy. "How is everything reading now? Did that get rid of the issue?"

Timothy grabbed his tablet and punched a bunch of keys. After a moment he showed them a map of the town. "Not only is it not showing an incursion, there isn't a single demon within a thousand miles. The red is all gone. The little specks of red are us standing here. You did good, dudes, really good."

Katie let out a deep breath. "Good, because I don't think I have it in me to go back in there again. At least not yet. Fighting her was one of the hardest things I've done. I would have died if Pandora and Juntto hadn't been there. When she got me in the side, I figured I was a goner."

Pandora scoffed. "I don't know if I have it in me to walk again. How are *you* doing, Juntto?"

Juntto grunted as he shrank back into Khal Drogo. "Good. I have a stiff neck, but other than that I could run a marathon."

Pandora and Katie looked at him. "We have mortal wounds, and you have a stiff neck. This is so unfair."

Korbin laughed and pulled Katie up to her feet. "We need to get you home. I think I am going to send Timothy back with you too. It's too dangerous out here for a non-infected."

Timothy closed his eyes and whispered loud enough for everyone to hear him, "Yes, thank God."

Katie nodded. "I think that might be a wise choice. Maybe once Juntto and I are rested and better we can help you finish this job for the general."

Korbin gave Pandora a hand to her feet. "That would be awesome. Until then, please keep your feet on the ground."

Katie laughed. She turned to Pandora. "Shortcut?"

Pandora yawned and stepped forward, swiping her hands to open a portal. Nothing happened. She frowned and took a wider stance, slashing her hand in front of her again. There was a slight flicker, but it quickly faded away. "Goddammit, *work*."

She waved her hands over and over, trying to open up a portal to hell, but nothing she did worked. Finally, she gave up. "I don't know what's going on. I guess my demonic powers are running a little low."

Katie gave her a serious look. "Okay, well, you just went through something seriously draining. There's a really good chance your body just needs to rest."

Pandora took a deep breath and looked down at her hands. She didn't want to say it out loud, but she couldn't help but wonder. Was this a result of battling Sasha or was it something else? She looked at Korbin briefly. He could tell she wasn't as confident as Katie was.

Timothy clapped his hands. "No big deal. I can't take the shortcut, so we have a chopper coming in ten. We can all ride together on the jet! It'll be like old times."

Pandora glanced at Katie as they followed Timothy and Juntto to the helo area. "I blame you for all this."

Katie scoffed. "Why? I didn't have anything to do with you being too weak."

"You wouldn't let me out."

"If I had, I would have been dead by now."

Timothy walked over to the girls. "Um, the chopper can only hold three of us."

Katie and Timothy stared at Pandora, who snapped her fingers and snarled, "Fine, I'll go back in my cage."

Katie rolled her eyes. "So damn dramatic."

"One day I will rise up against my oppressors."

"I feed you dozens of donuts a week. You're so oppressed."

25

The SUV pulled in front of Katie's condo in New York, and she let out a sigh of relief. She was finally home. Everyone climbed out of the car into a flurry of camera flashes from the mass of reporters waiting outside. Timothy was on his way to Las Vegas, but the rest of them were home. Two police officers held the crowd back as they walked through. Most of them cheered Katie, praising her and the others for their work, but, as usual, there were a few who wished Pandora would go back to hell. Normally Katie would snarl or flash red eyes to scare them, but tonight all she wanted was quiet.

They were exhausted. When they got to the top floor, Angie opened the door and jumped into Juntto's arms. "Oh, I like this look. I *knew* you liked Game of Thrones."

Juntto shrugged. "I like the Lannisters. They are ruthless."

Katie chuckled as she gave Angie a hug. "What are you guys going to do?"

Angie shook her head. "What do you want to do?"

Juntto rubbed his hands together with excitement. "I want to play video games. I need to get really good, because I heard about the most awesome thing."

"What's that?"

Juntto put his hands on his sides. "Video game competitions. Seriously, you can play against other people and win money and fame, but most importantly, a title."

Katie burst out laughing. "Wow, this shit is getting serious."

Angie forced a smile. "I mean, if that's what you want to do, I'm behind you. Of course, you will have to get good enough to at least beat *me*."

Juntto narrowed his eyes at Angie and turned to Katie. "I figured since I am already really good at it, why not get even better? I could conquer the entire video game world? I want to play against Kurtis Ling, Clement Ivanov, and maybe even learn DOTA 2 and work my way up to challenging Saahil Aurora. He is the champion of the world in that game. Apparently, he makes a shit-ton of money, too."

Katie shook her head. "I don't understand. You literally live a life where you have powers like a video game character and go out and fight battles like you're in a video game, but you do it all so you can come home and play video games?"

Juntto nodded. "Yeah, exactly."

Angie laughed and patted him on the arm, moving him across the hall to his room. "Come on, honey, let's get you cleaned up and plugged in. I think Katie could use some time to herself. A little quiet time away from you."

Angie winked at Katie and pushed him into his condo. Katie chuckled to herself as she opened her own door. She tossed her keys in the bowl Angie had put beside the door. She walked into her room and undressed, looking at the dried blood on her side. There was no scar or even a red mark to show where she had been stabbed.

Katie was impressed. *You do good work, Pandora.*

Pandora yawned. *I know. You owe me two dozen donuts.*

I think you earned them. Maybe this time you can come out of me and eat your own donuts.

Pandora got excited. *That would be awesome, but wait. Then I am taking on the negative health effects. You know what, I'll stick with enjoying them through you.*

Katie snorted shaking her head. *Gee, thanks, but next time I get laid, you're waiting in the hallway.*

Pandora gasped. *How dare you?*

Katie laughed and called Brock. He picked up his phone on the second ring. "Well, if it isn't the giant spider-killer. Let me tell you, you really amped up the morale in this building."

Katie smiled. "I'm glad. So the guys got to see her die?"

Brock laughed. "Oh, yeah. They replayed that shit over and over. From the spear through the heart all the way to her head coming to a stop in the courtyard. I think just seeing that will help them heal a little faster. How are you, though? I saw that nasty stab you got."

Katie sighed. "It hurt like a bitch, and I lost a bunch of blood. It was special metal, but luckily Pandora was out of me for the initial blow. Then she came in and healed me in no time. So, how do you like it in the armory?"

Brock let out a deep breath. "I really like being stationed in one place. This is the first time it's happened in my entire military career. And it already feels like home. It is a little quiet without you here, though."

Katie smiled to herself. "I'll be back soon. Oh, and I got your sword back."

Brock perked up. "That's awesome. I was really pissed that she had taken it from me."

Katie shook her head. "She didn't want to give it back, either. I'll bring it to you in person."

"That sounds perfect. Hey, I am about to walk into a security meeting. Can I call you back in a bit?"

Katie yawned. "Yep, you sure can. I may be asleep, but if not I will answer."

Katie hung up with Brock, but as soon as she did, there was a loud knock on the door. She sighed. She pulled her yoga pants and sweatshirt on and shuffled over, flinging it open. She assumed it would be Angie, but it wasn't. Instead, there were two men in black suits staring at her. She had never seen either of them before in her life. "Can I help you?"

The guy on the right nodded, his hands crossed in front of him. "The general wishes to see you in his office ASAP. If you could come with us?"

Katie eyed them and grabbed her keys. She followed the guys to a blacked-out SUV. "I could fly, you know?"

"Yes, ma'am, but we would appreciate it if you rode with us."

Katie didn't like it, but she climbed into the back. She knew before the thing took off she wasn't actually going to the general's office, but she didn't care. She had a feeling she knew exactly where they were headed.

Katie was led through the UN headquarters to a secret heavily armored bunker. It was dark down there, with security guards stationed about every fifteen feet. She walked to a checkpoint and stood waiting for the guards to let her through. They were speaking in hushed, angry tones. She knew what they were arguing about. Katie had strapped Tom to her hip before leaving the house.

She had one rule: no matter where she was going, she would always go prepared. The guard at the front held his hand over his gun tightly, his eyes flashing at Katie. "She cannot walk into these meetings with a gun."

The other guard patted him on the shoulder. "I was ordered to bring her here. She's got clearance. I was told not to disarm her, just show her into the Council room. That is Katie from Katie's Killers. Do you want to try to take a gun from her?"

The guard looked at her nervously and shook his head. Katie liked how it all went down. She no longer had to argue with people about her guns. They had accepted long ago that there was no talking her out of it. The general must have prepped them all before the meeting.

The guards opened the door and stepped to one side, standing at attention. Katie smiled and slowly walked into the room. There was a large oval table in the center with leaders from all over the world, just as she had suspected. It was a World Council meeting. Katie narrowed her eyes and peered down the line of men. Among them she found General Brushwood, President Dragos, the German Chancellor, and the President of Ghana. The general looked somber, but the others glared at her with such disdain that she almost felt uncomfortable.

General Brushwood stood up, and the rest followed suit. Katie walked to the empty chair next to him and took a seat. There was a low murmur among the men, and Katie wondered if she was the only woman to sit with the old bastards in one of their secret meetings. Either way, she knew something was coming she wasn't going to like. She could read the room.

Pandora wasn't having it. *You should seriously get up and leave. These bastards are going to try something fishy.*

Give them a chance. Maybe this is a thank-you thing.

Pandora scoffed. *Yeah, right. Bahahaha.*

The head of the secret council, President Putin, stood up and banged a gavel. "This secret meeting of the World Council is now in session. Our first order of business is, of course, the demon war. That is why we have asked Katie to join us. We are going to give our members a chance to voice their opinions."

President Dragos stood. "I will begin. It has come to my attention that Katie might be a serious liability. Ever since she became heavily involved in the war, she has taunted the higher demons, which led them to retaliate. Not only against my country but countries all over the world. There is no oversight with these mercenaries. They do what they want when they want, without any thought to what the repercussions might be for the rest of us."

General Brushwood grumbled, but he knew he had to hear them out.

President Dragos sat down, and the German Chancellor stood. "My concerns have to do with whether we can truly trust this mercenary. She has shown over and over she has no care for our historical artifacts, our cities, or our citizens. The money we pay her is good; we know that. But are her intentions good? This must be about more than just money. I do not trust that this is the case for Katie."

Katie lifted her eyebrows, not saying a word as the German Chancellor sat and the president of Ghana stood. "We have no threats in our country. However, I have watched as the demons have searched for this mercenary. They seek to hurt her, so they attack everyone but her. They kill women and children. They desecrate sacred temples. They destroy entire villages in a matter of seconds. Many times, Katie is hailed as a hero. She goes home to a hero's welcome while we dig small graves for our future generations lost to the Devil's hand. I fear she does more harm than good."

President Putin nodded thoughtfully. He gestured to the others. "Anyone else?"

They all shook their heads. Putin turned to Katie, who gave him her full attention. "It has become obvious to many of us that you do not have the world's best interests at heart. After we heard these stories, we were, of course, concerned. You have extraordinary gifts, but these gifts could seriously harm the world. You need someone regulating you, an independent body making sure you answer for your mistakes. Therefore, we have decided that you will no longer be a private entity. You are no longer on your own, but instead will be regulated under the World Council."

Pandora was livid. *Oh, hell no. I am not going to sit here with a man who poses topless on horses, the newest member of the Third Reich, the Romanian ballerina, and a bunch of scared, weak assholes and be told how I will live my life. They aren't fit to govern an infestation of pubic lice. Fuck this motherfucking shit, I will burn the whole place down around us.*

Katie took a deep breath. *Hold on. Just try to stay calm. We are going to say our piece. Just let it come at the perfect moment.*

The general stood up and cleared his throat. "If I may, I would like to speak in defense of Katie. I have worked with her for a long time. She should be given credit for bridging the relationship between military and mercenaries. That alone allowed us to acquire special weapons, ammunition, and insight on the battles raging around the world. Time after time she has put her life on the line to protect your countries and your people. Just this morning she killed a Leviathan who threatened the very existence of Romania as a country. She was not paid. She was there to rescue brave men and women trapped in circumstances beyond their control. It is an outrage that you would disrespect a true hero in this manner. I demand to know the name of this attorney, and I would like a full investigation opened on this very secret meeting."

Pandora could see that the general was getting upset. Frankly, she'd had enough of the rhetoric. She didn't need someone else putting their asses on the line for her. She and Katie were more than capable of standing up for themselves and facing the repercussions of those actions. Pandora took a deep breath and separated herself from Katie. The men around the table gasped and moved back.

Pandora was actually dressed this time. It was a meeting, after all. She paced the floor in black stiletto boots, scowling at the World Council with her red eyes. She suddenly slammed her hands on the table and snarled, "How *dare* you judge me! Humans have run this war for far too long. And to be quite frank, they are running it into the fucking ground. They have no ability to defeat the demons, they have no ability to understand them, and they barely have the ability to stay alive during an incursion."

Pandora stood up straight and held out her hand. Her angelic form whirled around her, and her wings spread wide behind her. Her crown of thorns was perched at a cocky angle on her head. She gripped the hilt of her sword and strode down the table, glaring at the men. Behind her, Katie summoned her angelic armor. Her wings spread wide behind her, and her shield shone like the sun.

The men of the council murmured, unnerved.

Pandora nodded appreciatively and continued, "This is the War of the Angels. You can fight beside me, you can follow my orders, or you can get the fuck out of my way. There is a reason that both Katie and I are angels. We did not give ourselves those titles. The God you cling to in your darkest moments gave us those titles, these wings, and this armor. With them comes the responsibility to beat the demons and send them straight back to hell. If you think for five seconds you will be allowed to rule me, you are grossly mistaken."

Pandora raised her voice. "This council is dissolved."

General Brushwood shook his head sadly.

President Dragos howled with rage. "You cannot dissolve this council! You don't have the authority!"

Pandora met President Dragos' eye and shook her head.

"I sacrificed my freedom so I could continue to save the people of this world. What have *you* done lately?"

The general moved around the table. "Katie, we can talk about this."

"We just did. This obviously isn't working anymore. I'll still fight the good fight, but I'll do it my way."

Katie took Pandora's hand, and they walked out of the room.

As they left, Pandora raised her other hand and flipped the council the bird.

Lieutenant Colonel Samuel Wilson lay on his prison cot reading his copy of *The Old Man and the Sea*. He sighed as he attempted to decipher the text through the pictures and graffiti drawn in the book. He did have his own cell, though. That was something. He had been given his own cell after assaulting a bunkmate. Wilson didn't mind sharing a room, but he was not at all willing to share his cell with some naïve idiot in there for going AWOL. No matter what sort of trouble he was in, he was still a lieutenant colonel who had proudly served his country for two decades.

He turned the page and paused as footsteps echoed down the hallway. A guard approached his cell door and stood at attention. "Colonel Wilson, you have a visitor."

Wilson peered at the guard, then set down his book.

They brought him into a private meeting room in cuffs. The small dark man inside stood up and gave him an oddly unnerving grin. Wilson frowned. "Who the fuck are you?"

He whistled when he spoke. That was because of his broken tooth, courtesy of a mean hook delivered by General Brushwood.

The man shook his hand and gestured for him to sit. "My name is Mr. Belly."

"Dumb name."

Belphegor shrugged inside his new lawyer skin. His old lawyer skin was attracting too much attention. He had chosen the name and had to admit it wasn't great, but it would do. "Nevertheless, it is my name. Mr. Belly. Rather jolly, I think. I'm your new legal counsel."

"I have a JAG lawyer."

"The World Council asked me to represent you. I am told that you were charged with working for a foreign power."

Wilson wrinkled his forehead. "World Council? That's General Brushwood's little boy-band. He hates my guts."

Belphegor tried to hide his glee. "Is it correct that you shot Katie of Katie's Killers right in the gut?"

Wilson chuckled. "That's correct. I'm a dangerous man." His face went cold. "So why the fuck would you put yourself in a room with me, then tell me you're buddies with General Brushwood?"

"Brushwood and I are hardly friends." Belphegor sighed and opened his briefcase. "You *are* a dangerous man. The charges against you are flimsy, and you have your men as character witnesses. Not to mention the time you've already served."

Wilson frowned. "Are you trying to get me out of here?"

"Oh, no, Colonel Wilson." Belphegor slid a few papers across the table. "I *am* getting you out of here. I've worked very hard to make sure the right people got the right things. Everything is in order now. I just need your signature."

Wilson didn't get it. "But...why?"

"Because you're a dangerous man. You took Katie on. That might make you the most dangerous man in the entire world. That's just the kind of man the World Council needs."

Belphegor handed him a pen. "Sign on the dotted line, please."

AUTHOR NOTES - MICHAEL ANDERLE

NOVEMBER 22, 2018

THANK YOU for not only reading this story but these *Author Notes* as well .

(I think I've been good with always opening with "thank you." If not, I need to edit the other *Author Notes*!)

RANDOM (*sometimes*) THOUGHTS?

Happy Thanksgiving, 2018!

I'm reminded by Ell Leigh Clarke (Ellie Clarke) that those who don't come from the United States won't think about a big holiday right at the end of November.

(Well, I believe some countries might, but I'm too lazy to go Google it right now. I have to get my exercises going so I have more room for the turkey. ;-))

Then, I have to "plump the pillow" and get ready for the annual After-Thanksgiving Turkey Nap (ATTN for short) while family is *still at the house*. It is actually a Marine-like effort to stay awake while paying attention to our loved ones, especially since the food we have overindulged is full of <insert scientific sounding word here> to create a huge chemical downer, singing lullabies in our mind to put us under. (*Editor's note: You mean tryptophan? Myth! It's that fourth helping of mashed potatoes.*)

Yes, for those fans who are thinking I overemphasized with the "Marine-like effort" I understand your concern that I am minimizing what Marines do.

I'm not.

I'm talking about the effort of listening to my mom, whom I love, speak about the comings and goings of her community instead of allowing my head to flop forward, the fourth helping of mashed potatoes acting like an airbag to stop my comatose self from smashing my nose. It is difficult for me.

That's all.

I salute you who have just made it through your own effort to mollify family while what you really want to do is curl up on any available horizontal surface, grab the nearest pillow, cat (pillow)—please, those demons wouldn't allow you to sleep on them, but the selfish little twits don't mind using ME as a bed, much less a pillow—or a rolled up coat.

Oh…I should probably talk books, too.

Today we have released the third act of the DAMNED series. Katie has changed Pandora, *or has she?* Can her ex-husband tempt them both back into the fold? If he does, will he live to regret it? (Can you imagine Pandora without donuts?)

Next Friday, we release *The Kurtherian Endgame* #3, *Through the Fire and Flame*. For those ready and waiting for a bit of ass-kicking with a different type of protagonist, we have it lined up.

Further, we are trying really hard to make the next release about four to six weeks (hopefully at most) beyond that. So, end of December / beginning of January 2019.

We already have the next book here in Katie's series on tap and ready to start, so we should have our next book to you here in December.

May EVERYONE reading have a good end of the year.

Join us on Facebook if you use that social media site.

Some of the funniest shit is dropped into the Protected by the Damned Facebook Group. It's the Group for those with twisted senses of humor (raising hand.) (*Editor's Note: Raising hand*)

HOW TO MARKET FOR BOOKS YOU LOVE

We are able to support our efforts with you reading our books, and we appreciate you doing this!

If you enjoyed this or ANY book by any author, especially Indie-published, we always appreciate if you make the time to review a book, since it lets other readers who might be on the fence to take a chance on it as well.

AROUND THE WORLD IN 80 DAYS

One of the interesting (at least to me) aspects of my life is the ability to work from anywhere and at any time. In the future, I hope to re-read my own *Author Notes* and remember my life as a diary entry.

Today I'm writing these author notes from my white leather chair at our place in La Puente, California. This home has been in my wife's family for decades, first purchased by her immigrant mom at least thirty-five years ago and later purchased by my wife from her mom. It is a very peaceful neighborhood where the neighbors look out for each other.

This morning, while half-way awake and half-way asleep, I heard the cooing of a dove…or the hoot of an owl. Frankly, I can't remember.

(No laughing! <grin> I need more Coke. I was asleep, remember?)

Anyway, it took me back to my time with my grandparents in Moulton, Tx. A time where I wanted nothing more during the Thanksgiving holidays as a schoolkid than freezing weather and the new set of books I had checked out of the school library.

If that happened? Then the parents were ok with me going back to the damned-cold room to cuddle up under an HONEST TO GOD feather bed (the kind where you could get stuck with a quill… cause the feathers came from something that was probably eaten in that household.)

I would LOSE myself reading. Life's worries washed away, and I was doing something amazing, something awesome, and something that didn't make me *work*.

I admit it. I wasn't the hardest-working child. Rather, I was working my intelligence to figure out how to hack getting out of work, or at least doing the work in less time.

Hacking is something I still do. Soon, you will see comments about "THE ZOO" or "The ZOO is coming…" Know that the kid who wanted to read all day is still at it.

Creating ways to get the stories he wants, at a velocity that makes him wish he could just sit in a comfortable chair, bed, lounge (whatever) and read through the holidays.

Now, I'm off to go practice my napping like the true man I am.

LOL

FAN PRICING

If you would like to find out what LMBPN is doing and the books we will be publishing, just sign up at http://lmbpn.com/email/. When you sign up, we notify you of books coming out for the week, any new posts of interest in the books and pop culture arena, and the fan pricing on Saturday.

Ad Aeternitatem,

Michael Anderle

CONNECT WITH MICHAEL TODD

Want more?

Find us On Facebook

https://www.facebook.com/Protected-by-the-Damned-193345908061855/

BOOKS BY MICHAEL TODD

PROTECTED BY THE DAMNED

Torn Asunder (1)

Killing Is My Business (2)

And Business Is Good (3)

Sit Down, Shut Up, And Pull The Trigger (4)

Welcome To The Jungle (5)

Metal Up Your Ass (6)

Dirty Deeds Done Dirt Cheap (7)

For Whom The Bell Tolls (8)

WAR OF THE DAMNED

Resurrection Of The Damned (1)

No Quarter (2)

Dark Is The Night (3)

Dim Glows The Horizon (4)

Waking The Leviathan (5)

Subversive Giants (6)

Juntto (7)

Redemption (8)

WAR OF THE ANGELS

A Sacred Pact (1)

DAMIAN'S CHRONICLES

Crucifix (1)

Renegade (2)

Apostle (3)

BOOKS WRITTEN AS MICHAEL ANDERLE

For a complete list of books by Michael Anderle, please visit:

www.lmbpn.com/ma-books/

All LMBPN Audiobooks are Available at Audible.com and iTunes

To see all LMBPN audiobooks, including those written by Michael Anderle please visit:

www.lmbpn.com/audible

www.ingramcontent.com/pod-product-compliance
Lightning Source LLC
LaVergne TN
LVHW091710070526
838199LV00050B/2335